ONCE LOST

(A RILEY PAIGE MYSTERY—BOOK 10)

BLAKE PIERCE

D1602715

ISBN: 978-1-64029-152-2

BOOKS BY BLAKE PIERCE

RILEY PAIGE MYSTERY SERIES

ONCE GONE (Book #1)
ONCE TAKEN (Book #2)
ONCE CRAVED (Book #3)
ONCE LURED (Book #4)
ONCE HUNTED (Book #5)
ONCE PINED (Book #6)
ONCE FORSAKEN (Book #7)
ONCE COLD (Book #8)
ONCE STALKED (Book #9)
ONCE LOST (Book #10)
ONCE BURIED (Book #11)

MACKENZIE WHITE MYSTERY SERIES

BEFORE HE KILLS (Book #1)
BEFORE HE SEES (Book #2)
BEFORE HE COVETS (Book #3)
BEFORE HE TAKES (Book #4)
BEFORE HE NEEDS (Book #5)
BEFORE HE FEELS (Book #6)

AVERY BLACK MYSTERY SERIES

CAUSE TO KILL (Book #1)
CAUSE TO RUN (Book #2)
CAUSE TO HIDE (Book #3)
CAUSE TO FEAR (Book #4)
CAUSE TO SAVE (Book #5)

KERI LOCKE MYSTERY SERIES

A TRACE OF DEATH (Book #1)
A TRACE OF MUDER (Book #2)
A TRACE OF VICE (Book #3)
A TRACE OF CRIME (Book #4)

PROLOGUE

Katy Philbin was giggling as she stepped carefully down the stairs,

Stop it! she told herself.

What was so funny, anyway?

What was she doing, giggling like a little girl—not like the seventeen-year-old she actually was?

She wanted more than anything in the world to act like a serious adult.

After all, *he* was treating her like an adult. He'd been talking to her like an adult all evening long, making her feel special and respected.

He'd even been calling her Katherine instead of Katy.

She really liked it when he called her Katherine.

She also liked the adult drinks he'd been making for her all evening—"Mai Tais," he called them, and they were so sweet that she could barely taste the alcohol.

And now she couldn't even remember how many she'd had.

Was she drunk?

Oh, that would be awful! she thought.

What would he think of her if she couldn't even handle a few icy, sweet-tasting drinks?

And now she was feeling extremely light-headed.

What if she fell down these stairs?

She looked down at her feet, wondering why they weren't moving as they should be. And why was the light so dim here?

To her embarrassment, she couldn't even remember exactly why she was here on this flight of wooden steps that seemed to get longer by the moment.

"Where're we going?" she asked.

Her words came out all fuzzy and sloppy but at least she'd managed to stop giggling.

"I told you," he said in reply. "I want to show you something."

She looked around for him. He was somewhere at the bottom of the stairs, but she couldn't see him. Just one lamp spilled a small pool of light in a corner far away.

But that light was enough to remind her where she was.

"Oh, yeah," she murmured. "Down'n your basement."

"Are you all right?"

"Yeah," she said, trying to convince herself that it was true. "I'll be right down."

She forced one foot to reach for the next step.

She heard him say, "C'mon, Katy. The thing I promised to show you is over here."

Dimly she realized …

He called me Katy.

She felt oddly disappointed, after a whole evening of being called Katherine.

"Be there in jus' a minnit," she said.

The slur in her words was getting worse.

And for some reason, she found that extremely funny.

She heard him chuckle.

"Are you having a good time, Katy?" he asked in a pleasant voice—a voice that she'd liked and trusted for many years.

"The besht," she said, giggling again.

"I'm glad."

But now the world seemed to be swimming around her. Hanging onto the railing, she sat down on the stairs.

He spoke again in a less patient voice.

"Hurry up, girl. I'm not going to stand here all day."

Katy pulled herself back to her feet, struggling to clear her head. She didn't like the tone of his voice now. But could she blame him for getting impatient? What was the matter with her, anyway? Why couldn't she get down these stupid stairs?

She was finding it harder and harder to focus on where she was and what she was doing.

She lost her grip on the railing and dropped down to sit on the step.

She wondered again—how many drinks had she had, anyway?

Then she remembered.

Two.

Only two!

Of course, she hadn't been drinking at all since that horrible night …

Not until now. But just two drinks.

For a moment she couldn't breathe.

2

Is it happening again?

She told herself sternly that she was being silly.

She was safe and sound here with a man she'd trusted all her life.

And she was making a fool of herself, and the last thing she wanted to do was make a fool of herself, especially around him, when he'd treated her so nicely and served her all those drinks and …

And now everything was foggy, blurred, and dark.

And she felt a strange nausea churning inside her.

"I'm not feeling sho good," she said.

He didn't reply, and she couldn't see him.

She couldn't see anything.

"I think I'd besht—better go home now," she said.

He still didn't say anything.

She reached out blindly, groping around in the air.

"Help me—me get up—off the shtairs. Help me go up the shtairs."

She heard his footsteps coming toward her.

He's going to help me, she thought.

So why was that churning, sick feeling getting worse by the second?

"D-d-rive me home," she said. "Could shyoo do that for me? Please?"

His footsteps stopped.

She could feel his presence right in front of her, even if she couldn't see him.

But why wasn't he saying anything?

Why wasn't he doing anything to help her?

Then she realized what that nauseous feeling actually was.

Fear.

She summoned up her last ounce of will, reached up and took hold of the railing, and pulled herself to her feet.

I have to leave, she thought. But she was unable to say the words aloud.

Then Katy felt a heavy blow to her head.

And then she didn't feel anything at all.

CHAPTER ONE

Riley Paige struggled to blink back tears. She was sitting in her office at Quantico, looking at a photo of a young woman who had a cast on her ankle.

Why am I punishing myself like this? she wondered.

After all, she needed to think about other things right now—especially a BAU meeting scheduled for just a few minutes from now. Riley was dreading that meeting, which might threaten her professional future.

In spite of that, Riley couldn't make herself look away from the picture on her cell phone.

She had snapped that picture of Lucy Vargas last fall, right here in the Behavioral Analysis Unit offices. Lucy's ankle was in a cast, but her smile was simply radiant, a dazzling contrast to her smooth brown skin. Lucy had just been injured on the first case she had worked with Riley and her partner, Bill Jeffreys. But Lucy had done great work, and she knew it, and so did Riley and Bill. That was why Lucy was smiling.

Riley's hand trembled a little as she held the cell phone in her hand.

Lucy was dead now—gunned down by a deranged sniper.

Lucy had died in Riley's arms. But Riley knew that Lucy's death hadn't been her fault.

She wished Bill felt the same way. Her partner was currently on mandatory leave and not doing at all well.

Riley shuddered as she remembered how things had unfolded.

The situation had been chaotic, and instead of shooting the sniper, Bill had shot an innocent man who was trying to help Lucy. Fortunately, the man wasn't badly injured, and no one blamed Bill for his actions, least of all Riley. Riley had never seen him so debilitated with guilt and trauma. Riley wondered how soon he could come back to work—or if he ever could.

Riley's throat tightened as she remembered holding Lucy in her arms.

"You've got a great career ahead of you," Riley had pleaded. *"Now stay with us, Lucy. Stay with us."*

But it was hopeless. Lucy had lost too much blood. Riley had felt the life ebbing away from Lucy's body until it was gone.

And now tears began to trickle down Riley's cheeks.

Her recollections were interrupted by a familiar voice.

"Agent Paige ..."

Riley looked up and saw Sam Flores, the lab technician with black-rimmed glasses. He was standing in her open office door.

Riley stifled a gasp. She hastily wiped away her tears and turned her cell phone face down on her desk.

But she could tell by Sam's stricken expression that he'd glimpsed what she'd been looking at. And that was the last thing she wanted.

A romance had been budding between Sam and Lucy, and he'd taken her death very hard. He still looked brokenhearted.

Now Flores looked at Riley sadly, but to Riley's relief he didn't ask what he'd just interrupted.

Instead he said, "I'm on my way to the meeting. You coming?"

Riley nodded, and Sam nodded back at her.

"Well, good luck, Agent Paige," he said, then continued on his way.

Riley muttered aloud to herself ...

"Yeah, good luck."

Sam seemed to realize she was going to need it for this meeting.

It was time to pull herself together and face whatever was coming next.

*

A little while later, Riley sat in the large conference room surrounded by more BAU personnel than she had expected, including technicians and investigators in a wide range of capacities. Not all of the faces were familiar, and not all of them were friendly.

I could really use an ally right now, she thought.

She certainly missed Bill's presence. Sam Flores sat nearby, but he looked too downcast to be of any help to her right now.

The least friendly face of all was Special Agent in Charge Carl Walder, who sat directly across the table from her. The man with the babyish, freckled face glanced back and forth between Riley and a written report in front of him.

He said in a sullen voice, "Agent Paige, I'm trying to understand what's going on here. We've granted a request to post agents at your house around the clock. This seems to have something to do with Shane Hatcher's recent activities, but I'm not sure exactly how or why. Please explain."

Riley gulped hard.

She'd known that this meeting was going to deal with her relationship with Shane Hatcher, a brilliant and dangerous escaped convict.

She also knew that a full and honest explanation would mean an end to her career.

It might even put her in prison.

She said, "Agent Walder, as you know, Shane Hatcher was last seen at a cabin that I own up in the Appalachian Mountains."

Walder nodded and waited for Riley to say more.

Riley knew she had to choose her words very carefully. Until recently, she and Hatcher had had a secret pact. In return for helping Riley on an intensely personal case, Riley had agreed to let Hatcher hide away in the cabin she had inherited from her father.

It had been a pact with a devil, and Riley looked back on it with shame.

Riley continued, "As you also know, Hatcher escaped an FBI SWAT team that surrounded my cabin. I have reason to think he might turn up at my home."

Walder squinted at her suspiciously.

"Why do you think that?"

"Hatcher is obsessed with me," Riley said. "Now that he's been spotted, I'm fairly sure he'll try to reach out to me. If so, the agents around my house have got a good chance of capturing him."

Riley cringed a little inside.

It was a half-truth at best.

The real reason she wanted agents around her house was to protect her and her family.

Walder sat drumming his fingers on the table for a moment.

"Agent Paige, you say that Hatcher's obsessed with you. Are you sure that obsession isn't mutual?"

Riley bristled a little at the insinuation.

She was relieved when her immediate superior, Brent Meredith, spoke up. Meredith cut a daunting presence as always with his black, angular features and his stern look. But Riley's relationship with Meredith had always been respectful, even friendly. He'd often been her ally in difficult times.

She hoped that he'd be one right now.

He said, "Chief Walder, I think that Agent Paige's request for agents at her home was well-founded. We mustn't pass up even the faintest possibility of bringing Hatcher to justice."

"Yes," Walder said. "And I am not satisfied with the fact that we knew exactly where he was but he still got away." Walder drew himself up in his chair, stared directly at Riley, and asked, "Agent Paige, did you warn Hatcher about the SWAT team that was closing in around him?"

Riley could hear a gasp in the room.

Not many people would have the nerve to ask her such a question. But Riley had to suppress a laugh. This was one question she could answer truthfully. It was why she had reason to fear Hatcher now.

"No, I did not," Riley said firmly, meeting Walder's gaze with a glare.

Walder dropped his eyes first. He turned to Jennifer Roston, a young African-American woman with short straight hair who sat looking at Riley with intense dark eyes.

"Do you have questions, Agent Roston?" he asked.

Roston said nothing for a moment. Riley waited somewhat anxiously for her reply. Roston had been assigned to bring Shane Hatcher to justice. Roston was new to the BAU and eager to make her mark. Riley didn't think she could count on the new agent to be her ally.

Roston hadn't taken her eyes off Riley during the whole meeting so far.

"Agent Paige, would you mind explaining the exact nature of your relationship with Shane Hatcher?"

Riley bristled again.

She wanted to say …

Yes, I mind. I mind very much.

Roston's tactic was becoming clear to Riley.

Some days ago Roston had privately interrogated Riley about this very topic in this very room.

Now Roston clearly intended to ask her the same questions all over again, hoping to catch Riley in a contradiction. Roston expected Riley to crack under the pressure of a large meeting like this. And Riley knew from hard experience not to underestimate her. Roston was highly skilled with mind games.

Say as little as possible, she told herself. *Be extremely careful.*

*

After the meeting broke up, everyone left the room except Riley.

Now that it had ended, Riley felt too badly shaken to get up from her chair.

Roston had asked her familiar questions—for example, how often Riley had communicated with Hatcher, and how. She'd also asked about the death of Shirley Redding, a real estate agent who had gone to the cabin against Riley's wishes and had died there. The police didn't suspect foul play, but Riley was sure that Hatcher had murdered her for intruding on his territory. Riley sensed that Roston also suspected the truth.

Through all of Roston's questions, Riley had responded with familiar lies.

She could tell that Roston was far from satisfied.

This isn't over, she thought with a chill. How long could she hope to conceal the whole truth about her relationship with Hatcher?

But a much more terrifying worry also weighed on her.

What was Shane Hatcher going to do now?

She knew he felt bitterly betrayed that she hadn't warned him about the approaching SWAT team. In fact, he had deliberately allowed himself to be seen at the cabin, allowed the FBI to close in, just to test her loyalty.

From Hatcher's perspective, she had failed that test.

She remembered a text message he had sent to her afterward …

"You will live to regret it. Your family might not."

She knew Hatcher too well not to take his threats seriously.

Riley sat at the big table clenching her hands together anxiously.

How did I let it come to this? she wondered.

Why had she allowed her relationship with Hatcher to continue even after his escape from prison?

Something Walder had just said echoed in her mind …

"You say that Hatcher's obsessed with you. Are you sure that obsession isn't mutual?"

Now that she was sitting here alone, she couldn't deny the truth behind Walder's question.

Hatcher had fascinated Riley ever since she first met him in Sing Sing, seeking out his considerable expertise as a self-taught criminologist. He still fascinated her now that he was at large— fascinated her with his brilliance, his ruthlessness, and his strange capacity for loyalty. In fact, Riley felt an uncanny bond with him— a bond that Hatcher did everything he could to strengthen and manipulate.

It was just like Hatcher had sometimes told her:

"We're joined at the brain, Riley Paige."

Riley shuddered at the thought.

She hoped that at long last she had broken that bond.

But had she also brought the wrath of Shane Hatcher upon the people she loved most?

Just then Riley heard a voice behind her.

"Agent Paige …"

Riley turned and saw that Jennifer Roston had just stepped back into the room.

"I think that you and I need to talk some more," Roston said, sitting down at the table across from Riley.

Riley's mind flooded with dread.

What trick might Roston have up her sleeve now?

CHAPTER TWO

Riley and Jennifer Roston sat looking at each other across the conference room table in silence for almost a full minute.

The suspense was almost more than Riley could take.

Finally Roston said, "That was quite a performance you just gave, Agent Paige."

Riley felt stung and angry.

"I don't need this," she growled.

She started to get up from her chair to leave.

"No, don't go," Roston said. "Not without hearing what I've got on my mind."

Then with an odd smile, she added, "You might be surprised."

Riley felt as though she knew perfectly well what Roston had in mind.

She had set her mind on destroying Riley.

Nevertheless, Riley stayed seated. Whatever was going on between her and Roston, it was high time to settle it. And besides, she was curious.

Roston said, "First of all, I think we got off to a bad start. There have been some misunderstandings. I never meant for us to be enemies. Please believe me. I admire you. A lot. I came to the BAU eager to work with you."

Riley was a little taken aback. Roston's facial expression and tone of voice seemed perfectly sincere. The truth was, Riley had been deeply impressed by everything she'd heard about Roston. Her academy scores were said to be astonishing, and she'd already won commendations for field work in Los Angeles.

And now, sitting here looking at her, Riley was impressed anew with Roston's demeanor. The woman was short but compact and athletic, and she radiated energy and enthusiasm.

But now seemed no time for Riley to heap praise on the new agent. There had simply been too much tension and mistrust between them.

After a pause, Roston said, "I think we've got a lot to offer each other. Right now. In fact, I'm pretty sure we both want exactly the same thing."

"What's that?" Riley asked.

Roston smiled and tilted her head a little.

"To put an end to Shane Hatcher's criminal career."

Riley didn't reply. It took moment for Riley to register that Roston's words were perfectly true. She no longer considered Shane Hatcher to be an ally. In fact, he was a dangerous enemy. And he had to be stopped before he did harm to any of Riley's loved ones.

To do that, he would have to be caught or killed.

"Tell me more," Riley said.

Roston tucked her chin on her hand and leaned toward Riley.

"I'm going to say a few things," she said. "I'd like you to listen without saying anything in reply. Don't deny or agree with what I say. Just listen."

Riley nodded uneasily.

"Your relationship with Shane Hatcher continued even after he escaped Sing Sing. In fact, it became more intense than ever. You've communicated with him more than once—several times, I'm pretty sure, occasionally in person. He's helped you on official cases, and he's helped you in more personal ways. Your relationship with him has become—what's the word? Symbiotic."

It took Riley considerable self-control not to react to any of this.

All of it was, of course, absolutely true.

Roston continued, "I'm pretty sure you were aware of his presence at your cabin. In fact, you probably agreed to it. But the death of Shirley Redding was no accident. And it wasn't part of your bargain. Hatcher has gotten out of control, and you want nothing more to do with him. But you're scared of him. You don't know how to break the connection."

An unsettling silence fell between Riley and Roston. Riley wondered how she knew all this. It seemed downright uncanny. But Riley didn't believe in mind reading.

No, she's just one hell of a detective, Riley thought.

This new agent was extremely smart, and her instincts and intuition seemed to be as strong as Riley's.

But what was Roston trying to do right now? Was she setting a trap, trying to get Riley to confess all that had gone on between her and Hatcher?

Somehow, Riley's gut told her otherwise.

But did she dare trust her?

Roston was smiling enigmatically again.

"Agent Paige, do you think I don't know how you feel? Do you think I don't have secrets of my own? Do you think I haven't gotten in over my head, made a pact with someone I shouldn't have? Believe me, I know exactly what you're dealing with. You took a chance, and rules sometimes need to be broken. So you broke them. Not many agents have your guts. I really do want to help."

Riley studied Roston's face without replying. She was again struck by the younger agent's sincerity.

Riley could feel a grim smile forming at the corners of her mouth. Apparently something dark lurked inside Roston, as it did in herself.

Roston said, "Agent Paige, when I first started working on the Hatcher case, you gave me access to all the computer files you had relating to him. Except for one titled 'THOUGHTS.' It was listed in the summary, but I couldn't find it. You told me you'd deleted it. You said it was just rough notes and redundant stuff."

Roston leaned back in her chair, seeming to relax a little.

But Riley was anything but relaxed. She'd rashly deleted the file called THOUGHTS, which actually contained vital information about Hatcher's financial connections—connections that allowed him to remain at large and wield considerable power.

Roston said, "I'm pretty sure you've still got that file."

Riley suppressed a shudder of alarm. The fact was, she had kept the file on a thumb drive. She'd often thought about simply erasing it, but somehow she couldn't bring herself to do so. Hatcher's spell over her had been strong. And just maybe she'd thought she might need to use that information someday herself.

Instead of erasing it, she'd been carrying it around in a state of indecision.

It was in Riley's purse right now.

"I'm pretty sure that file is important," Roston said. "In fact, it might contain information that I need to put Hatcher away once and for all. And we both want that to happen. I'm sure of it."

Riley gulped.

I mustn't say anything, she thought.

But didn't everything Roston said make perfect sense?

That thumb drive might well be the key to freeing Riley from Shane Hatcher's clutches.

Roston's expression softened more.

"Agent Paige, I'm going to make you a solemn promise. If you give me that information, nobody will ever know that you ever withheld it. I won't tell a soul. Never."

Riley felt her resistance collapse.

Her every instinct assured her of Roston's sincerity.

She silently reached into her purse, took out the thumb drive, and handed it to the younger agent. Roston's eyes widened slightly, but she didn't say a word. She just nodded and put the drive in her pocket.

Riley felt a desperate need to break the silence.

"Do you wish to discuss anything else, Agent Roston?"

The younger agent chuckled a little.

"Please, call me Jenn. All my friends do."

Riley squinted uncertainly as Roston got up from her chair.

"Mind you, I won't presume to call you anything except Agent Paige. Not until you feel comfortable otherwise. But please. Do call me Jenn. I positively insist."

Roston left the room, leaving Riley sitting there in astonished silence.

*

Riley settled down to catch up with paperwork in her office. Whenever she wasn't working on a case, it seemed as though tons of bureaucratic tedium awaited her and didn't let up until she went out into the field again.

It was always unpleasant. But today she had an especially hard time focusing on what she was doing. She grew more and more worried that she'd just made a terribly foolish mistake.

Why on earth had she just handed that file over to Jennifer Roston—or "Jenn," as she now insisted Riley call her?

It was nothing less than a confession of obstruction on Riley's part.

Why had she given it to this particular agent when she'd never shown it to anyone else? How could an ambitious young agent do anything other than report Riley's transgression to her superiors—maybe even to Carl Walder himself?

Any minute now, Riley might find herself under arrest.

Why hadn't she just erased the file?

Or she could have gotten rid of it, as she had done with the gold chain Hatcher had given her. The chain had been a symbol of her bond with Hatcher. It had also contained a code for contacting him.

Riley had thrown it away in a frantic effort to free herself of him.

But for some reason, she hadn't been able to bring herself to do the same with the thumb drive.

Why?

The financial information it contained was surely enough to at least limit Hatcher's movements and activities.

It might just be enough to stop him for good.

It was a riddle, as were so many aspects of her relationship with Hatcher.

While Riley was sorting papers on her desk, her cell phone rang. It was a text message from an unknown number. Riley's gasped when she saw what it said.

Did you think this would stop me? Everything is already moved. You can't say you weren't warned.

Riley found it hard to breathe.
Shane Hatcher, she thought.

CHAPTER THREE

Riley stared at the text message, panic rising inside her.

It wasn't hard to guess what had happened. Jenn Roston had opened the file as soon as she and Riley had parted. Jenn had found out what was in it and had already gotten right to work trying to shut down Hatcher's operation.

But in his message, Hatcher himself defiantly announced that Jenn hadn't succeeded.

Everything is already moved.

Shane Hatcher was still at large, and he was angry. With his financial resources intact he might be more dangerous than ever.

I've got to answer him, she thought. *I've got to reason with him.*

But how? What could she possibly say that wouldn't infuriate him more?

Then it occurred to her that Hatcher might not fully understand what was happening.

How could he know that it was Roston sabotaging his network, not Riley? Maybe she *could* make him understand at least that much.

Her hands shook as she typed in a reply.

Let me explain.

But when she tried to send the text, it was marked "undeliverable."

Riley groaned with despair.

Exactly the same thing had happened the last time she'd tried to communicate with Hatcher. He'd sent her a cryptic message, then cut her off. She used to be able to communicate with Hatcher by video chat, text, and even phone calls. But those days were over.

Right now, she had no way at all of reaching him.

But he could still reach her.

The second sentence of his new message was especially chilling.

"You can't say you weren't warned."

Riley flashed back to what he had written the last time she had communicated with him.

"You will live to regret it. Your family might not."

Riley gasped and said aloud …

"My family!"

She fumbled with her cell phone as she punched in her home number. She heard it ring, then keep on ringing. Then the outgoing message came on, her own voice.

It was all Riley could do to keep from screaming.

Why wasn't anyone answering? The schools were on spring break. Her kids were supposed to be home. And where was Riley's live-in housekeeper, Gabriela?

Just before the outgoing message ended, she heard the voice of Jilly, the thirteen-year-old that Riley was in the process of trying to adopt. Jilly sounded breathless.

"Hey, sorry, Mom. Gabriela went to the grocery store. April and Liam and I were out in the backyard kicking a soccer ball around. We're expecting Gabriela to get back any minute."

Riley realized she'd been holding her breath. She made a conscious effort to start breathing again.

"Is everything all right?" she asked.

"Sure," Jilly said with a shrug in her voice. "Why wouldn't it be?"

Riley struggled to calm herself down.

"Jilly, could you go and look out the front window for me?"

"OK," Jilly said.

Riley heard a few footsteps.

"I'm looking," Jilly said.

"Is the van with the FBI agents still out there?"

"Yeah. And so is the one in the alley. I just saw it when I was in the backyard. If that Shane Hatcher guy comes around, those guys are sure to catch him. Is something wrong? You're kind of scaring me."

Riley forced a laugh.

"No, nothing's wrong. I'm just—being a mom, I guess."

"OK. I'll see you later."

The call ended, but Riley's worry was still surging inside her. She went down the hall and straight to Brent Meredith's office. She stammered, "Sir, I—I need to take the rest of the day off."

Meredith looked up from his work.

"May I ask why, Agent Paige?" he asked.

Riley opened her mouth, but no words came out. If she explained that she'd just gotten a threat from Shane Hatcher, wouldn't he insist on seeing the message? How could she show it to him without admitting that she'd just given the file to Jenn Roston?

Meredith looked concerned now. He seemed aware that something was wrong that Riley couldn't talk about.

"Go," he said. "I hope everything is all right."

Riley's heart flooded with gratitude at Meredith's understanding and discretion.

"Thank you, sir," she said.

Then she hurried out of the building and got in her car and drove home.

*

As she neared her townhouse in a quiet Fredericksburg neighborhood, she was relieved to see that the FBI van was indeed still there. Riley knew there was another van stationed in the alley. Although the vehicles were unmarked, they were hardly inconspicuous. But there was nothing to be done about that.

Riley parked her car in her driveway, walked over to the van, and looked inside the open passenger window.

Two young agents were sitting in the front seats—Craig Huang and Bud Wigton. Riley's spirits lifted a little. She thought highly of both agents, and she'd worked with Huang several times recently. Huang had been a little too gung-ho for Riley's liking when he first came to the BAU, but he was rapidly maturing into an excellent agent. She didn't know Wigton as well, but he had an excellent reputation.

"Anything going on?" Riley asked them through the window.

"Not a thing," Huang said.

Huang sounded bored, but Riley felt relieved. No news was definitely good news as far as she was concerned. But was it too good to last?

"Mind if I have a look inside?" Riley asked.

"Be our guest," Huang said.

The side door to the windowless van slid open, and Riley stepped inside to find another agent, Grace Lochner, stationed inside. Riley knew that Grace also had a sterling reputation at the BAU.

Lochner was seated in front of a battery of video screens. She turned toward Riley with a smile.

"What have you got going here?" Riley asked.

Seeming eager to show off the technology at her disposal, Lochner pointed to a couple of screens that showed overhead views of the neighborhood.

She said, "Here we've got real-time satellite images showing all the comings and goings within a half mile of here. Nobody can get near here without us noticing."

Laughing a little, Lochner added, "I'm glad you live in a quiet neighborhood. It gives us less traffic to keep track of."

She pointed out several more screens showing street-level activity.

She said, "We've hidden cameras around the neighborhood to see what's going on closer up. We can check license plates of any vehicle that comes near here."

A voice crackled over an intercom.

"Have you guys got a visitor?"

Lochner answered, "Agent Paige just stopped by to say hello."

The voice said, "Hello, Agent Paige. This is Agent Cole, in the vehicle around back of your house. I've got Agents Cypher and Hahn with me too."

Riley smiled. Those were all familiar names of well-respected agents.

Riley said, "I'm glad to have you on the job."

"Our pleasure," Agent Cole said.

Riley was impressed by the communication between the two vans. She could see the van behind her house in a couple of Lochner's screens. Obviously, nothing could happen to either team without the other team knowing about it immediately.

Riley was also pleased by the display of weaponry stocked inside the van. The team had enough firepower to fight off a small army if necessary.

But she couldn't help but wonder—was it enough to fight off Shane Hatcher? She left the van and walked on toward her house, telling herself not to worry. She couldn't imagine even Shane Hatcher thwarting all this security.

Still, she couldn't help remembering the text message she had just received.

You can't say you weren't warned.

CHAPTER FOUR

When Riley stepped inside her house, the place seemed eerily empty.

"I'm home," she called out.

But nobody replied.

Where is everybody? Her alarm started to turn into panic.

Was it possible that Shane Hatcher had slipped through all that security after all?

Riley struggled not to imagine what might have happened if he had. Her pulse and breathing quickened as she hurried to the family room.

All three kids—April, Liam, and Jilly—were there. April and Liam were playing chess and Jilly was playing a video game.

"Didn't you hear me?" she asked.

All three looked up at her with blank expressions. They had obviously all been concentrating on what they were doing.

She was about to ask the kids where Gabriela was when she heard her housekeeper's voice behind her.

"Are you home, *Señora* Riley? I was downstairs and I thought I heard you come in."

Riley smiled at the stout Guatemalan woman.

"Yes, I just got in," she said, breathing easier now.

With a welcoming nod and a smile, Gabriela turned and headed toward the kitchen.

April looked up from the game she was playing with Liam.

"Is everything OK, Mom? You look kind of agitated."

"I'm fine," Riley said.

April turned her attention back to the game.

Riley took a moment to marvel how mature her fifteen-year-old daughter looked. April was slender, tall, and dark-haired, with Riley's hazel eyes. April had been through more than her share of life-threatening danger during the last few months. But she seemed to be doing very well these days.

Riley looked over at Jilly, a smaller girl with olive skin and big dark eyes. Riley was in the process of adopting her. At the moment,

Jilly was sitting in front of a large screen blasting bad guys away.

Riley frowned a little. She didn't like violent video games. As far as she was concerned, they made violence—especially gun violence—seem both too attractive and too sanitized. She believed they had an especially bad influence on boys.

Still, Riley considered, maybe these games were harmless compared to Jilly's own experience. After all, the thirteen-year-old had survived real-life horrors. When Riley had found Jilly, she had been trying to sell her body out of sheer desperation. Thanks to Riley, Jilly had a chance at a better life.

Liam looked up from the chessboard.

"Hey, Riley. I was wondering …"

He hesitated before asking his question.

Liam was the newcomer to the household. Riley had no plans to adopt the tall, gangly kid with red hair and blue eyes. But she had rescued him from a drunken father who had beaten him up. He needed a place to live right now.

"What is it, Liam?" Riley asked.

"Is it OK if I go to a chess competition tomorrow?"

"Could I go too?" April asked.

Riley smiled again. Liam and April had been dating when Liam had come to live down here in the family room, but they had promised to keep that relationship on hold for the time being. They had to be *hermanos solamente,* as Gabriela had put it—brother and sister only.

Riley liked Liam, all the more so because of the positive influence the bright boy had on April. He'd gotten April interested in chess and foreign languages and schoolwork in general.

"Of course you can go, both of you," she said.

But then she felt a renewed burst of worry. She got out her cell phone and found some photos of Shane Hatcher and showed them to all three kids.

"But you've got to watch out for Shane Hatcher," she said. "You've got these pictures on your own phones. Always remember exactly what he looks like. Contact me right away if you see anyone who looks anything like him."

Liam and April looked at Riley with surprise.

"You've told us all this before," Jilly said. "And we've looked at those pictures a thousand times. Has something changed?"

Riley wavered for a moment. She didn't want to scare the kids. But she felt that they needed to be warned.

"I got a message from Hatcher a little while ago," she said. "It was …"

She hesitated again.

"It was a threat. That's why I want you all to be especially on your guard."

To Riley's surprise, Jilly grinned at her.

"Does this mean we get to stay home from school when spring break is over?" she asked.

Riley was startled by Jilly's nonchalance. She also briefly wondered—maybe Jilly had the right idea. Should she keep the kids out of school? And should Liam and April not go to that chess competition tomorrow?

Before she could think things through, April said, "Don't be silly, Jilly. Of course we're going to keep right on going to school. It's not like we can put our lives on hold."

Then turning to Riley, April added, "It's not a real threat. Even I know that. Remember what happened in January?"

Riley remembered all too well. Hatcher had saved April and Riley's ex-husband, Ryan, from a killer bent on revenge against Riley. She also remembered how Shane Hatcher had delivered the killer bound and gagged for Riley to deal with at her own discretion.

April went on, "Hatcher wouldn't hurt us. He went to a lot of trouble to save me."

Maybe April's got a point, Riley thought. At least where she and the other kids are concerned. But she was still glad that the agents were stationed outside.

April shrugged a little and added, "Life goes on. We've all got to keep doing what we do."

Jilly said, "And that goes for you too, Mom. It's a good thing you got home early. You've got plenty of time to get ready for tonight."

For a second, Riley couldn't remember what Jilly meant.

Then it came back to her—she had a date tonight with her handsome former neighbor, Blaine Hildreth. Blaine was the owner of one of the nicest casual restaurants here in Fredericksburg. He was planning to come by and pick Riley up and treat her to a wonderful dinner.

April hopped to her feet.

"Hey, that's right!" she said. "Come on, Mom. Let's go upstairs and I'll help you choose something to wear."

*

Later that evening, Riley was sitting on the candlelit patio at Blaine's Grill, enjoying wonderful weather, excellent food, and charming company. Across the table from her, Blaine cut a handsome figure as always. He was just a little younger than Riley, lean and fit, with a slightly receding hairline that he wasn't the least bit vain about.

Riley also found him to be a pleasant conversationalist. As they ate a delicious dinner of rosemary chicken pasta, they chatted about current events, memories of long-ago times and travels, and goings-on in Fredericksburg.

Riley was delighted that their talk never once turned to her work at the BAU. She was in no mood to even think about that. Blaine seemed to sense that and steer clear of the subject. One thing Riley really liked about Blaine was his sensitivity to her moods.

In fact, there was very little about Blaine that Riley didn't like. True, they'd had a bit of a spat not long ago. Blaine had tried to make Riley jealous over a woman friend, and he had succeeded all too well. Now they were both able to laugh about how childish they'd both been.

Maybe it was partly the wine, but Riley felt warm and relaxed inside. Blaine was comfortable company—fairly recently divorced like Riley, and anxious to get on with life without quite knowing how.

Dessert finally arrived—Riley's favorite, raspberry cheesecake. She smiled a little as she remembered how April had secretly called Blaine before an earlier date to alert him to some of Riley's favorite things, including raspberry cheesecake and her favorite song—"One More Night" by Phil Collins.

As she enjoyed her cheesecake, Riley talked about her kids, especially how Liam was settling in.

"I was a little worried at first," she admitted. "But he's an awfully good kid, and we all love having him around the house."

Riley paused for a moment. It felt positively luxurious to have someone to talk to about her domestic doubts and worries.

"Blaine, I don't know what I'm going to do with Liam in the long run. I just can't send him back to that drunken brute of a father, and God only knows what's become of his mother. But I don't see how I can legally adopt him. Taking in Jilly has been

23

really complicated and it's not settled yet. I don't know if I can do it again."

Blaine smiled at her sympathetically.

"You'll just take things one day at a time, I guess," he said. "And whatever you do, it will be the best thing for him."

Riley shook her head a bit sadly.

"I wish I knew that for sure," she said.

Blaine reached across the table and took hold of her hand.

"Well, take my word for it," he said. "What you've already done for Liam and Jilly is wonderful and generous. I admire you so much for it."

Riley felt a lump form in her throat. How often did anyone ever say anything like that to her? She was often praised for her work in the BAU, and had even received a Medal of Perseverance recently. But she was not accustomed to being praised for simple human things. She hardly knew how to take it.

Then Blaine said, "You're a good woman, Riley Paige."

Riley felt tears well up in her eyes. She laughed nervously as she wiped them away.

"Oh, look what you've done," she said. "You've made me cry."

Blaine shrugged, and his smile grew even warmer.

"Sorry. Just trying to be brutally honest. The truth sometimes hurts, I guess."

They laughed together for a few moments.

Finally Riley said, "But I haven't asked about your daughter. How's Crystal doing?"

Blaine looked away with a bittersweet smile.

"Crystal's doing just great—good grades, happy and cheerful. She's away right now for spring break, at the beach with her cousins and my sister."

Blaine sighed a little. "It's only been a couple of days, but it's amazing how fast I start missing her."

It was all Riley could do not to start crying all over again. She'd known all along that Blaine was a wonderful father. What might it be like to be in a more permanent relationship with him?

Careful, she told herself. *Let's not rush things.*

Meanwhile, she had almost finished her raspberry cheesecake.

"Thank you, Blaine," she said. "It's been such a lovely evening."

Gazing into his eyes, she added, "I hate to see it end."

Gazing back at her, Blaine squeezed her hand.

"Who says it has to end?" he asked.

Riley smiled. She knew her smile was enough to answer his question.

After all, why should their evening end? The FBI was guarding her family and no new killer was demanding her attention.

Maybe it was time to enjoy herself.

CHAPTER FIVE

George Tully didn't like the looks of one patch of ground over by the road. He didn't exactly know why.

Nothing to worry about, he told himself. The morning light was probably just playing tricks on him.

He took a deep breath of fresh air. Then he stooped down and picked up a handful of loose soil. As always, it felt soft and luxurious. It also smelled good, rich with nutrients from past corn harvests—husks and ears plowed back into the soil.

Good old black Iowa dirt, he thought as bits of it trickled down between his fingers.

This land had been in George's family for years, so he'd known this fine soil all his life. But he never got tired of it, and his pride in farming the richest land in the world never waned.

He looked up across fields that stretched as far as he could see. The earth had been tilled for a couple of days now. It was ready and waiting for corn kernels dusted purple with insecticide to be placed where each new cornstalk would soon appear.

He'd held off on the planting until today to make sure of the weather. Of course there was never any way to be certain that a frost wouldn't come even this late in the year and ruin the crop. He could remember a freak April blizzard back in the '70s that had taken his father by surprise. But as George felt a breath of warm air and looked up at some high clouds streaking across the sky, he felt as confident as he could hope to feel.

Today's the day, he thought.

As George stood watching, his field hand Duke Russo came driving a tractor that dragged a forty-foot-long planter behind it. The planter would seed sixteen rows at a time, thirty inches apart, one kernel at a time, deposit fertilizer on top of each one, cover the seed, and roll on its way.

George's sons, Roland and Jasper, had been standing in the field awaiting the tractor's arrival, and they walked toward it as it rumbled along one side of the field. George smiled to himself. Duke and the boys made a good crew. There was no need for George to hang around for the actual planting. He waved at the three men, then turned to head back to his truck.

But that odd patch of earth near the road caught his attention again. What was wrong over there? Had the tiller missed that patch? He couldn't imagine how that could have happened.

Maybe a groundhog had been digging there.

But as he walked toward the spot, he could see that no groundhog had done this. There was no opening, and the soil was patted down.

It looked like something had been buried here.

George growled under his breath. Vandals and pranksters sometimes gave him trouble. A couple of years ago, some boys from nearby Angier stole a tractor and used it to demolish a storage shed. More recently, others had spray-painted obscenities on fences and walls and even cattle.

It was infuriating—and hurtful.

George had no idea why the kids would come out of their way to give him trouble. He'd never done any harm to them that he knew of. He'd reported the incidents to Joe Sinard, Angier's police chief, but nothing ever got done about it.

"What have those bastards done this time?" he said aloud, tapping the soil with his foot.

He figured he'd better find out. Whatever was buried here might wreck his equipment.

He turned toward his crew and waved for Duke to stop the tractor. When the engine was off, George yelled to his sons.

"Jasper, Roland—fetch me that shovel in the tractor cab."

"What's wrong, Pop?" Jasper called back.

"I don't know. Just do it."

A moment later, Duke and the boys came walking toward him. Jasper handed his father a shovel.

As the group watched curiously, George prodded the soil with his shovel. As he did, a strange, sour smell met his nostrils.

He felt a wave of instinctive dread.

What the hell's under here?

He turned over a few shovels full of dirt until he struck something solid but soft.

He shoveled more carefully, trying to uncover whatever it was. Soon something pale came into view.

It took a few moments for George to register what it was.

"Oh, Lord!" he gasped, his stomach churning with horror.

It was a hand—a young woman's hand.

CHAPTER SIX

The next morning, Riley watched as Blaine fixed a breakfast of eggs Benedict with fresh squeezed orange juice and rich, dark coffee. She reflected that passionate lovemaking was not limited to ex-husbands. And she realized that waking up in comfort with a man was something new.

She felt grateful for this morning, and grateful to Gabriela, who had assured her she would take care of everything when Riley had phoned her last night. But she couldn't help but wonder if a relationship like this would survive, given the many other complications of her life.

Riley decided to ignore that question and focus on the delicious meal. But as they ate, she soon noticed that Blaine's mind seemed to be elsewhere.

"What's the matter?" she asked him.

Blaine didn't reply. His eyes roamed about uneasily.

She felt a flash of worry. What was the problem?

Was he having second thoughts about last night? Was he less contented with this than she was?

"Blaine, what's wrong?" Riley asked, her voice shaking a little.

After a pause, Blaine said, "Riley, I just don't feel … *safe*."

Riley struggled to make sense of what Blaine had said. Was all the warmth and affection they'd shared since their date last night suddenly gone? What had happened between them to change everything?

"I—I don't understand," she stammered. "What do you mean, you don't feel safe?"

Blaine hesitated, then said, "I think I need to buy a gun. For home protection."

His words jolted Riley. She hadn't expected this.

But maybe I should have, she thought.

Sitting across the table from him, she could see a scar on his right cheek. He'd gotten that scar last November in Riley's own home, trying to protect April and Gabriela from an attacker bent on revenge.

28

Riley remembered the terrible guilt she'd felt at seeing Blaine unconscious in a hospital bed after it was over.

And now she felt that guilt all over again.

Would Blaine ever feel safe with Riley in her life? Would he ever feel that his daughter could be safe?

And was a gun what he really needed to make him feel safer?

Riley shook her head.

"I don't know, Blaine," she said. "I'm not a great fan of civilians keeping weapons in their homes."

As soon as the words were out, Riley realized how patronizing they sounded.

She couldn't tell from Blaine's expression whether he was offended or not. He seemed to be waiting for her to say more.

Riley sipped her coffee, gathering her thoughts.

She said, "Did you know that statistically, home weapons are more likely to lead to homicides, suicides, and accidental deaths than successful home defense? In fact, gun owners are generally at greater risk of becoming homicide victims themselves than people who don't own guns."

Blaine nodded.

"Yeah, I know all about that," he said. "I've been doing some research. I also know about Virginia's self-defense laws. And that this is an open-carry state."

Riley tilted her head with approval.

"Well, you're already better prepared than most people who decide to buy a gun. Even so …"

Her words trailed off. She was reluctant to say what was on her mind.

"What is it?" Blaine asked.

Riley took a long, deep breath.

"Blaine, would you want to buy a gun if I wasn't part of your life?"

"Oh, Riley—"

"Tell me the truth. Please."

Blaine sat staring into his coffee for a moment.

"No, I wouldn't," he finally said.

Riley reached across the table and held Blaine's hand.

"That's what I thought. And I'm sure you can understand how that makes me feel. I care for you a lot, Blaine. It's terrible to know that your life is more dangerous because of me."

"I get that," Blaine said. "But I want *you* to tell me the truth about something. And please don't take this wrong."

Riley silently braced herself for whatever Blaine was about to ask her.

"Are your *feelings* really a good argument against my buying a gun? I mean, isn't it a fact that I'm in more danger than the average citizen, and that I ought to be able to defend myself and Crystal— and maybe even you?"

Riley shrugged a little. She felt sad to admit it to herself, but Blaine was right.

If a gun would make him feel more safe and secure, he ought to have one.

She was also sure that he'd be as responsible as a gun owner could possibly be.

"OK," she said. "Let's finish breakfast and go shopping."

*

Later that morning, Blaine walked into a gun store with Riley. Right away Blaine wondered if he was making a mistake. He couldn't guess how many fearsome weapons were on the walls and in glass cases. He'd never even fired a gun before—unless he counted the BB gun he'd had as a kid.

What am I getting into? he thought.

A large, bearded man in a plaid shirt was moving about among the merchandise.

"How can I help you folks?" he asked.

Riley said, "We're looking for some home protection for my friend."

"Well, I'm sure we've got something here that will suit you," the man said.

Blaine felt awkward under the man's gaze. He guessed that it wasn't every day when an attractive woman brought her boyfriend in here to help him choose a weapon.

Blaine couldn't help but feel embarrassed. He even felt embarrassed about feeling embarrassed. He'd never thought of himself as the kind of man who felt insecure about his masculinity.

As Blaine tried to snap himself out of his awkwardness, the gun seller eyed Riley's own sidearm with approval.

"That Glock Model 22 you've got there's a fine piece, ma'am," he said. "A law enforcement professional, are you?"

Riley smiled and showed him her badge.

The man pointed to a row of similar weapons in a glass case.

"Well, I've got your Glocks right over here. Pretty good choices, if you ask me."

Riley looked at the weapons, then looked at Blaine, as if to ask his opinion.

Blaine couldn't do anything but shrug and blush. He wished he'd put the same time into researching weapons as he had into statistics and laws.

Riley shook her head.

"I'm not sure a semiautomatic is quite what we're in the market for," she said.

The man nodded.

"Yeah, they're kind of complicated, especially for someone new to guns. Things can go wrong."

Riley nodded in agreement, adding, "Yeah, things like misfires, stovepipe jams, double feed, failure to eject."

The man said, "Of course, those aren't real problems for a seasoned FBI gal like you. But for this feller, maybe a revolver is more the style you're looking for."

The man escorted them to a glass case full of revolvers.

Blaine's eyes were drawn to some of the guns with shorter barrels.

At least they looked less intimidating.

"What about that one there?" he said, pointing to one.

The man opened the case, took out the gun, and handed it to Blaine. The weapon felt strange in Blaine's hand. He couldn't decide whether it was heavier or lighter than he'd expected.

"A Ruger SP101," the man said. "Good stopping power. Not a bad choice."

Riley eyed the weapon doubtfully.

"I think we're looking for something with maybe a four-inch barrel," she said. "Something that absorbs the recoil better."

The man nodded again.

"Right. Well, I think maybe I've got just the thing."

He reached into the case and took out another larger pistol. He handed it to Riley, who examined it with approval.

"Oh, yeah," she said. "A Smith and Wesson 686."

Then she smiled at Blaine and handed him the gun.

"What do you think?" Riley said.

This longer weapon felt even stranger in his hand than the smaller weapon had. All he could do was smile at Riley sheepishly.

She smiled back. He could see by her expression that she'd finally registered how awkward he was feeling.

She turned to the owner and said, "I think we'll take it. How much does it cost?"

Blaine was stunned by the price of the weapon, but was sure that Riley knew best whether he was getting a fair deal.

He was also rather stunned by how easy it was to make the purchase. The man asked him for two proofs of identity, and Blaine offered him his driver's license and his voter registration card. Then Blaine filled out a short, simple form consenting to a background check. The computerized check took only a couple of minutes, and Blaine was cleared to buy his weapon.

"What kind of ammo do you want?" the man asked as he started to ring up the sale.

Riley said, "Give us a box of Federal Premium Low Recoil."

Just moments later, Blaine was a somewhat baffled gun owner.

He stood looking down at the daunting weapon, which lay on the counter in an open plastic case, nestled in protective foam. Blaine thanked the man, shut the case, and turned to leave.

"Wait a minute," the man said cheerfully. "Don't you want to try her out?"

The man led Riley and Blaine through a door in the back of the store that opened into a startlingly large indoor shooting range. Then he left Riley and Blaine to themselves. Blaine was just as glad that nobody else was there at the moment.

Riley pointed out the list of rules on the wall, and Blaine read them carefully. Then he shook his head uneasily.

"Riley, I don't mind telling you …"

Riley chuckled a little.

"I know. You're a little overwhelmed. I'll talk you through it."

She led him over to one of the empty booths, where he put on ear and eye protection gear. He opened the case with the pistol, careful to keep it pointed downrange before he even picked it up.

"Do I load it?" he asked Riley.

"Not yet. We'll do some dry fire practice first."

He took the pistol into his hands, and Riley helped him find the proper position—both hands on the gun handle but with fingers clear of the cylinder, elbows and knees slightly bent, leaning slightly forward. In a few moments, Blaine found himself aiming his pistol at a vaguely human shape on a paper target about twenty-five yards downrange.

"We're going to practice double action first," Riley said. "That's when you don't pull back the hammer with every shot, you do all the work with the trigger. That will give you a good sense of how the trigger feels. Pull the trigger back smoothly, then let it go just as smoothly."

Blaine practiced with the empty gun a few times. Then Riley showed him how to open the cylinder and fill it with shells.

Blaine took up the same stance as before. He braced himself, knowing that the gun would kick a good bit, and carefully aimed at the target.

He pulled the trigger and fired.

The sudden backward force startled him, and the gun leaped in his hand. He lowered the gun and looked toward the target. He couldn't see any holes in it. He fleetingly wondered how on earth anyone could hope to aim a weapon that jumped so sharply.

"Let's work on your breathing," Riley said. "Breathe in slowly while you aim, then breathe out slowly, drawing back the trigger so that you fire exactly when you've fully exhaled. That's when your body is most still."

Blaine fired again. He was surprised at how much more control he felt.

He looked downrange and saw that he had at least hit the paper target this time.

But as he prepared to take another shot, a memory flashed through his mind—a memory of the most terrifying moment of his life. One day when he'd still been living next door to Riley, he'd heard a terrible racket next door. He'd rushed over to Riley's townhouse and found the front door partially open.

A man had thrown Riley's daughter on the floor and was attacking her.

Blaine had rushed toward them and pulled the man off April. But the man was too strong for Blaine to subdue, and Blaine was badly beaten before he finally lost consciousness.

It was a bitter memory, and for a moment it brought back a feeling of heart-sickening helplessness.

But that feeling suddenly evaporated as he felt the weight of the gun in his hands.

He breathed and fired, breathed and fired, four more times until the cylinder was empty.

Riley pushed a button that brought the paper target up to the booth.

33

"Not bad for your first time," Riley said.

Indeed, Blaine could see that those last four shots had at least landed within the human shape.

But he realized that his heart was pounding, and that he was overcome with a strange blend of feelings.

One of those feelings was fear.

But fear of what?

Power, Blaine realized.

The feeling of power in his hands was staggering, like nothing he'd ever felt before.

He felt so good that it positively scared him.

Riley showed him how to open the cylinder and pop out the empty shells.

"Is that enough for today?" she asked.

"Not on your life," Blaine said breathlessly. "I want you to teach me everything there is to know about this thing."

Riley stood smiling at him as he reloaded.

He could still feel her smile as he aimed at a fresh target.

But then he heard Riley's cell phone ring.

CHAPTER SEVEN

When Riley's cell phone started ringing, Blaine's last shots were still ringing in her ears. Reluctantly, she pulled out her phone. She had hoped to have an uninterrupted morning with Blaine. When she looked at the phone she knew she was about to be disappointed. The call was from Brent Meredith.

She'd been surprised at how much she was enjoying teaching Blaine to shoot his new pistol. Whatever Meredith wanted, Riley felt sure it was going to interrupt the best day she'd had in a long while.

But she had no choice but to take the call.

As usual, Meredith was brusque and to the point.

"We've got a new case. We need you on it. How fast can you get to Quantico?"

Riley suppressed a sigh. With Bill on leave, Riley had hoped to have some time off until the pain of Lucy's death eased a little.

No such luck, she thought.

No doubt she would be leaving town shortly. Did she have enough time to run home and see everybody and change clothes?

"How about an hour?" Riley asked.

"Make it shorter. Meet me in my office. And bring your go bag."

Meredith ended the call without waiting for a reply.

Blaine was standing there waiting for her. He pulled off his eye and ear protection gear and asked, "Something to do with work?"

Riley sighed aloud.

"Yeah, I've got to get to Quantico right away."

Blaine nodded without complaint and unloaded the gun.

"I'll drive you there," he said.

"No, I'm going to need my go bag. And that's in my car at home. I'm afraid you need to drop me off at my place. I'm also afraid we're in a bit of a hurry."

"No problem," Blaine said, carefully putting the new weapon in its case.

Riley gave him a kiss on the cheek.

"It sounds like I'm going to be leaving town," she said. "I hate that. I've had such a wonderful time."

Blaine smiled and kissed her back.

"I've had a wonderful time too," he said. "Don't worry. We'll pick up where we left off as soon as you get back."

As they left the shooting range and exited through the gun store, the owner called a hearty goodbye to them.

*

After Blaine dropped her off at her house, Riley dashed inside to explain to everyone that she was leaving. She didn't even have time for a change of clothes, but at least she had showered at Blaine's house this morning. She was relieved that her family seemed unruffled by her sudden change in plans.

They're getting used to getting along without me, she thought. She wasn't sure she really liked that idea, but she knew it was a necessity in a life like hers.

Riley checked that everything she needed was in her car and then made the short drive to Quantico. When she arrived at the BAU building, she headed straight for Brent Meredith's office. To her dismay, she encountered Jenn Roston walking in the same direction down the hall.

Riley and Jenn made eye contact for just a fleeting moment, then they both hastened on in silence.

Riley wondered whether Jenn felt as awkward right now as she did. Just yesterday they'd had an uncomfortable meeting, and Riley was still uncertain whether she had made a terrible mistake in giving Jenn that thumb drive.

But Jenn probably wasn't worried about it, Riley figured.

After all, Jenn had had the upper hand yesterday. She'd controlled the situation brilliantly to her own advantage. Had Riley ever known anyone who had been able to manipulate her that way?

She quickly realized—of course she had.

That person was Shane Hatcher.

Still walking and still facing straight ahead, the younger agent spoke quietly. "It didn't pan out."

"What?" Riley asked, without breaking her own stride.

"The financial information on the thumb drive. Hatcher used to have funds stored in those accounts. But the money has all been moved out, and the accounts are closed."

Riley resisted the impulse to say, *"I know."*

After all, Hatcher had said as much yesterday in his threatening text message.

For a moment Riley didn't know what to say. She kept walking without comment.

Did Jenn think that Riley had double-crossed her by slipping her a phony file?

Finally Riley said, "That file was all I've got. I'm not holding out on you."

Jenn didn't reply. Riley wished she had some idea whether she believed her.

She also wondered—if she had put that information to use earlier on, might Hatcher be behind bars right now? Or even dead?

When they reached the door to Meredith's office, Riley stopped, and so did Jenn.

Riley felt a touch of alarm.

Jenn was obviously going to Meredith's office too.

Why was the new agent in on this meeting? Had she told Meredith about Riley withholding information?

But Jenn just stood there, still making no eye contact.

Riley knocked on Meredith's door, and then she and Jenn went inside.

Chief Meredith was sitting behind his desk, looking as intimidating as usual.

He said, "Sit, both of you."

Riley and Jenn obediently sat down in chairs in front of the desk.

Meredith was quiet for a moment.

Then he said, "Agent Paige, Agent Roston—I'd like each of you to meet your new partner."

Riley stifled a gasp. She glanced at Jenn Roston, whose dark brown eyes had widened at the news.

"That had better not be a problem," Meredith said. "The BAU is overloaded with cases right now. With Agent Jeffreys on leave and everybody else on assignment, you get each other. Consider it settled."

Riley realized that Meredith was right. The only other agent she might really want to work with right now was Craig Huang, but he was busy watching her home.

"This is fine, sir," Riley said to Meredith.

Jenn said, "I'll be honored to work with Agent Paige, sir."

Those words surprised Riley a little. She wondered if Jenn really meant them.

"Don't get too excited," he said. "This case probably won't amount to much. Just this morning, a teenage girl's body was found buried in farmland near Angier, a small town in Iowa."

"A single murder?" Jenn asked.

"Why is this a case for the BAU?" Riley asked.

Meredith drummed his fingers on his desk.

"My guess is it probably isn't one," he said. "But another girl went missing earlier from the same town, and she still hasn't been found. It's a small, quiet place where this sort of thing just doesn't happen. Folks there say that neither girl was the type who might run away or take up with strangers."

Riley shook her head doubtfully.

"So what makes anybody think this a serial?" she asked. "Without another body, isn't that a little premature?"

Meredith shrugged.

"Yeah, that's the way I see it. But the police chief in Angier, Joseph Sinard, is in a panic about it."

Riley's forehead crinkled at the sound of the name.

"Sinard," she said. "Where have I heard that name before?"

Meredith smiled a little and said, "Maybe you're thinking of the FBI's executive assistant director, Forrest Sinard. Joe Sinard is his brother."

Riley almost rolled her eyes. It made sense now. Somebody high in the FBI food chain was being pestered by a relative in the heartland, so the case had gotten kicked to the BAU. She'd been stuck with politically driven investigations like this in the past.

Meredith said, "You two need to go out there and see if there's even a case to look at."

"What about my work on the Hatcher case?" Jenn Roston asked.

Meredith said, "We've got plenty of folks working on that—technicians and fact-finders and such. I assume they've got access to all your information."

Jenn nodded.

Meredith said, "They can spare you for a few days. If this even takes that long."

Riley's feelings were decidedly mixed. Aside from not being sure about whether she wanted to work with Jenn Roston, she didn't much look forward to wasting her time on a case that probably didn't even need BAU help.

She'd rather be helping Blaine learn to shoot.

Or doing other things with Blaine, she thought, suppressing a smile.

"So when do we leave?" Jenn asked.

"As soon as possible," Meredith said. "I've told Chief Sinard not to move the body until you get there. You'll fly into Des Moines, where Chief Sinard's people will meet you and drive you to Angier. It's about an hour from Des Moines. We have to get the plane fueled up and ready to go. In the meantime, don't go too far. Takeoff will be in less than two hours."

Riley and Jenn left Meredith's office. Riley went straight to her own office, sat down for a moment, and looked around aimlessly.

Des Moines, she thought.

She'd only been there a few times, but it was where her older sister, Wendy, lived. Riley and Wendy, estranged for years, had gotten in touch last fall when their father was dying. Wendy, not Riley, had been with Daddy when he died.

Thinking about Wendy stirred up guilt over that as well as other disturbing memories. Daddy had been hard on Riley's sister, and Wendy had run away when she was fifteen. Riley had been just five. After their father died, they had vowed to keep in touch, but so far that had amounted to a video chat.

Riley knew she should visit Wendy if she had the chance. But obviously not right away. Meredith had said that Angier was an hour away from Des Moines and that the local police would pick them up at the airport.

Maybe I can see Wendy before I come back to Quantico, she thought.

Right now, she had a little time to kill before the BAU plane took off.

And there was someone she wanted to see.

She was worried about her longtime partner, Bill Jeffreys. He lived near the base, but she hadn't seen him for several days. Bill was suffering from PTSD, and Riley knew from her own experience how tough recovery could be.

She took out her cell phone and typed a text message.

Thought I'd stop by for a few minutes. U home?

She waited a few moments. The message was marked

"delivered" but not yet read.

Riley sighed a little. She didn't have time to wait for Bill to check his messages. If she wanted to see him before she left, she had to drop by right now and just hope he was home.

*

It was only a few minutes' drive from the BAU building to Bill's little apartment in the town of Quantico. When she parked her car and started toward the building, she noticed again what a depressing place it was.

There was nothing especially wrong with it as apartment buildings went—it was an ordinary red brick building, not a tenement or anything like that. But Riley couldn't help remembering the nice suburban home where Bill had lived until his divorce. In comparison, this place had no charm at all and now he lived alone. It wasn't a happy situation for her best friend.

Riley walked into the building and headed straight toward Bill's second-story apartment. She knocked on the door and waited.

No reply came. She knocked again and still got no response.

She took out her cell phone and saw that the message was still unread.

She felt a burst of worry. Had something happened to Bill?

She reached for the doorknob and turned it.

To her alarm, the door was unlocked, and it swung open.

40

CHAPTER EIGHT

Bill's apartment looked like it had been burglarized. Riley froze in the doorway for a moment, about to draw her gun in case an intruder was still here.

Then she relaxed. Those things strewn about everywhere were food wrappers and dirty plates and glasses. The place was a mess, but it was a personal mess.

She called out Bill's name.

She heard no answer.

Then she called out again.

This time she thought she heard a groan from a nearby room.

Her heart pounded again as she hurried through the doorway into Bill's bedroom. The room was dim and the blinds were closed. Bill was lying on the unmade bed, wearing rumpled clothes and staring up at the ceiling.

"Bill, why didn't you answer when I called?" she asked somewhat irritably.

"I did," he said in a near-whisper. "You didn't hear me. Could you stop being so loud?"

Riley saw a nearly empty bourbon bottle sitting on the nightstand. Suddenly the whole scene became clear. She sat down on the bed beside him.

"I had kind of a rough night," Bill said, trying to force a feeble chuckle. "You know what that's like."

"Yeah, I do," Riley said.

After all, despair had driven her to her own binges and ensuing hangovers.

She touched his clammy forehead, imagining how sick he must feel.

"What set you off drinking?" she asked.

Bill groaned.

"It was my boys," he said.

Then he fell silent. Riley hadn't seen Bill's two sons for a while. She guessed that they must be about nine and eleven years old by now.

"What about them?" Riley asked.

"They came over to visit yesterday. It didn't go well. The place was a mess, and I was so irritable and edgy. They couldn't wait to go home. Riley, it was awful. I was awful. One more visit like that, and Maggie won't let me see them again. She's looking for any excuse to cut them out of my life for good."

Bill made a noise that sounded almost like a sob. But he didn't seem to have the energy to cry. Riley suspected he'd done plenty of crying alone.

Bill said, "Riley, if I'm no good as a father, what good am I? I'm no good as an agent, not anymore. What's left?"

Riley felt a stab of sadness in her throat.

"Bill, don't talk like that," she said. "You're a great father. And you're a great agent. Maybe not today but every other day of the year."

Bill shook his head wearily.

"I sure didn't feel like much of a dad yesterday. And I just keep hearing that shot. I keep remembering running into that building, seeing Lucy lying there bleeding."

Riley felt her own body tremble a little.

She, too, remembered all too well.

Lucy had entered an abandoned building unaware of any danger, only to be taken down by a sniper's bullet. Following close behind her, Bill had mistakenly shot a young man who had been trying to help. By the time Riley got there, Lucy had used her last ounce of strength to kill the sniper with multiple rounds.

Lucy had died moments later.

It had been an awful scene.

Riley couldn't remember many worse situations in her entire career.

She said, "I got there even later than you did."

"Yeah, but you didn't shoot an innocent kid."

"It wasn't your fault. It was dark. You had no way of knowing. Besides, that kid's doing all right now."

Bill shook his head. He held up a shaky hand.

"Look at me. Do I look like the kind of guy who can ever get back to work?"

Riley was almost angry now. He truly did look terrible—certainly not like the shrewd, brave partner she'd learned to trust with her life, nor the handsome man she'd felt rashly attracted to from time to time. And all this self-pity didn't become him.

But she sternly reminded herself …

I've been there. I know what it's like.

And when she'd been like this, Bill had always been there to get her through it.

Sometimes he'd had to be tough on her.

She figured he needed a bit of that toughness right now.

"You look like hell," she said. "But the condition you're in right now—well, you did to yourself. And you're the only one who can fix it."

Bill looked up into her eyes. She sensed that he was really paying attention to her now.

"Sit up," she said. "Pull yourself together."

Bill creakily pulled himself up and sat on the edge of the bed next to Riley.

"Has the agency assigned you a therapist?" she asked.

Bill nodded.

"Who is he?" Riley asked.

"It doesn't matter," Bill said.

"It sure as hell does matter," Riley said. "Who is he?"

Bill didn't reply. But Riley was able to guess. Bill's assigned psychiatrist was Leonard Ralston, known better to the public as "Dr. Leo." She felt herself flush with anger. But she wasn't angry with Bill now.

"Oh, my God," she said. "They've stuck you with Dr. Leo. Whose idea was that? Walder's, I'll bet."

"Like I said, it doesn't matter."

Riley wanted to shake him.

"He's a quack," she said. "You know that as well as I do. He's into hypnosis, recovered memories, all sorts of discredited crap. Don't you remember last year, when he persuaded an innocent man that he was guilty of murder? Walder likes Dr. Leo because he's written books and been on TV a lot."

"I'm not letting him mess with my head," Bill said. "I won't let him hypnotize me."

Riley was trying to keep her voice under control.

"That's not the point. You need someone who can *help* you."

"And who might that be?" Bill asked.

Riley didn't have to think about it for more than a few seconds.

"I'm going to make you some coffee," she said. "When I get back, I expect you to be on your feet and ready to get out of this place."

On her way to Bill's kitchen, Riley looked at her watch. She had little time to spare before the plane would be ready. She had to act quickly.

She took out her cell phone and punched in the personal number for Mike Nevins, a forensic psychiatrist in DC who worked for the Bureau from time to time. Riley considered him to be a close friend, and he had helped her through several of her own crises in the past, including a terrible case of PTSD.

When Mike's phone started ringing, she put her cell phone on speaker, left it on the kitchen counter, and started setting up Bill's coffeemaker. She was relieved when Mike answered the phone.

"Riley! It's great to hear from you! How are things? How is that growing family of yours?"

The sound of Mike's voice was refreshing, and she could almost see the fussy, well-dressed man and his pleasant expression. She wished she could chat with him and catch up with things, but there wasn't time for that.

"I'm fine, Mike. But I'm in a hurry. I've got to catch a plane shortly. I need a favor."

"Name it," Mike said.

"My partner, Bill Jeffreys, is going through a rough time right now after our last case."

She could hear a note of genuine concern in Mike's voice.

"Oh dear, I heard about that. Terrible thing, the death of that young protégé of yours. Is it true that your partner has been put on leave? Something to do with shooting the wrong man?"

"That's right. He needs your help. And he needs it right away. He's drinking, Mike. I've never seen him this bad."

There was a short silence.

"I'm not sure I understand," Mike said. "Hasn't he been assigned a therapist?"

"Yeah, but he's not doing Bill any good."

Now there was a note of caution in Mike's voice.

"I don't know, Riley. I'm generally not comfortable taking patients who are already under someone else's care."

Riley felt a flash of worry. She didn't have time to deal with Mike's ethical scruples right now.

"Mike, they've assigned him to Dr. Leo."

Another silence fell.

I'll bet that did the trick, Riley thought. She knew perfectly well that Mike despised the celebrity therapist with all his heart.

44

Finally Mike said, "When can Bill come in?"

"What are you doing right now?"

"I'm in my office. I'll be tied up for a couple of hours but I can be available after that."

"Great. He can get there by then. But please let me know if he doesn't show up."

"I'll do that."

As they ended the call, coffee was trickling into the carafe. Riley poured a cup and went back to Bill's bedroom. He wasn't there. But the door to the adjoining bathroom was closed, and Riley could hear Bill's electric razor on the other side.

Riley rapped on the door.

"Yeah, I'm decent," Bill said.

Riley opened the door and saw that Bill was shaving. She set the coffee down on the edge of the sink.

"I made you an appointment with Mike Nevins," she said.

"For when?"

"Right now. As soon as you can get out of here and drive there. I'll text you his office address. I've got to go."

Bill looked surprised. Of course, Riley hadn't told him anything about being in a hurry.

"I've got a case in Iowa," Riley explained. "The plane's waiting right now. Don't skip out on Mike Nevins. I'll find out about it, and there will be hell to pay."

Bill grumbled, but then said, "OK, I'll get there."

Riley turned to leave. Then she thought of something she wasn't sure she should bring up.

Finally she said, "Bill, Shane Hatcher's still on the loose. There are agents posted around my house. But I got a threatening text from him, and nobody knows about it except you. I don't *think* he'd attack my family, but I can't be sure. I wonder if maybe …"

Bill nodded.

"I'll keep an eye on things," he said. "I need to do something useful."

Riley gave him a quick hug and left the apartment.

As she walked toward her car, she checked her watch again.

If she didn't run into any traffic, she'd make it to the airstrip in time.

Now she had to start thinking about her new case, but she wasn't particularly worried about it. This one probably wouldn't take long.

After all, how could a single small-town murder demand much in the way of time and effort?

CHAPTER NINE

Even as she walked across the tarmac toward the plane Riley started psyching herself up for her new case. But there was one thing she needed to do before she got too wrapped up in it.

She sent a text to Mike Nevins.

Text me when Bill shows up. Text me if he doesn't.

She breathed a sigh of relief when Mike responded immediately.

Will do.

Riley told herself that she'd done all she could do for Bill right now, and it was up to him to make the most of her help. If anybody could help Bill deal with the things that were tormenting him, Riley was sure that Mike could.

She climbed the steps into the cabin, where Jenn Roston was already seated and working on her laptop computer. Jenn glanced up and nodded as Riley sat down across the table from her.

Riley nodded back.

Then Riley looked out the window during takeoff and as the plane climbed to cruising altitude. She didn't like the chilly silence between her and Jenn. She wondered if maybe Jenn didn't like it either. These flights were normally a good time to talk over details of a case. But there was really nothing to say about this one yet. The body had just been found that morning, after all.

Riley took a magazine out of her bag and tried to read, but she couldn't focus her attention on the words. Having Jenn sit across from her quietly like that was too distracting. Instead, Riley just sat there pretending to read.

The story of my life these days, she thought.

Pretending and lying were becoming all too routine.

Finally Jenn looked up from her computer.

"Agent Paige, I meant what I said at the meeting with

47

Meredith," she said.

"Pardon?" Riley asked, looking up from her magazine.

"About being honored to work with you. It's been a dream of mine. I've followed your work ever since I started at the academy."

For a moment, Riley didn't know what to say. Jenn had said much the same thing to her before. But again, Riley couldn't tell from Jenn's expression whether she was sincere.

"I've heard great things about you," Riley said.

As noncommittal as it sounded, at least it was true. Under different circumstances, Riley would have been thrilled at the chance to work with a smart new agent.

Riley added with a weak smile, "But I wouldn't get my expectations up if I were you—not for this case."

"Right," Jenn said. "It's probably not even a case for the BAU. We're liable to fly back to Quantico tonight. Well, there will be others."

Jenn turned her attention back to her computer. Riley wondered whether she was working on the Shane Hatcher files. And of course, she worried anew that she shouldn't have given Jenn that thumb drive.

But as she sat there thinking about it, she realized something. If Jenn had really meant to double-cross her by asking for that information, wouldn't she have used it against her already?

She remembered what Jenn had said to her yesterday.

"I'm pretty sure we want exactly the same thing—to put an end to Shane Hatcher's criminal career."

If that was true, Jenn really was Riley's ally.

But how could Riley be sure? She sat there considering whether she should broach the subject.

She hadn't told Jenn about the threat she had received from Hatcher.

Was there really any reason not to?

Might Jenn actually be able to help her in some way? Maybe, but Riley still didn't feel ready to take that step.

Meanwhile, it seemed downright weird that her new partner still called her Agent Paige while insisting that Riley call her by her first name.

"Jenn," she said.

Jenn looked up from her computer.

"I think you should call me Riley," Riley said.

Jenn smiled a little and turned her attention back to her

computer.

Riley set her magazine aside and stared out the window at the clouds below. The sun was shining brightly, but Riley didn't find it cheerful.

She felt terribly alone. She missed having Bill around to trust and confide in.

And she missed Lucy so much that she ached inside.

*

When the plane taxied into the Des Moines International Airport, Riley was able to check her cell phone. She was pleased to see that she'd gotten a message from Mike Nevins.

Bill's here with me right now.

It was one less thing to worry about.

A police car was waiting outside the plane. Two cops from Angier introduced themselves at the base of the boarding steps. Darryl Laird was a gangly young man in his twenties, and Howard Doty was a much shorter man in his forties.

Both had stunned expressions on their faces.

"We're sure glad you're here," Doty told Riley and Jenn as the two cops escorted them to the car.

Laird said, "This is whole thing is just …"

The younger man shook his head without finishing his thought.

These poor guys, Riley thought.

They were just regular small-town cops. Murders were surely few and far between in a small Iowa town. Maybe the older cop had handled one or two homicides at one time or other, but Riley guessed that the younger one hadn't been through anything like this before.

As Doty started to drive, Riley asked the two cops to tell her and Jenn whatever they could about what had happened.

Doty said, "The girl's name was Katy Philbin, seventeen years old. A student at Wilson High. Her parents own the local pharmacy. Nice girl, everybody liked her. Old George Tully came across her body just this morning when he and his boys were getting ready to do the spring planting. Tully's got a farm just a short way out of Angier."

Jenn asked, "Any idea how long she'd been buried there?"

"You'll have to ask Chief Sinard about that. Or the medical examiner."

Riley thought back to what little Meredith had been able to tell them about the situation.

"What about the other girl?" she asked. "The one who went missing earlier?"

"Holly Struthers is her name," Laird said. "She was ... uh, I guess she *is* a student at our other high school, Lincoln. She's been missing for about a week. The whole town had been hoping she'd just turn up sooner or later. But now ... well, I guess we've got to keep on hoping."

"And praying," Doty added.

Riley felt an odd chill when he said that. She couldn't begin to guess how often she'd heard people say that they were praying that a missing person would turn up safe and sound. She never had the impression that prayer helped one way or the other.

Does it even make people feel better? she wondered.

She couldn't imagine why or how.

It was a bright, clear afternoon when the car left Des Moines and headed out onto a wide highway. Soon Doty exited onto a two-lane road that stretched over the slightly rolling countryside.

Riley felt a strange, gnawing feeling in her stomach. It took her a few moments to realize that her feeling had nothing to do with the case—at least not directly.

She often felt this way whenever she had a job to do in the Midwest. She didn't normally suffer from a fear of open spaces—agoraphobia, she thought it was called. But vast plains and prairies stirred up a unique kind of anxiety in her.

Riley didn't know which was worse—the sheer flat plains she'd seen in states like Nebraska, stretching out as far as the eye could see, or monotonous rolling prairie like this, the same farmhouses, towns, and fields seeming to appear over and over again. Either way, she found it unsettling, even a little nauseating.

Despite the Midwest's reputation as a land of wholesome, all-American values, it somehow didn't surprise her that people committed murder here. As far as she was concerned, the countryside alone would be enough to drive a person crazy.

Partly to get her mind off the landscape, Riley took out her cell phone to text her whole family as a group—April, Jilly, Liam, and Gabriela.

Got here safely.

She thought for a moment, then added …

Miss you all already. But I'll probably be back before U know it.

*

After about an hour on the two-lane highway, Doty turned the car off onto a gravel road.

As he kept on driving, he said, "We're coming up on George Tully's land now."

Riley looked around. The landscape looked exactly the same—huge stretches of unplanted fields interrupted by gullies, fences, and lines of trees. She did notice a single large house in the midst of it all, standing next to a ramshackle barn. She figured that must be where Tully lived with his family.

It was an odd-looking house that appeared to have been added onto and cobbled together over the years, probably for quite a few generations.

Soon a medical examiner's vehicle came into sight, parked on the shoulder of the road. Several other cars were parked nearby. Doty parked right behind the examiner's van, and Riley and Jenn followed him and his younger partner out onto a recently tilled field.

Riley saw three men standing over a dug up spot. She couldn't see what had been found there, but she did glimpse a bit of brightly colored clothing fluttering in the spring breeze.

That's where she was buried, she realized.

And at that moment, Riley was hit by a strange gut feeling.

Gone was any sense that she and Jenn would have nothing to do here.

They had work to do—a girl was dead and they wouldn't stop until the killer was found.

CHAPTER TEN

Two people were standing by the freshly revealed body. Riley headed straight toward one of them, a brawny man about her own age.

"Chief Joseph Sinard, I assume," she said, offering her hand.

He nodded and shook her hand.

"Folks around here just call me Joe,"

Sinard indicated an obese, bored-looking man in his fifties who was standing beside him, "This is Barry Teague, the county medical examiner. You two are the FBI folks we've been expecting, I guess."

Riley and Jenn produced their badges and introduced themselves.

"Here's our victim," Sinard said.

He pointed down into the shallow hole, where a young woman lay carelessly splayed, wearing a bright orange sundress. The dress was hitched up over her thighs, and Riley could see that her underwear had been removed. She wasn't wearing any shoes. Her face was unnaturally pale, and her open mouth still had dirt in it. Her eyes were wide open. The soiled body was dull in color, no longer the shade of any living human being.

Riley shuddered a little. She seldom felt any emotion when seeing a dead body—she'd seen far too many of them over the years. But this girl reminded her too much of April.

Riley turned toward the medical examiner.

"Have you come to any conclusions, Mr. Teague?"

Barry Teague crouched down next to the hole, and Riley crouched next to him.

"It's bad—real bad," he said in a voice that expressed no emotion at all.

He pointed to the girl's thighs.

"See those bruises?" he asked. "Looks to me like she was raped."

Riley didn't say so, but she felt sure that he was correct. Judging from the smell, she also guessed that the girl had died the night before last, and that she'd been buried here for most of that time.

She asked the ME, "What do you think was the cause of death?"

Teague let out an impatient-sounding growl.

"Don't know," he said. "Maybe if you federal folks let me haul the body out of here and do my job, I might be able to tell you."

Riley bristled inside. The man's resentment of the FBI's presence was palpable. Were she and Jenn Roston going to face a lot of local resistance?

She reminded herself that it had been Chief Sinard who called in the request. At least she could count on Sinard's cooperation.

She told the ME, "You can take her away now."

She got to her feet and looked around. She saw an elderly man some fifty feet away, leaning against a tractor and staring straight toward the body.

"Who's that?" she asked Chief Sinard.

"George Tully," Sinard said.

Riley remembered that George Tully was the owner of this land.

She and Jenn walked over to him and introduced themselves. Tully seemed barely to notice their presence. He kept staring toward the body as Teague's team carefully got ready to move it.

Riley said to him, "Mr. Tully, I understand that you found the girl."

He nodded dully, still not taking his eyes off the body.

Riley said, "I know this is hard. But could you please tell me what happened?"

Tully spoke in a vague, distant-sounding voice.

"Not much to tell. Me and the boys came out this morning early for planting. I noticed something odd about the soil there. The look of it bothered me so I started to dig … and then there she was."

Riley sensed that Tully wasn't going to be able to tell her much.

Jenn said, "Do you have any idea when the body might have been buried here?"

Tully shook his head mutely.

Riley looked around for a moment. The field seemed to have been recently tilled.

"When did you till this field?" she asked.

"Day before last. No, the day before that. We were just getting started seeding it today."

Riley turned this over in her mind. It seemed consistent with her guess that the girl had been killed and buried the night before last.

Tully squinted as he continued to stare ahead.

"Chief Sinard told me her name," he said. "Katy—her last name was Philbin, I think. Odd, I didn't recognize that name. I didn't recognize her either. Time was …"

He paused for a moment.

"Time was when I knew pretty much all the families in town, and their kids too. Times have changed."

There was a numb, aching sadness in his voice.

Riley could feel his pain now. She felt sure he'd lived on this land all his life, and so had his parents and grandparents and great-grandparents, and he'd hoped to pass the farm down to his own children and grandchildren.

He'd never imagined something like this could possibly happen here.

She also realized something else—that Tully had been standing in exactly this same spot for hours, staring with horrified disbelief at the poor girl's body. He'd found the body in the early morning, reported it, and then hadn't been able to make himself move from this spot. Now that the body was being taken away, maybe he'd leave soon.

But Riley knew that the horror wouldn't leave him.

His words echoed through her head …

"Times have changed."

He must have felt as though the world had gone mad.

And maybe it has, Riley thought.

"We're terribly sorry this happened," Riley told him.

Then she and Jenn headed back toward the excavated spot.

Teague's team now had the covered body up on a gurney. They were awkwardly moving it over the tilled soil toward the medical examiner's vehicle.

Teague approached Riley and Jenn. He spoke in that seemingly perpetual monotone of his.

"In answer to your question, how'd she die … I got a better look, and she'd been bludgeoned, hit more than once. So that's it."

Without another word he turned and walked away to join his team.

Jenn let out a scoff of annoyance.

"Well, it sounds like the examination is done as far as he's concerned," she said. "He's a real sweetheart."

Riley shook her head in dismayed agreement.

Then she walked toward Chief Sinard and asked, "Was anything else found with the body? A handbag? Cell phone?"

"No," Sinard said. "Whoever did it must have kept those."

"Agent Roston and I need to meet with the girl's family as soon as possible."

Chief Sinard frowned a little.

"That's going to be pretty rough," he said. "Her dad, Drew, was just out here a little while ago to identify the body. He was in pretty bad shape when he left."

"I understand," Riley said. "But it's really necessary."

Chief Sinard nodded, took a key out of his pocket, and pointed to a nearby car.

"I figure you two are going to need your own transportation," he said. "You can use my car as long as you're here. I'll drive on ahead in a police vehicle and show you where the Philbins live."

Riley let Jenn take the keys and drive. Soon they were following Sinard's police car toward the town of Angier.

Riley asked her new partner, "What are your thoughts at this point?"

Jenn drove in silence for a moment as she seemed to mull the question over.

Then she said, "We know that the victim was seventeen years old—within the age range of about half of the victims of this kind of crime. It's still an unusual case. Most victims of serial sexual predators are prostitutes. This one may fall into the ten percent who are victims of acquaintances of one kind or another."

Jenn paused again.

Then she added, "More than half of these kinds of murders are by strangulation. But blunt force trauma is the second most frequent cause of death. So in that sense this murder may not be atypical. Still, we've got a lot to learn. The most important question is whether we're dealing with a serial killer."

Riley nodded grimly in agreement. Jenn wasn't saying anything she didn't already know, but whatever her misgivings might be about her new partner, at least she was well informed. And they were both facing the possibility of a terrible answer to that last question, both hoping the answer was "no."

In a matter of minutes they were following Sinard into Angier and driving down Main Street. Riley saw nothing to distinguish it from other Main Streets she'd seen throughout the Midwest—bland and characterless rows of shops, some of them old and some of them new. She detected no hint of charm or quaintness. Riley had much the same feeling about the town as she'd had during the drive across the rolling prairie—a sense of something dark lurking behind the veneer of Midwestern wholesomeness.

She almost gave voice to her thoughts. But she quickly reminded herself that it wasn't Bill who was at her side, but a young woman she barely knew and still didn't know if she could trust.

Would Jenn Roston share Riley's feelings, or even want to hear them?

Riley had no way of knowing, and it bothered her.

It was hard not having a partner she could talk to freely, expressing ideas as they came whether they made sense or not. She missed Bill more with every passing minute—and Lucy as well.

The victim's family lived in an older but well-kept brick bungalow on a quiet street with large trees in the yard. The curb and the driveway were crowded with parked vehicles. Riley guessed the Philbins had a lot of visitors at the moment.

Sinard stopped his marked patrol car in the street and got out. He gestured Jenn toward a small parking space and stood giving directions to help her squeeze the car into place. Once the car was parked, Riley and Jenn got out and walked toward the house. Chief Sinard was already on his way to the front door, his patrol car still double-parked in the street.

Riley wondered—were they going to meet an innocent grieving family and many sincere and well-meaning friends and loved ones?

Or were they about to encounter people who might be capable of murder?

Either way, Riley always dreaded this kind of visit.

CHAPTER ELEVEN

For several long moments, Riley couldn't put her finger on what struck her as odd about the house where Katy Philbin had lived. As soon as she and Jenn walked in through the front door she had felt a tinge of unease.

As Riley had expected, the living room was crowded with people—well-wishing friends and neighbors, most of them women. In typical small-town style, the community was pulling together to help a family in a time of crisis.

So why did the scene strike her as somehow strange?

Then Riley realized—everything seemed uncannily organized and proper. All the people appeared to be wearing their Sunday best. They had brought food and had arranged it on the dining room table, and everybody was either tending to assigned tasks or eating and talking in hushed voices.

It reminded Riley of many funeral receptions she'd been to, the kind of event that might take place after a burial. It hardly seemed possible that Katy Philbin's desecrated body had been found just this morning. How had this orderly gathering come together so spontaneously and quickly?

It's that kind of town, she reminded herself.

Riley felt weirdly out of place in this world where everybody seemed to know just what to do at any given moment and for any occasion. It had been a long, long time since she'd lived in this kind of community—not since she'd been a child, really. And she was far from comfortable about being here in this kind of setting.

All this neighborly activity seemed too rehearsed, too automatic, for Riley's liking. After all, the girl's death hinted that something evil lurked beneath this veneer of rural propriety and decency. She couldn't shake off an irrational feeling that all this kindness and good will was an enormous lie.

Riley and Jenn followed close behind Chief Sinard. He was saying kind things to everybody as he moved among them, and he obviously knew everybody by name.

Sinard struck Riley as truly the perfect small-town police chief.

He also had the ruddy complexion of a man who had been exposed to all the weather that the Midwest had to offer. Riley felt sure he'd lived in this part of the country—perhaps this very town—all his life.

Riley remembered that his brother was Forrest Sinard, the FBI's executive assistant director. She'd met Forrest Sinard a few times, and he'd struck her as witty and urbane, hardly the rural type at all. She wondered how two brothers had wound up following such different paths in their lives.

A man and woman seated in the back of the room were the center of everyone's attention. Chief Sinard introduced Riley and Jenn to Katy's parents, Drew and Lisa Philbin.

Lisa seemed barely aware of the two agents' presence.

"Why not?" she kept asking her husband. "Why can't I?"

"It's best not to, honey," Drew kept saying, holding her hands tightly. "Believe me, it's best."

"If not now, when?"

"I don't know. Soon maybe. Not yet."

Riley understood what was going on right away. She remembered Chief Sinard mentioning that Drew had been to George Tully's field to identify his daughter's body. Now his wife wanted to see the body too, but Drew wanted to spare her the horror—at least for the time being.

Lisa looked all around in tearful confusion.

"She's my daughter, and I'm her mother," she said, choking back a sob. "Katy needs me. Where is she?"

Riley felt a pang of sympathy.

Denial, she thought.

It was going to take a while before the reality of Lisa's daughter's death sank in.

Meanwhile, Riley guessed that she and Jenn ought to address most of their questions to Drew.

She said, "Mr. Philbin, we're terribly sorry for your loss, and we hate to disturb you. But my colleague and I need to ask you a few questions."

Still holding his wife's hands tightly, Drew simply nodded.

"When did you notice that your daughter had gone missing?" Riley asked.

Drew knitted his brow as if trying to remember.

Shock, Riley thought.

Although he had accepted the reality of his daughter's death,

Riley knew that he was still struggling with confusion. She worried whether he might find it difficult to answer even the simplest questions.

"Last night, I think," he said. "No, the night before last."

Lisa appeared to be emerging from her fog of denial at least a little. She said, "Yes, it was the night before last. She was out late for a club meeting at her school. We expected her late, but she didn't come home at all."

"Did you report her missing?" Jenn asked.

Lisa and Drew looked at each other uncertainly.

"We did—didn't we?" Lisa asked her husband.

Drew stammered, "Y-yes. We called Chief Sinard … I can't remember exactly …"

Riley looked at Chief Sinard, who said, "It was Lisa who called me. She called last night. I put out a local alert online."

Riley noticed that Jenn seemed to react to this information with suspicion. They knew that Katy had almost certainly been killed Wednesday night. She hadn't come home, but her parents hadn't reported her missing until last night, Thursday night.

Jenn asked Lisa, "You mean you waited a full day? Didn't you know that another girl had already gone missing?"

Lisa's eyes darted among Jenn's, Riley's, and Chief Sinard's faces.

She replied, "We did hear about that. But we didn't actually know her. And she just ran away, didn't she? It was … it had … nothing to do with us … with Katy … Did it?"

Riley knew there was nothing she could say in reply. After all, as far as anybody knew at this point, Holly really had run away and might turn up at any time.

But that didn't stop her partner from asking questions.

Speaking rather sharply, Jenn said, "I'm afraid I don't understand. Why wait so long? Didn't you start worrying when she didn't show up Wednesday night?"

Riley started to cut her partner off, but she told herself that Jenn's suspicion was understandable. At this point, every person they met—especially male—might be Katy's killer. That might even include Drew Philbin.

But Riley also worried that Jenn might let her suspicion get the best of her. She was definitely not as skillful at questioning as Lucy had been. Even Bill had been better at putting others at ease. Riley knew that she herself tended to be blunt sometimes and she had depended on her partners to be friendlier.

Lisa seemed to be on the verge of panic.

She stammered, "I … we … this isn't …"

Drew gently interrupted his wife.

"What Lisa means to say is that this has happened before. I don't mean that Katy was ever gone for *this* long. But she stayed out until the wee hours of the morning once before without calling home. We thought she was doing something like that again."

Lisa nodded and chimed in, "And we *did* call other people yesterday morning—her ex-boyfriend, some of her friends, even a couple of her teachers."

"But not Chief Sinard?" Jenn asked.

Lisa looked shaken and ashamed.

"We just … we didn't think …"

Before Jenn could prod Lisa and Drew with more questions, Riley touched her on the shoulder to quiet her. She ignored the sidewise glance that Jenn gave her. Riley had a pretty good idea why the couple might not have called the police chief right away, but now was no time to get into it.

Riley asked the couple, "Did Katy mention being frightened of anything or anybody recently? Was anything making her uneasy?"

Lisa and Drew looked thoughtful for a moment.

"Not exactly," Lisa said. "But she hadn't been herself lately. She'd been quiet, stayed in her room a lot, and she seemed … I don't know, sad or upset about something. She wouldn't tell me what it was all about."

Drew shook his head.

"Lisa's right," he said. "She was behaving oddly. She used to be so happy and enthusiastic about everything—school, sports, friends."

Lisa said, "We kept waiting for her to pull out of it. Whenever I asked her what was the matter, she said it was nothing."

Lisa paused for a moment. Then she said, "I think she changed when she broke up with Dustin."

Riley's attention quickened.

"Her boyfriend?" Riley asked.

"That's right," Drew said. "Dustin Russo."

"Did she say what the breakup was about?" Riley asked.

Lisa shrugged slightly.

"No. She wasn't telling us much of anything around then."

Riley asked, "Did anything about Dustin's behavior worry the two of you?"

"Not really," Drew said. "I mean, he's a kid. He's just a regular teenage kid."

"Did Katy keep a diary?"

"If she did, it would be on her laptop. We never snooped."

"Of course," Riley said. "But we'll need to go over it."

Drew was silent for a moment, then said, "Anything that might help. It's upstairs, in …"

"I'll have someone pick it up," Riley said.

Then Riley looked at Jenn, whose mind seemed to be elsewhere. But Riley knew they needed to find the kid and talk to him.

Riley said to the couple, "Thanks so much for your help. I know this is terribly difficult."

She handed Drew her FBI card.

"Please call me if you think of anything else you think we should know. We're terribly sorry for your loss."

As Riley and Jenn turned away from the couple, they saw that Chief Sinard was now surrounded by houseguests, who were asking him all kinds of questions. Riley and Jenn managed to push among them and pull him aside.

Riley asked him, "Do you know a boy named Dustin Russo?"

Chief Sinard nodded.

"Yeah, Rae and Derek Russo's boy," he said. "He was dating Katy the last I heard."

"What are your impressions of him?" Riley asked.

"We need to talk to him," Jenn said.

Chief Sinard looked at his watch.

"Well, school's out, so we can probably catch him at home. I'll drive ahead of you and take you there."

Riley didn't especially want Sinard along for the interview. She and Jenn would do better without him. Fortunately, it wasn't hard to think of an excuse.

"No, you're needed here," she said, indicating the people who had surrounded him. "Just give us his address and directions to his house."

After Chief Sinard jotted down the information, Riley said, "Oh, and Drew said that Katy's laptop is upstairs. Would you have someone pick it up? We should check it out."

"I'll do that," Sinard said, then turned back to the questioning guests.

Riley and Jenn left the house and walked to the car. Saying nothing and looking grim, Jenn got into the driver's seat.

Without comment, Riley took the passenger's seat. She glanced over at the younger agent, wondering why she was sensing tension between them. She remembered that Jenn had gotten quiet while they were talking to the Philbins. She wasn't sure what was wrong and she wasn't sure she wanted to know.

As Jenn drove, Riley gazed out the side window, wondering whether their partnership was going to work out.

The question worried her. She hoped she'd have more of an answer to it after they'd dealt with Dustin Russo.

But right now she couldn't help but think she might be better off working this case on her own. Or with someone else.

Riley missed Bill and Lucy more and more.

But she couldn't think about that now.

Possibly—just possibly—they were on their way to meet a young murderer.

CHAPTER TWELVE

Jenn Roston was quietly seething as she drove toward the Russo house. Riley had cut her short during the interview, and it really pissed her off. Should she just let it go, or should she mention it?

Finally Jenn said to Riley, "You wouldn't let me ask the questions I wanted to ask."

"When was that?" Riley said.

"It was when the Philbins couldn't explain why they hadn't called Chief Sinard earlier. I'm sure they were hiding something. We needed to put more pressure on them. You went too easy on them."

To Jenn's surprise, Riley let out a small chuckle.

"So are you thinking Drew Philbin raped and killed his own daughter?" she asked.

"Aren't you?" Jenn asked. "I mean, isn't it a possibility?"

"It might be. We sure haven't eliminated him as a suspect."

Jenn was starting to feel confused now. She said, "They didn't call Chief Sinard for a full day. That seemed weird. I wanted to know why. Didn't you? Maybe we could have cracked this case right then and there."

Riley laughed a little again and asked, "Did you ever live in a small town, Jenn?"

Jenn wondered what Riley's question had to do with the matter at hand.

"No," she said. "I was a city kid, born and raised in Richmond."

She glanced and saw that Riley was looking reflectively out the window.

"Well, I grew up in some small towns," Riley said. "One was a little town called Slippery Rock, up in the Appalachian Mountains. It had a population of a few hundred. Whenever my father and I walked by the liquor store, he'd go inside and buy whiskey—lots of it, he drank a lot."

Riley paused for a moment, seemingly lost in memory.

"I'd look in the window when Daddy was in there. I never, ever saw anybody else in there except old Mr. Stalnaker, who owned the store. He'd always talk to Daddy for a while—he never seemed to have anybody else to talk to."

Riley laughed again.

"Well, I was really little and didn't know any better, so one time I asked Daddy, 'Doesn't anybody in Slippery Rock drink except you?' He laughed. That surprised me, because he was a bitter man and didn't laugh a lot …"

Riley's voice faded away. For a moment, Jenn wondered if she was going to finish her story.

Then she said, "He told me, 'Sure, kid. Most of the men in this shit hole of a town drink more than I do. It's just they don't buy their liquor at Mr. Stalnaker's place. Their wives won't let them. They have to drive on over to Lyons or Tryon and buy their booze there.'"

Riley chuckled.

"It was a town full of drunks, and everybody knew that everybody else drank, but they were also decent churchgoers, and they didn't dare be seen in a liquor store. Not Daddy, of course. He didn't give a damn what anybody thought."

Riley fell silent. It took Jenn a few moments to understand the point she was making.

Finally Jenn said, "I think I get it. In a small town like this, appearances are everything."

Riley nodded and said, "Angier's a bigger town than Slippery Rock. But it's still rural America. We're in a place where appearances can be a lot more important that what's really going on *behind* those appearances. At least to the locals."

Jenn turned that over in her mind as she continued to drive. She had never lived in a small town, but she had certainly known people to whom appearances were all-important.

Then she said, "So … Drew and Lisa Philbin were worried about their daughter when she didn't show up that first night and all the next day. But they were also worried what people might think if they knew about it. The first night, they probably didn't call anybody. The next day they called only a handful of people at first—the boyfriend, friends, teachers. But …"

Riley nodded and finished Jenn's thought.

"But not Chief Sinard, at least not right away. They knew he'd put the word out, and everybody would find out about it. And of course, that's exactly what happened when they reported Katy missing."

It all seemed clear to Jenn now.

Why hadn't she been able to figure it out before?

Because I'm not Riley Paige, she thought. She realized that she simply lacked the wide range of experience with people that an agent needed.

Then Riley asked, "Do you still think Drew Philbin is our killer?"

Jenn shrugged a little.

"I don't know. We still can't count him out."

"Anything else?"

Jenn paused, putting her thoughts together.

She reasoned out loud, "I don't think we're dealing with a serial killer. The disposal of the body was too sloppy, too amateurish."

"Well," Riley said, "some serials don't conceal the body at all. They just dump them or even display them. I've seen victims left hanging in chains or made up to look like dolls."

Jenn remembered learning about those cases during her classroom days.

She said, "But a killer who doesn't want people to even know a murder has been committed does conceal the body. I just think that a serial would probably do a better job of it. And I've got a gut feeling about the boyfriend. Katy's death sounds like a lovers' spat turned really mean."

"What about the other missing girl?"

"I think she'll probably turn up alive any day now."

"Maybe we'll know more soon," Riley said. Then in a softer voice she added, "Towns like this give me the creeps."

They were only a few blocks from the Russo house now. As she kept driving, Jenn mulled over everything that Riley had just said.

It was all very insightful, of course—but what else did she expect from Riley Paige?

But this was also the first time Riley had opened up to her about anything personal.

Is she starting to trust me? Jenn wondered.

Riley had actually told Jenn very little that she didn't already know. Jenn had studied Riley's life in great detail—including her childhood as a military brat spent in small towns like Slippery Rock

65

and Lanton, Virginia. She knew about Riley's cases.

She didn't know all of Riley's personal secrets. But she did know a lot more about Riley than Riley realized.

A lot more than she knows about me, Jenn thought wryly.

After all, Jenn had secrets of her own.

*

Riley felt uneasy during the rest of the ride. She wondered why she'd told Jenn all that about herself and her father.

She hadn't meant to let her guard down like that. But it was all too easy to forget that it wasn't Bill who was in the car beside her.

At least she hadn't shared any damaging information.

And it didn't have anything to do with Shane Hatcher.

Still, Riley decided that she'd better put her guard back up. For the time being, she just hoped that she and Jenn could work effectively together on whatever was going to happen next. After all, Jenn had just said that she had a gut feeling that the Russo kid was their killer.

Riley's own gut hadn't told her much of anything just yet. But Jenn was a talented young agent. And if she was right, they might be on the verge of making an arrest.

They soon pulled up to the house and parked. The Russos lived in a neighborhood much like the one they had just visited, with perfect lawns and small, comfortable, well-kept houses.

Riley and Jenn got out of the car, walked up to the front door, and knocked. They were greeted by an anxious-looking woman wearing an apron. She was about Riley's age. Riley and Jenn produced their badges and introduced themselves.

"Are you Dustin Russo's mother?" Riley asked.

"Yes," the woman said. "I'm Rae Russo."

"Is Dustin at home?"

"Yes."

"We'd like to talk to him if that's possible."

The woman looked uncertain for a moment.

Then she said, "Come on in."

Riley and Jenn followed her into an immaculately tidy little home.

The woman called her son's name upstairs. No one answered.

She called again, "Dustin, it's the FBI. They want to talk to you."

Still no one answered.

The woman shook her head worriedly.

"He came home from school a little while ago and shut himself up in his room first thing, without saying a word to me. He's been like that for days now—in a terrible mood, not like himself at all."

Riley's nerves started to prickle.

"We really do need to talk to him," she said.

"What about?" Rae Russo asked.

Jenn said, "Are you aware that Katy Philbin was found dead this morning?"

Rae's eyes widened with alarm.

"Oh, yes. It's just awful. But surely you don't think—"

"We just need to talk to your son," Riley said.

Rae Russo nervously led them up the stairs. Then she knocked on the bedroom door.

"Dustin, these people really need to talk to you."

Still there was no answer.

Riley wondered—was he even in there? If so, might he be dangerous?

Riley's hand hovered near her weapon and silently signaled Jenn to do the same.

She knew they had to be ready for anything.

CHAPTER THIRTEEN

Riley managed to resist the temptation to draw her weapon.

She said to Rae, "Open the door, please."

Rae hesitated, then nodded nervously and turned the doorknob and pushed the door open.

It was a small dormer room, with the typical clutter of an adolescent occupant. Lying on the bed was a muscular teenager with a crew cut—Riley remembered Chief Sinard mentioning that Dustin was a football player.

His eyes were closed and he didn't seem to notice that anyone had entered. Riley quickly realized why. Even from the doorway, she could hear the blare of music he was listening to on a headset.

His mother called his name again. His eyes snapped open and he sat up and took off his earphones. He looked at his visitors with a blank expression.

"What's up?" he asked in a dull-sounding voice.

Riley and Jenn showed their badges and introduced themselves again. The boy scratched his head. If he was surprised, Riley could hardly detect it. He had a broad, bulky, immobile face with beady eyes.

Riley silently gestured for Rae Russo to leave the room, which she did, closing the door behind her.

Riley said to Dustin, "I take it you know about what happened to Katy Philbin."

"Yeah, kind of," Dustin said, scratching himself idly. "Everybody was talking about it at school. Bummer."

Riley and Jenn exchanged glances.

Jenn said, "You don't sound too broken up about it. Weren't you two dating recently?"

He shrugged and said, "She broke up with me."

Jenn stepped toward him and spoke in a sharp voice.

"Does that mean she deserved what happened to her?"

Riley started worrying anew. Jenn sounded like she might be jumping to conclusions already. After their visit to the Philbins', Riley knew that Jenn's interviewing skills were limited. And

68

Riley's own weren't exactly nuanced. Neither of them was likely to coax answers out of a reluctant witness.

If only Bill or Lucy were here, she thought.

Dustin's face didn't register any particular emotion.

"Huh-uh," he said. "What happened to her was awful. She was a really nice girl. She was …"

He seemed to be searching for the right word.

"Pretty," he finally said. "Everybody liked her. I liked her a lot."

Then he sat staring again.

Jenn asked, "Where were you on Wednesday night?"

"What time?" Dustin asked.

"All of it," Jenn said, moving still closer to him. "From when school let out until the next morning."

Dustin shrugged a little.

"Right here," he said. "I don't go out much anymore. I don't feel like it. You can ask my mom."

Riley noticed Jenn glancing toward the dormer window. She knew what Jenn was thinking. It would have been possible for Dustin to slip out the window without his mother noticing. But the window faced the street. How likely was it that he could have gotten out unnoticed?

In a sleepy neighborhood like this, Riley couldn't discount the possibility.

When Dustin spoke again, Riley heard a slight tremor in his voice.

"I don't know what happened," he said. "She was so happy, so much fun to be with. Then one day she was all different. I couldn't tell whether she was angry or sad, but she didn't want to be around me anymore."

Riley was slightly startled.

Was Dustin still in denial that his girlfriend had been murdered?

Or was something else going on here?

Riley asked, "Do you think whatever was bothering her had anything to do with her murder?"

"I don't know. Maybe. I just don't know."

Riley noticed that Jenn was staring at her. Riley guessed she was wondering whether they were going to arrest this boy, or at least treat him like a suspect. Riley still hadn't made up her mind.

She said to Dustin, "So you don't know why she changed?"

"No idea," Dustin said.

"Do you know anybody who might know?"

Dustin squinted with thought.

"Yeah, maybe. Daisy Kinney and Taylor McGrath are—
were—Katy's best friends. She talked to them about pretty much
everything."

"Where might we find them?" Riley asked.

Dustin looked over at the clock on his nightstand.

"Well, if you head over to the school right now, you might
catch them. They're on the soccer team, like Katy was. They've got
a game this afternoon against Cobbtown High School. It ought to be
wrapping up right about now."

Riley quickly assessed the situation, then made a decision.

"Thanks for talking to us," she said. "Let us know if you think
of anything we should know. Meanwhile, we need for you to stay in
town."

Dustin shrugged again.

"I'll be here," he said. "I'm not going anywhere."

Jenn looked aghast.

She wants to slap the cuffs on him here and now, Riley thought.

But that just wasn't going to happen.

Riley turned to leave the room, and Jenn reluctantly followed.

Before they got out the door, Dustin said, "If you're going to
talk to Daisy and Taylor, ask them if they know why Katy broke up
with me. I really want to know."

As they headed toward the stairs, Jenn said in a whisper,
"Riley!"

"Not now," Riley whispered back.

Dustin's mother was standing at the bottom of the stairs,
looking as worried as before. She seemed a bit relieved when Riley
asked her for directions to Wilson High School.

When they left the house and got into the car, Jenn spoke
sharply.

"Riley, what the hell are we doing?"

"We don't have anything on him," Riley said. "We can't arrest
him."

Jenn started the car and started to drive.

"Shouldn't we bring him in for further questioning?" Jenn
asked.

"He won't tell us anything else."

"Isn't he a flight risk?"

"He's not," Riley said.

"How do you know?"

Riley didn't reply. The truth was, she didn't have any rational reason to think Dustin Russo wouldn't leave town the first chance he got. But somehow, she couldn't imagine him going far outside of that room.

"What do you make of him?" Jenn asked.

Riley shrugged a little.

"He's a jock. Not an especially bright one. Other than that, I couldn't say. What do *you* make of him?"

Jenn shook her head uneasily.

"Something's wrong with that kid," Jenn said. "His emotional responses were so inappropriate. He seemed a whole lot more upset about breaking up with Katy than he was that she'd been killed."

Riley couldn't help but agree with Jenn's assessment. Still, she had a different perspective on Dustin's reactions.

She said, "You haven't spent a lot of time with teenagers, have you?"

Jenn let out a scoffing laugh and said, "Well, I *was* one—and not very long ago. Not that that gives me any particular insights." She fell quiet for a moment, then added, "I was certainly a pain in the ass."

Riley looked out the window, remembering what she'd been through with April, then Jilly, and what she might yet have to face with Liam. Although April and Jilly seemed pretty stable now, they'd both gone through turbulent and rebellious phases. There had been times when Riley had felt like motherhood was an impossible job and she'd half-wished she could just quit. And as much as she liked Liam, she still didn't feel as though she knew him at all well.

Riley said, "Well, based on my own experience, you can only be sure of one thing about teenagers—that you can't be sure of anything at all. They're all different, and they're all mysteries, at least as far as adults are concerned."

Riley paused to think a little more. She remembered that odd tremor in Dustin's voice.

"Then one day she was all different," he'd said.

Riley said, "I can't say I'm surprised when a teenager reacts to tragedy in an emotionally inappropriate way. Their emotions are all over the place and don't make a lot of sense. A lot of the time they don't know what they're thinking or feeling themselves. Dustin might be grieving his heart out and not even know it himself."

"Or he might just be a cold-blooded killer," Jenn said in a tight voice. "And a rapist too. Jesus, Riley. I don't know. I think you might have made a big mistake back there."

Riley suppressed a sigh. This kind of thing often happened whenever she had to work with someone new. A new partner always had a hard time learning to trust Riley's gut feelings.

Worse still, Jenn's doubts were starting to get to her.

What if she's right? Riley wondered.

Riley's instincts weren't infallible, after all. She'd made some mistakes over the years.

What if she'd made one just now, leaving Dustin unattended?

Steady, she told herself. *Keep your head in the game.*

If she let self-doubt kick in, she'd lose her ability to get a sense of the case. She couldn't let that happen. If they were actually tracking a serial killer, more lives might well be at stake.

CHAPTER FOURTEEN

As Jenn pulled their car into the school parking lot, Riley felt unsettled by the sight of cheerful teenage girls climbing onto a yellow bus. The soccer game had apparently just ended, and the kids looked so innocent, so unsuspecting.

Do they have any idea of the evil that's out there? Riley wondered.

Surely they had heard about Katy Philbin's death by now. But Riley reminded herself that kids were like that. The horror wasn't real to them. They were too young to grasp it. And their innocence made them all the more vulnerable.

She saw that COBBTOWN HIGH was written across side of the bus, so she knew that the girls boarding it were on the visiting team. Jenn parked the car, and she and Riley walked toward the stands where spectators were still milling around. Although there were smiles among the group, they seemed subdued. It was obvious that the news was sinking in to the town's collective psyche.

The nearby Wilson High School looked old and quaint in comparison to the modern school where April went. The whole scene gave Riley the eerie feeling that she'd stepped back in time to the years of her own childhood, or maybe into some kind of 1950s sitcom. Everything seemed so wholesome. She didn't even see any kids wearing kinky outfits or flaunting rebellious attitudes.

As Riley and Jenn approached, some people gave them curious looks. For the moment, she considered it just as well that the whole town not know she and Jenn were FBI agents.

So without identifying herself, she quietly asked a couple for directions to the home team's locker room. Smiling pleasantly, they indicated a little brick building near the stands. Outside the building, a man wearing a coach's uniform was still being congratulated by a few people. Riley and Jenn waited for a quiet moment to approach him.

When they introduced themselves, the man let out a gasp of relief.

"The FBI!" he said. "Oh, thank God! Chief Sinard told me he'd

73

put in a call for you. He and his people feel so overwhelmed. You made here it in no time at all."

He shook hands with both Riley and Jenn.

"I'm Judd Griggs, the soccer coach. I can't tell you how glad I am that you're here."

He was a big, kindly bear of a man. Riley took an immediate liking to him.

"We're terribly sorry about the circumstances," Riley said.

"Yes," Griggs said with faraway, sorrowful look. "I'm—we're all—it's just so hard to believe. Katy was such a wonderful, special girl—a real star in every way, a leader too. The other girls on the team just loved her and looked up to her."

He swallowed hard.

Then he said, "I thought about canceling today's game. But the girls wouldn't hear of it. They wanted to play this one for Katy. They said they wanted to make her proud."

His voice sounded thick with emotion.

"I was worried about how they'd feel if they had a bad game. It just seemed like so much pressure. But they were amazing. We tied Cobbtown one-to-one, and that's a great team. It looks like we've got a chance at the playoffs this year. If only Katy could be here too …"

His words trailed off.

"I'm sorry," he said. "This is just such a terrible day."

Riley's heart went out to him. He obviously cared a lot about the girls on his team. The pain of Katy's loss must have been unbearable to him.

Then Jenn said, "Mr. Griggs, could you tell us where you were and what you were doing on Wednesday night?"

Riley winced.

Is she going to treat every man she meets like a suspect? she wondered.

Griggs seemed distraught enough to her as it was.

Riley hastily said, "Mr. Griggs, I'm sorry—"

"No, no need to apologize," Griggs said. "You're doing your job, I understand. I was home with my wife all evening, watching TV mostly. I don't know if that's very helpful. If there's anything I can do to confirm that, I'll do my best. I'll do anything— *anything*—I can to help."

Jenn looked like she wanted to press him some more, but Riley quieted her with a frown. Jenn didn't look happy about it.

Riley asked Griggs, "Do you know a girl named Holly Struthers?"

He thought for a moment, then asked, "I don't think so. Is she a Wilson student?"

"No," Riley said. "She's enrolled in Lincoln High."

"Then I probably wouldn't have met her unless she plays on their soccer team," he said. "I did hear something about a girl in town going missing. Is that the name?"

"Yes, she has been reported missing."

"Do you think her disappearance had anything to do with …?"

"We don't think anything just yet," Riley said. "For all we know, Holly still might turn up just fine."

The coach shrugged slightly and added, "From what I've heard, some folks think she just ran off with a boy or something. Good Lord, I hope it's not something worse."

Riley wished she could reassure him. And as she always felt when interviewing distraught people, she wished she didn't have to cause him further anguish.

She hesitated, then said, "Mr. Griggs—"

"Please, call me Judd."

"Judd, did you notice any changes in Katy's mood or behavior recently?"

Judd Griggs thought for a moment.

"Now that you mention it—maybe so. I'm not sure I should talk about it, since I don't really know what happened. Or if anything happened."

"Anything you can tell us will be helpful," Riley said.

Judd looked out over the soccer field.

"Awhile back the girls had a party after a big victory. I didn't go—I always let them celebrate among themselves. But at practice the next day, Katy seemed different—subdued and quiet, not really herself. I kept waiting for her to snap out of it, but she never did."

Riley asked, "Did it affect how she played the game? Did she lose her enthusiasm?"

Judd knitted his brow.

"No, if anything, she worked harder—too hard, I thought. She pushed herself like she never had. But she wasn't enjoying it anymore."

Judd looked down at the ground and shook his head.

"I should have talked to her," he said. "I should have asked what it was all about. Maybe if I'd gotten her to tell me …"

He seemed on the verge of tears now.

Riley hated that he felt this way. She wanted to assure him that it wasn't his fault. But she'd learned long ago that too much empathy could distract her from her work. It wasn't her job to become the local therapist. The people who had known and loved Katy were going to have to look to someone else for help.

Besides, he might well be right. If he *had* talked to Katy, maybe she'd be alive today.

Riley glanced toward the door to the locker room.

She asked, "Is your team still in there?"

Judd nodded.

"Yeah. I guess you need to talk with them too. Go easy on them, OK? They just had a good game, in spite of what's happened. It's a shame they have to be reminded, but you've got to do your job."

As Riley and Jenn started to walk toward the locker room, Judd called after them.

"Agent Paige, Agent Roston … you don't think anything like this is going to happen again, do you?"

He had an imploring expression now. Riley felt a deep pang of sympathy for him. All he wanted was a word of reassurance.

But she had no reassurance to offer him, so she just turned away.

As she and Jenn walked toward the locker room door, Jenn said, "Let me ask the questions in there."

A bit surprised, Riley turned toward Jenn.

She could see by her expression that the younger agent was annoyed about how Riley had kept her from asking Judd Griggs questions.

As much as she disliked Jenn's interviewing style, she couldn't very well stop her from doing it altogether.

She's got to learn sometime, Riley thought.

Riley said, "Just remember—the girls aren't suspects." It didn't seem likely that any teenage girl in this town had killed a friend and buried her.

Jenn looked a little insulted at having been told what was obvious. But Riley didn't much care.

They continued on into the steamy locker room. The girls were mostly dressed and getting ready to leave. There was some chatter and some giggles, but the mood was pretty subdued for a team that had just played a good game.

Jenn and Riley produced their badges and introduced themselves.

The girls' eyes widened and most sat down on the locker room benches.

"Is this about what happened to Katy?" one girl asked.

"That's right," Jenn said. "We're really sorry about your loss. We just hope you can answer a few questions."

Riley was glad that Jenn started with a note of sympathy. But there wasn't a lot of warmth in her voice. She was sorry that Jenn had never had a chance to learn from Lucy.

But Riley managed to keep quiet. The upside of letting Jenn doing the talking was that she could watch the girls' faces and gauge their reactions. Right now, they seemed understandably anxious.

Jenn asked, "Does anybody have any idea who might have wanted to hurt Katy?"

The girls looked nervously at each other and shook their heads. Some of them said no.

"When was the last time any of you saw her?" Jenn asked.

The girls murmured to each other for a moment, trying to remember.

Then one girl said, "It was after practice on Wednesday. We all went over to the Burger Shanty to get something to eat."

Another said, "Katy left before the rest of us did."

"Did she say where she was going?" Jenn asked.

"No," the second girl said. "But I saw her through the window heading toward the bus stop. So I guess she was planning to take the bus home. That's what she usually did."

Jenn seemed to think for a moment.

Then she said, "Coach Griggs said something about a party you all had recently."

Riley noticed a sudden change in the girls' expressions. They looked more alarmed than before.

What's it all about? she wondered.

Jenn continued, "He said that Katy's mood changed after the party. Do any of you know why?"

The girls said "no" in a hushed, nervous chorus.

Riley scanned their faces carefully as she let Jenn keep on asking a few more routine questions. Their anxiety at the mention of the party lingered even when they went on to other topics. Riley was sure that at least some of them knew something.

She was also sure that they weren't going to open up in a group.

She remembered the names of the girls Dustin had mentioned—the girls who were especially close to Katy.

When Jenn seemed to be finished asking questions, Riley said, "Thanks, girls. You've been a great help. Are Daisy Kinney and Taylor McGrath here?"

Two girls sitting together on a bench suddenly looked especially anxious.

"I'm Daisy," one said.

"I'm Taylor," the other said.

Riley said, "We'd like to talk to the two of you alone. The rest of you may leave. Again, my partner and I are terribly sorry for your loss."

All of the other girls left the locker room.

Daisy and Taylor sat on the bench looking terrified.

"Are we in some kind of trouble?" Daisy asked.

"My folks are expecting me outside," Taylor said.

Riley said nothing. She looked each of the girls in the eyes. She saw a world of trepidation there.

"Something happened at that party," Riley said.

The girls said nothing.

"We need for you to tell us what happened," Riley said.

Taylor forced a shrug.

"I sure don't know anything," she said.

Daisy nudged her friend with her elbow.

"Taylor," Daisy said.

"Daisy doesn't know anything either," Taylor said.

"Taylor," Daisy said again.

Taylor looked at Daisy sharply.

"Daisy, no. Katy made us promise. We're not supposed to tell anybody. Ever."

A sob rose up in Daisy's throat.

"She's dead, Taylor. We've got to say something."

Riley felt a tingle deep inside.

These girls knew something—and whatever it was, it was dark and ugly.

CHAPTER FIFTEEN

The girls' faces had reddened. Watching them closely, Riley suspected they were feeling both fear and shame. She could see that Taylor was still reluctant to talk. But Daisy was crying a little and looked like she wanted to tell the truth.

Riley said, "I need the two of you to tell me everything about that party."

The girls were silent for a long tense moment.

Then Daisy blurted, "The party was at Taylor's house."

Taylor let out a groan of dismay.

"Daisy, don't do this."

"We've got to tell them the truth, Taylor," Daisy said.

Then turning toward Riley and Jenn, Daisy said, "We'd just played a great game against Blenker. Everybody wanted to celebrate. Taylor's parents were away, so we had the party in her rec room."

Jenn asked, "Was there drinking?"

"Well, yeah," Taylor said defensively. "It's not against the law."

"Actually, it is against the law," Jenn said.

Riley gritted her teeth a little.

The last thing she needed was for Jenn to raise irrelevant issues.

Riley said, "We're not here about your drinking. You're not in trouble for that. Not this time. This is all about Katy and whatever happened to her. Were there any boys at the party?"

"Some," Daisy said. "Mostly from school. Katy was waiting for her boyfriend to show up—Dustin Russo. But he was really late. So she kind of started flirting with another guy. We didn't know him real well, an older guy who lives over in Manton, calls himself 'Trip.' He comes around Angier and hangs around from time to time."

Daisy paused for a moment.

"Well, Katy was drinking some, which wasn't really her style, and she normally wouldn't have anything to do with a creep like

Trip. But I think she was just mad at Dustin, and she was maybe trying to make him jealous. Well, there was a lot going on, and I guess Katy and Trip slipped out without my noticing it."

"I didn't notice it either," Taylor said.

Daisy continued, "A while later Katy came back to the party. She seemed really out of it, kind of messed up. She was really upset, and Taylor and I asked her why, but she wouldn't tell us. When Dustin finally showed up, she tried to act like nothing had happened. But a few days later she broke up with him."

Now Taylor seemed more willing to talk.

She said, "Katy started acting weird after that. Not doing homework, cutting classes. That wasn't like her at all. And she started pushing herself real hard at soccer—way too hard, it really scared the rest of us. It was like she was trying to let off steam, or get rid of her anger, or trying to hurt herself."

Taylor fell silent for a moment.

"You'd better tell them, Taylor," Daisy said.

Taylor's voice was thick with emotion now.

She shook her head.

"I should have figured it out right way. I guess I kind of knew it, but didn't want to admit it. When the party was over, after I'd cleaned up the rec room and gone upstairs to bed, I noticed that my room was kind of messed up. A couple of things were knocked over, and the bedspread was rumpled. Somebody had been in there. But I just kept telling myself it wasn't important."

Taylor gulped hard.

"But Katy kept getting worse and worse, and I just couldn't help wondering …"

Her words trailed off.

Daisy started talking now.

"One day after school, Taylor told me about the bedroom, and I said we really needed to talk to Katy and find out what happened. So we found her and took her aside and really made sure that she tell us."

Now Taylor was starting to cry. She said, "Katy wasn't sure what happened or how. She guessed that Trip had put something in her drink. She didn't even remember going out of the rec room with him. The next thing she knew she was in the bedroom and Trip was having sex with her. When it was over he just put his pants back on and laughed and left her there."

Taylor wiped away a tear.

She said, "We tried to tell her it wasn't anything important. I mean, she was on the pill like the rest of us, so she wasn't going to get pregnant. As long as the guy didn't have any STDs she'd be all right."

Taylor shrugged and added, "It was like I told her, it was just sex."

Riley shuddered. The whole thing made her feel sick inside—not just what the guy had done to Katy, but how these girls had dealt with it.

"Just sex," she thought.

Did they even fully understand that their friend had been raped?

Riley now knew that her ugly feelings about Angier had been right all along.

It was anything but the picture-perfect '50s sitcom town.

There was plenty of darkness behind those doors.

Daisy looked anxiously back and forth at Riley and Jenn.

"Do you think this had anything to do with what happened to her? Please tell us no. Because if we could have done something to stop it but didn't …"

Riley didn't reply. It now seemed more than likely that Trip was their suspect. But the truth was, she didn't know whether the girls could have prevented Katy's death. All she knew was that she felt sickened by the whole thing.

In Riley's silence, Jenn spoke up.

"Tell us more about Trip. Is that his real name?"

Taylor shrugged again and blew her nose on a tissue.

"I don't know. I don't think so. Do you, Daisy?"

"I doubt it," Daisy said. "Like I said, he was an older guy, and he was a real bullshitter. He kept telling kids that he was scouting Angier to make an independent movie, and that he might want some of us to act in it. Some of our friends believed him. I sure didn't."

Riley was on the verge of asking why Taylor had let him in to her party. But she quickly realized—Trip had convinced enough of the local kids that he was cool that Taylor wouldn't make him leave. She might also have been scared of him.

Riley asked, "Do you have any idea where Trip really lives?"

Daisy and Taylor looked at each other.

Taylor said, "Sometimes he said he was from Minneapolis, sometimes from Chicago."

Daisy said, "I don't think he lived in either of those places. He was just full of bullshit."

Riley thanked the girls for their help, and she and Jenn left the locker room. There were few people around the stadium now. Riley and Jenn headed for the car, where Riley called Chief Sinard's cell phone number.

She said, "Chief Sinard, I don't want to get your hopes up, but my partner and I think we have a suspect. Have you heard of a young man who hangs around Angier who calls himself 'Trip'?"

She heard Sinard let out a grunt of disapproval.

"I sure have. He's a bad sort. He mixes with the local kids bragging and telling them crazy lies about himself. We think it's a ruse to sell drugs, but we haven't been able to prove it. We try to keep an eye on him, hoping he'll slip up some day and we can nail him."

Riley briefly wondered—had Trip been selling drugs at the girls' party?

If so, Taylor and Daisy had said nothing about it.

But it was hardly something to worry about right now.

"Do you know his real name?" she asked Sinard.

"Yeah, it's Ivan Crozier."

"What about an address?"

"Let me look."

Riley waited for a few moments.

Then Sinard said, "He lives over in Manton, about twenty miles west of Angier. The address I've got is 420 Bennett Drive."

Riley ended the call and entered the address into GPS service on her cell phone. When the directions came up, Jenn started to drive.

*

Riley's spirits sank when Jenn drove up to the address.

As it turned out, 420 Bennett Drive was a trailer park.

Jenn asked, "How are we supposed to know which trailer Ivan Crozier lives in?"

Riley wondered the same thing. Doubtless individual homes were marked with letters or something, but the overall street address was the only information they had.

"I guess we've just got to ask around," Riley said.

They parked and got out of the car. Riley saw that this trailer park was shabby and dilapidated. Some of the trailers looked like they'd been long abandoned—or if they weren't, it seemed to her that they should have been.

A pair of unshaven middle-aged men wearing tattered work clothes came sauntering toward them.

They didn't look at all friendly.

One of them smiled at Riley and Jenn, tipping his baseball cap and leering and grinning at them through an incomplete set of crooked yellow teeth.

"What can we do for you lovely ladies?" he asked.

Before Riley could say anything, she heard another man's voice behind her.

"Hey, boys—it looks like these gals is cops!"

Riley turned around and saw another man stooping behind the car Chief Sinard had lent them. He was peering at the license plate. Riley remembered that the word OFFICIAL appeared on the plate.

"Cops!" the man who hadn't spoken yet said. "I don't believe it. You girls are much too pretty to be cops. And where are your uniforms?"

Curious neighbors were starting to emerge from the trailers—several more tough-looking men and three or four women, one of them holding a baby. As they stood gawking, they reminded Riley of dirt-poor rural hillbillies she had encountered in Appalachia. Her memories of people like that were far from pleasant.

She took out her badge.

"We're Special Agents Paige and Roston, FBI."

All of the faces around them darkened.

"FBI," the man who'd spoken first growled.

"Goddamn feds," the man standing next to him said.

"Ladies, I do think you've got the wrong address," the man behind the car said.

There were more men than before, and they started to crowd in around Riley and Jenn.

Riley's hand hovered near her weapon.

"Keep cool," she whispered to Jenn. "But be ready for anything."

CHAPTER SIXTEEN

The circle of men closed in threateningly around Riley and Jenn. Although Riley wasn't sure how she and her new partner would fare in an unarmed brawl with this rough group, she didn't want to use her weapon, and she was determined not to show fear.

She said in a sharp, loud voice, "My partner and I are looking for a man named Ivan Crozier. He calls himself 'Trip.' Do you know him? Does he live around here?"

To Riley's surprise, the men all stopped in their tracks.

She noticed some of them smiling grimly at one another.

"You're FBI—and you're looking for Trip?" one said.

"That's right," Riley said.

Several of the men let out a burst of sardonic laughter. Even a couple of the women joined in.

"We know Trip, all right," one man said.

An obese, middle-aged woman said, "What's this about, drugs or something?"

Riley knew better than to answer her question.

"We've got our own business with him," Riley said.

Another woman pointed and said, "Trip lives down that way, in Trailer Q."

The circle of men opened, leaving Riley and Jenn room to move.

"Go ahead, go in after him," one said.

"Knock yourself out," said another. "Good luck."

There was a general murmur of amused agreement. The obese woman let out a mean-spirited cackle.

Riley actually felt more worried than before. What did these men know that she and Jenn didn't know? Perhaps Trip wasn't alone in that trailer. Perhaps he had an arsenal of weapons like the lone wolf she had arrested in California.

She also didn't know whether the people clustered around them might be working with Trip. They were clearly an angry bunch but she hadn't determined where their anger was focused.

All of those unknowns meant that she and Jenn could be

84

heading into a dangerous trap. But Riley didn't see that they had any choice.

Apparently Jenn felt the same way, because she started walking in the direction of Trip's trailer.

Riley stopped her and said, "Let's do this my way. Give me the car key."

With a slightly puzzled look, Jenn gave Riley the key.

"Come on," Riley said. Jenn followed her back to the car and they both got in.

Riley drove through the maze of mobile homes until they got to one with letter Q roughly painted on the door. This trailer was in such bad shape that she found it hard to believe anyone lived there. But there was a battered car parked in front.

Riley pulled up tightly behind the car, leaving no room for it to pull out. She and Jenn got out of their car and walked onto the stoop outside the door. Riley knocked sharply.

"We're looking for Ivan Crozier. Are you at home?"

A voice answered from inside.

"What do you want?"

"We just want to talk to you."

"If you're selling something, go away."

"That's not it," Riley said. "We just want to talk."

After a pause, the voice grumbled, "Shit."

Riley heard footsteps, and then the flimsy metal door rattled open.

Inside the door stood a thin, groggy-looking man wearing an undershirt and pajama bottoms. He was about thirty, and he had a punkish haircut with shaved sides and an unkempt top. His hair was dirty, and judging from his smell he badly needed a shower.

Riley fleetingly wondered why the kids in Angier found this guy to be cool.

He must clean up well, she figured.

Riley and Jenn pulled out their badges and introduced themselves.

Trip rolled his eyes, which looked dilated. Riley guessed he was pretty stoned right now.

"FBI," he said in an unsteady, distant-sounding voice. "Crap. What's this all about?"

"We'd like to ask you a few questions about Katy Philbin?"

"Katy who?" Trip asked.

Jenn said, "We think you know who she is."

Trip just stared around blankly, squinting in the bright daylight.

"She lives over in Angier," Riley said.

Trip nodded.

"Oh, yeah. Katy. What about her?"

"We'd like to come in and talk to you about that," Riley said.

Trip smirked a little.

"I don't have to let you in, do I?" he said.

Riley took an intimidating step into his personal space—a tactic that had worked for her in countless situations like this.

"Why wouldn't you?" she said. "If you've got nothing to hide?"

Trip nervously backed away, and Riley and Jenn stepped into the trailer. They found themselves in a long, narrow hallway that contained a rudimentary kitchen area. She guessed that two doors on the right-hand end led to a bedroom and a bathroom.

To her left was what looked like a living room.

Riley nodded in that direction.

"Maybe we could go sit down," she said.

Again, she stepped a little too close to Trip for his comfort.

He backed away unsteadily, then started to lead Riley and Jenn down the hallway.

As they followed him, Riley began to worry.

Something seemed off about this situation.

Trip didn't seem dangerous—at least not at the moment. So what had the neighbors been up to, eagerly sending Riley and Jenn here?

The one thing Riley knew for sure was that the neighbors hated them for being feds.

Now she wondered if they had directed them here as a ruse. Might they be preparing some kind of an ambush outside?

Riley whispered to Jenn as they walked, "Keep an eye out a window."

"Looking for what?" Jenn whispered back.

"You'll know it if you see it."

The little living room was sparsely furnished with a couple of chairs, a table, and an unlighted lamp. The furnishings looked so battered and seedy that Riley doubted whether Trip had even bought them at a thrift shop. It seemed more likely that he'd scavenged them from junkyards.

He might well be a drug dealer, but he didn't strike Riley as a very successful one. He probably just sold drugs to support his own

86

habit. Judging from his thin, drawn face and pallid skin, she guessed he might be into heroin.

Riley and Jenn sat down on a ragged chair while Trip squatted onto a little three-legged stool. Jenn moved toward the window.

Riley flashed a fake smile at him.

"We hear that you go by the name of Trip," she said. "Is it OK for us to call you Trip?"

He shrugged.

"It's what everybody else calls me."

Riley asked, "What do you do for a living, Trip?"

"I'm an independent filmmaker," Trip said, sounding more alert now—even a bit enthusiastic. "You may have heard of my work. I've won awards at some of the best festivals. My best-known work is a movie called *Origami Lace.* It was a huge hit at Sundance."

It was such a brazen lie that Riley was starting to feel fascinated.

She remembered what Daisy had said about him …

"… a real bullshitter."

Daisy had definitely gotten that right.

Riley shook her head and said, "Sorry, it doesn't ring a bell."

Jenn said, "Not with me either."

Out of the corner of her eye, Riley could see that Jenn was keeping watch through the filthy window.

Trip said, "What about the girl?"

"Maybe you should tell us," Riley said.

"I don't know what you're talking about," Trip said.

Riley couldn't tell whether he was lying or not.

She said, "Her body was found this morning in a cornfield near Angier. She'd been raped and murdered."

Riley noticed barely any change in Trip's expression.

"That's bad," he said.

Still looking out the window, Jenn said, "We understand something happened between the two of you at a party not long ago."

Trip snickered a little.

"Yeah, she was kind of all over me. Not that I minded. I liked her. We really clicked. I thought maybe we might have a future together."

He seemed to be coming to life more and more as he thought about Katy.

"Did you ever have that kind of a thing? Where you meet someone and it feels like fate pulled you together? I felt that way about Katy, and she told me she felt the same way about me. But now …"

He shook his head.

"It's just too bad," he said.

Riley studied his expression, which was now pretty cheerful.

One lie after another, Riley thought.

She'd dealt with bullshit artists like him before. Based on her experience, she'd found them surprisingly easy to interview or interrogate. That was because they loved to talk and she could almost count on every single statement they made to be a lie. They could be informative in a negative sort of way.

Almost everything was a lie, Riley reminded herself. After all, few things in her line of work were ever that simple and easy.

Riley said, "Katy's friends said you drugged her at that party and raped her."

Trip looked completely indifferent.

"Who told them that?" he asked.

"Katy."

"It's not true. Do I look like the kind of guy who needs to drug girls to get them have sex with him?"

Yes, that's exactly what you look like, Riley thought. But there was no point in saying so aloud.

Riley said, "Katy was killed on Wednesday night. Can you tell us where you were then, from dusk until dawn?"

Trip grinned and got up from his stool.

"Sure. I was in Des Moines. I can prove it."

He walked across the room to a Formica table covered with bills and miscellaneous papers. He dug around looking through them.

Meanwhile, Riley noticed a change in his attitude.

As he rummaged through papers, he kept glancing up at a plywood cabinet hanging on the wall above the table. It was locked with a padlock.

Something was in there—something he didn't want them to see.

Riley felt sure of it.

He managed to find the paper he was looking for and stepped over to Riley and handed it to her.

It was, in fact, a bill with his name on it from a motel in Des

Moines.

It indicated that he had checked in on Tuesday and left on Thursday.

Convenient, Riley thought.

But it was hardly proof of his innocence. If he'd wanted to set up an alibi in advance, someone else could have gone to Des Moines in his place using his name.

But was this guy shrewd enough to plan ahead like that?

Trip didn't sit back down. He was pacing anxiously now, back and forth in front of that cabinet.

She asked, "What do you keep in that cabinet, Trip?"

He flashed her a weak smile.

"Film equipment," he said. "The tools of my trade."

Like almost everything else he'd been saying, it was a lie, and Riley knew it.

She smiled and said, "Would you show them to me? I've always been fascinated by filmmaking."

"A funny thing—I lost the key," he said.

Riley realized that Jenn was standing beside her now. The talk about the cabinet seemed to have gotten her attention, and she'd left her post at the window.

Riley was annoyed with her.

She wanted to tell her to go back and do as she'd been told.

Jenn stepped toward the cabinet.

"Are you sure it's really locked?" Jenn said. "Looks like it might be open to me."

Riley tingled all over with alarm.

What was Jenn going to do, break into the cabinet with her bare hands?

Riley thought that it wouldn't be hard to do. For that matter, either of them could pick that lock pretty quickly. But that would be a disaster—an illegal search that would lead to trouble and get them nowhere. Any evidence would be inadmissible.

Riley stepped toward Jenn and reached out to touch her arm. Then everything happened fast.

Trip moved between Jenn and the cabinet. He gave the young agent a sharp, unexpected push. Jenn fell backward against Riley, and they both tumbled to the floor. With surprising agility, Trip darted around them and into the hallway.

As Riley and Jenn scrambled to their feet, they heard the trailer door slam.

"What the hell did you think you were doing?" Riley said.

"Bending the rules," Jenn said. "Don't tell me you never do it too."

Riley knew they didn't have time to argue.

"Come on," she said. "He's getting away."

She and Jenn tore out of the trailer in time to see Trip hesitating outside his car. It seemed to be taking a moment for him to realize that Riley's vehicle was very effectively blocking his.

When he looked up and saw Riley and Jenn, the skinny young man took off on foot and disappeared behind the next trailer. Riley and Jenn dashed after him.

At that moment, she heard a man's voice call out.

"Hey, boys—the FBI girls are after our boy!"

Damn, Riley thought.

The neighbors were surely about to come to Trip's rescue.

Things were about to get messy.

CHAPTER SEVENTEEN

In pursuit of the fleeing suspect, Riley and Jenn rounded the back of the next trailer. They pulled up in surprise at what they encountered there.

The two agents almost ran into the backs of a circle of people. The neighbors who had confronted them earlier had surrounded Trip, but they didn't seem to be protecting him.

Riley pushed her way between two women in the circle. At that moment, she saw the biggest of the men body-slam Trip. Then the same man stooped over the wailing figure on the ground, raised his fist, and punched him in the head.

The onlookers, both women and men, all cheered loudly.

The situation became brutally clear to Riley. The neighbors had turned vigilante.

Trip's very life was now in danger.

"We've got to stop this," Riley said to Jenn, who had pushed her way up beside her.

Jenn nodded in agreement and reached for her pistol.

"No weapons," Riley said.

Jenn looked at Riley with an incredulous expression.

"Are you kidding me?" Jenn said.

Riley knew all too well how deadly a situation like this could turn if weapons were drawn. This crowd was far too riled up to stop account of a threat to shoot. Even a warning shot might not stop them. Other weapons would surely appear and matters could get out of control in mere seconds. Someone could get killed.

But Riley didn't have time to explain.

"I mean it," she snapped.

Jenn didn't look happy, but she seemed to understand.

Riley flung herself inside the circle of angry people.

"Break it up, all of you!" she shouted.

Most of them stepped back, looking disappointed.

But the man who had thrown Trip down was ignoring her, hitting Trip in the face repeatedly.

Riley grabbed him from behind by the shoulders and pulled

him hard. He was an enormous man, and Riley couldn't budge him. Then she saw Jenn hurry around in front of him and give him a sharp kick to the chest. The man hurtled onto his back.

Now those who had been standing back were furious. A couple of other guys rushed forward to pick up where the big man had left off.

Riley said sharply to Jenn, "You take the guy on the right."

Riley rushed at the nearer assailant and gave him a swift punch in the solar plexus. The man buckled over, and Riley could hear the air rush out of his lungs. She turned in time to see Jenn take the other man down with a kick to the groin.

The small crowd was yelling curses at Riley and Jenn now.

Riley wondered if they were going to need their weapons after all. She yelled over their voices.

"What do you people think you're doing?"

One of the men yelled back, "We're doing what's got to be done."

A woman holding a baby yelled, "We were sure that Trip was dealing drugs. You FBI folks coming here proved it. We've got kids growing up here. We won't put up with it."

"Let us do our job," Riley said.

"Your job!" snorted one woman in contempt.

A man yelled, "Ain't that just like you feds," a man said. "You beat up a couple of us good citizens for no good reason, but you won't touch a hair on this punk's head. You'll just haul him in for a good talking-to, and he'll say he didn't do anything wrong, and you'll say you believe him and let him go."

The crowd was getting louder now.

Riley shouted, "That's not what's going to happen! Listen to me! We're going to arrest him on suspicion of sexual assault and murder."

The shouting died down. The men and women looked surprised.

"You heard me," Riley said. "We're definitely not letting him go with a slap on the wrist."

There was a general murmur among the crowd. Everybody seemed to agree to let Riley and Jenn make the arrest.

Riley breathed more easily. She turned to Jenn and said, "Cuff him and read him his rights."

Trip lay curled up on the ground whimpering, his face bleeding from the blows he had taken. Jenn handcuffed his hands behind him and began to read him his rights.

Meanwhile, a woman stepped toward Riley.

"Psst," the woman said to her. "Did you find the drugs in his trailer?"

Riley was too puzzled by the question to reply. Then she recognized the woman.

She was the obese woman who had asked earlier …

"What's this about, drugs or something?"

Riley squinted at the woman, not knowing what to say.

The woman let out a low cackle.

She said, "Well, maybe you just didn't look hard enough. Maybe you should go poke around some more."

For a moment, Riley hesitated. The woman seemed to be making a point that she thought was important.

She looked over at Jenn to see if she had things under control. A couple of the guys were actually helping her now, pulling Trip up on his feet. Everyone seemed perfectly happy with the outcome.

"Get him into the car," Riley said to Jenn. "I'll be right back."

Riley hurried back to Trip's trailer and went inside. She headed straight for the little living room at the end of the trailer.

Sure enough, the plywood cabinet now stood wide open. Inside were bags of powder and lots of little plastic bottles.

The woman must have sneaked in here and broken the lock.

Riley stood there staring for a second, trying to grasp the situation.

Had she just gotten lucky?

After all, she had hardly conducted an illegal search of the premises. She'd simply stumbled across Trip's drug supply by accident.

Anyway, now didn't seem like the time to mull over the legal ramifications. And she couldn't just leave stuff like this here.

She took out her cell phone and snapped several pictures of the drugs in the cabinet. Then she picked up a plastic wastebasket, emptied its contents onto the floor, and loaded all the drugs into it, careful not to add her own fingerprints to what might already be on them.

She went back outside in time to see Jenn pushing Trip into the back seat of the car.

The obese woman stepped toward Riley again.

Winking, she said, "My name's Ethel Burney, by the way. Pleased to make your acquaintance."

She turned and walked away.

Jenn called out to Riley from the car, "What have you got there?"

Riley looked into the pail, shrugged, and said, "You won't believe it when I tell you. Come on, let's take this punk to the police station."

CHAPTER EIGHTEEN

An hour or so later, Riley stood beside Chief Sinard outside the interview room in the Angier police station. The two of them were watching and listening as Jenn interviewed Ivan "Trip" Crozier, who sat shackled to a heavy table.

Trip showed the beating he'd gotten back at the trailer park. His face was bruised and bandaged. But Riley couldn't bring herself to feel sorry for him.

He's scum, all right, she thought. The world was certainly a better place without him on the streets.

But was he the killer they were looking for? Riley was still trying to figure that out.

It was clear that Jenn, who was asking all the right questions, was trying to figure that out too.

She said, "You claim to have been in Des Moines on the night of Katy Philbin's murder."

"Yeah," Trip said.

"What were you doing in Des Moines?"

"Business."

"What kind of business?"

"Scouting locations. Did I tell you I'm an independent filmmaker?"

Riley could sense Jenn's brain clicking away as she probed for Skip's weak spot. So far Jenn hadn't been able to find it. Still, the young agent was doing good work. Riley felt sure she couldn't do any better herself.

"Can anybody confirm your whereabouts?" Jenn asked.

Trip shrugged.

"I dunno, I'll have to think," he said.

A silence fell.

"Well?" Jenn asked.

Trip sneered a little.

"I said I'll have to think. Ask me later when I've had time to think about it."

Riley knew that he was toying with Jenn. So far, he hadn't

asked for a lawyer. Riley knew he would do so eventually, probably before the day was over. Meanwhile, he was just having some fun wasting the taxpayers' time and money.

He hardly seemed like the stoned-out loser that they had found in the trailer park. He was obviously both shrewd and mischievous. Riley was finally starting to see why the local kids had been attracted to him. He was sardonically cool in a way that teenagers could appreciate.

As Jenn continued asking questions, Chief Sinard spoke to Riley quietly.

"About those drugs you found …"

Riley smiled a little. She had shown the chief her photos of the open cabinet, and the drugs were now checked in as evidence.

"Yeah, I know how that looks." Riley said. "But I told you the truth. We found the cabinet open."

Chief Sinard shook his head.

"I want to believe you," he said. "But you can bet this punk is going to accuse you of an illegal search. That could spoil the only charge we can make against him at this point. He's already complaining about police brutality."

Riley almost laughed.

The idea that she and Jenn would have bothered pulverizing this guy in order to arrest him seemed patently absurd, and she was sure the chief knew it.

"I'll tell you what, Chief," Riley said. "If he starts making a fuss about it, look up a woman named Ethel Burney. She lives in the trailer park. I think she'll be glad to explain about the drugs."

After all, Riley now realized that the woman had given her name for exactly that reason.

A pretty smart woman, Riley thought. Ethel probably knew that she wasn't likely to get charged with any crime. Even if that happened, she'd probably think it was worth it to get rid of a neighbor like Trip.

Riley half wanted to stop back at the trailer park and thank Ethel for what she'd done. But she knew that would be a bad idea.

Riley added, "Ethel might also confirm what Agent Roston and I said about how the guy got beaten up."

"I hope so," Chief Sinard said with a sigh.

Riley listened as Jenn kept prodding Skip with questions— good questions. But Jenn was still getting nowhere with him.

Finally Skip leaned back in his chair, smiling smugly.

"I think I'm ready for a lawyer now," he said.

It was what Riley had expected, of course. Even so, she stifled a groan of annoyance.

In a town like this, a lawyer wouldn't be available until tomorrow.

There was nothing left for them to do today.

*

Evening had set in by the time Riley was able to stretch out on the bed of her motel room on the outskirts of Angier. Looking back, she found it hard to believe all that had happened today—from the discovery of Katy Philbin's body to the wild rescue and arrest of Trip Crozier. Had she and Jenn really flown out here from Quantico just this morning?

Riley felt exhausted—but far from satisfied.

Bored and achy, she glanced around the room. It looked exactly like many rooms she'd been in over the years. She could almost swear she'd seen the same bland paintings of rivers and trees a thousand times before.

The room struck Riley as just like the town of Angier—ugly beneath a cheap veneer of respectability.

There was a knock on the door, and Riley called "Come in." Jenn entered carrying a box of pizza and a six-pack of beer.

Riley smiled and sat up.

"Now why didn't I think of that?" she asked.

She and Jenn sat down on a rather uncomfortable couch and put the pizza and beer on the coffee table in front of them.

"You did good work today," Riley said after taking her first bite of pizza.

Jenn scoffed at the compliment.

"You mean when I got us both knocked down in Trip's trailer? Yeah, that was real smooth of me."

"I'm talking about how you questioned Trip."

Jenn shook her head.

"It's not like I got anything out of him," she said. "You could have done better."

"No," Riley said. "I couldn't."

After feeling vaguely at odds with Jenn all day, it felt good to be able to say something positive about her. And the truth was, Riley was feeling comfortable with her right now. She wasn't sure exactly why.

I'd better enjoy it while it lasts, Riley thought.

She also reminded herself that she'd better be careful what she told her.

"Do you think we've got our guy?" Jenn asked, sipping on her beer.

Riley shook her head.

"I wish I knew."

"Does your gut tell you anything?"

Riley sat quietly, mulling over her feelings.

"No," she said. "What about your gut?"

"I've got nothing," Jenn said. "So what do we do now?"

Riley thought for a moment.

"So far, we don't even know if we're looking for a serial killer. We don't know of any connection between Katy and Holly, and for all we know, Holly might still wind up alive."

Riley paused to think a little more.

"Tomorrow let's go talk to Holly's parents. If it's obvious that her disappearance isn't connected with Katy's death, we've really got no further business here. It's not an FBI case after all. We'll fly back to Quantico tomorrow."

"What if another girl gets murdered?" Jenn asked.

Riley shivered a little. That was precisely the question she'd been trying not to ask herself. It was a grim irony that another life would have to be lost before the FBI could declare it an actual serial case.

"Let's just hope that doesn't happen," Riley said.

Riley and Jenn ate and drank in silence for a little while.

Finally Jenn said, "I guess it's none of my business, but …"

She paused for a moment. Then she said, "I wish you'd tell me more about Shane Hatcher. Your relationship with him, I mean. I'm just curious about it. Your rapport with him, your chemistry. It's something of a legend, you know—how you teamed up with a convicted murderer to solve crimes."

Riley was surprised that she didn't resent the question. She sensed Jenn wasn't trying to trap her. She actually seemed to be genuinely curious.

"What was it like, working with him?" Jenn asked. "Do you wish you could work with him again someday? Would you want to?"

Riley shook her head.

"Jenn—" she began.

"I know, it's none of my business. I'm sorry for asking."

"No, it's not that really ... it's just that I keep asking myself those questions, and I still don't know the answers. It's all an enigma to me."

Riley took a long sip of her beer.

"He scares me, but he fascinates me," she said. "You've heard of the proverbial moth and the flame?"

"Yeah," Jenn said with a sigh. "I know all about that."

Riley turned toward Jenn and glimpsed a faraway look in the young agent's eye.

She's got her own secrets, Riley thought, not for the first time.

Was Jenn ever going to tell Riley about them? Did Riley even want to know those secrets?

At last the two agents finished their pizza. Four beers were left in the six-pack, but neither of them wanted more. Jenn picked them up and went back to her room. Riley had just stretched out on her bed again when her cell phone buzzed.

It was a text message from an unknown number.

It said ...

You're a long way from home.

Her skin crawled when she realized that it was another message from Shane Hatcher.

She typed back frantically.

Where are you? What do you mean?

But once again, when she tried to send the text, it was marked "undeliverable."

Riley could only guess that Hatcher was sending these texts with disposable phones that he discarded right away.

She sat staring at the text. Like so many of Shane Hatcher's communications, it was riddling and mysterious.

But it certainly seemed like a warning.

I really am a long way from home, Riley thought.

Was her family in danger right now? She remembered Bill's promise before she'd come out here ...

"I'll keep an eye on things."

She punched in his phone number and was relieved when he

answered.

"Hey, Riley. How's the case going?"

Riley was on her feet pacing now.

"OK, I guess. We've got a suspect, anyway. But that's not why I'm calling. I just got a text from Hatcher."

"Another threat?"

"With Hatcher it's hard to tell. How are things at my house?"

"Fine. I just got home from driving by there. I talked to Wigton and Lochner in their van out front. They've not noticed anything unusual. I call them every couple of hours or so to check on things."

Riley breathed a sigh of relief.

"Bill, thanks for doing this. I can't tell you how grateful I am."

"Like I said this morning, I need to do something useful."

Riley sat down on the edge of the bed.

"How did things go with Mike Nevins?"

"Fine," Bill said.

His tone of voice sounded a little flatter now.

"How are you feeling?"

"Better."

"Tell me more."

Bill laughed a little. His laughter sounded a little forced.

"Don't be a mother hen. Just trust me, I'm feeling better, OK?"

She sensed he was making an effort to sound cheerful. But she knew better than to nag him about his state of mind. He'd only get less communicative. She thanked him again, and they ended the call.

Then she punched in her home phone number.

April answered.

"Hi, Mom. Catch any bad guys yet?"

"Yeah, one. We don't know yet whether he's the one we're looking for. How is everything at home?"

"Fine, I guess."

Riley's brain was fumbling around, trying to think of questions to ask without frightening April.

"And Jilly, she's OK? And Liam?"

April laughed a little at the worry in Riley's voice.

"We're all fine—Gabriela too. She fixed a great meal—*pollo en crema,* chicken in cream. Wish you could have been here for that."

Riley managed to laugh a little.

"Yeah, me too. Well, just give everybody my love."

"When do you think you'll be back?"

"I'm not sure. Maybe tomorrow. I miss you."

April laughed some more.

"Hey, you've only been gone a day."

"Yeah, I know. I'm just having one of those 'mom' spells, I guess. Give my love to everybody."

She and April ended the call, and Riley lay back down on the bed again.

She was stiff and sore and tired. A hot shower would surely make her feel better. But even then, she wouldn't be fully relaxed, and she wouldn't stop worrying.

Hatcher's text kept flashing through her mind.

You're a long way from home.

She asked herself what the hell she was doing here anyhow.

Maybe tomorrow the missing girl would turn up alive and she could just go back home.

CHAPTER NINETEEN

Camryn Mays was in her little apartment doing her nails when she heard her cell phone's ringtone.

Don't answer it, she told herself.

Who could it possibly be that she'd want to talk to?

Hardly anybody in Angier, surely, and she didn't know anybody who lived anywhere else except her brother, and he never phoned her.

She hated living in Angier—more on some mornings than on others.

Today she wanted to get out of this town so bad she could taste it.

The ringtone stopped, and Camryn finished painting her nails and blew on them to make them dry a little faster. They'd be dry in plenty of time for her lunchtime shift at Vern's Café. She just hoped they wouldn't get chipped today from handling dishes and flatware.

The other servers called the lunch shift the "run and gun" shift. Customers came and went too fast for the servers to do much more than take their orders and dump their food in front of them.

There was no time to chat with customers—and that was fine with Camryn.

Nobody in Angier had anything interesting to say.

Yesterday had been no exception. All the talk had been about how Katy Philbin had been found dead.

Camryn knew she should feel sad and shocked about it, but she couldn't quite manage it. She remembered Katy from back before she'd graduated from Wilson High. Camryn had considered Katy stupid and shallow. Her taste in boyfriends proved it. What did she ever see in that jock Dustin Russo, anyway?

He's such a jerk, she thought.

In fact, she felt sure that Dustin had killed Katy. Who else would have bothered?

But the last Camryn had heard, Dustin hadn't been arrested.

The police in this town are so stupid.

Of course, nobody wanted to suspect a high school football

hero. Sports and jocks—nobody at Wilson High had ever talked about anything else. Camryn hadn't been interested in that kind of thing at all. Being an African-American student in such a white school made her feel all the more isolated.

She was so glad she was through with that school.

Not that she was all that crazy about Angier Community College. There weren't a lot of black students there either, and even the professors weren't very interesting to talk to. But at least it was a step up toward getting out of this town and going to a four-year college.

And after that, what?

Well, with a business degree, she could move away and make a comfortable life for herself.

She envied her brother, who had already finished college and was living in Cedar Rapids. Somehow, it had been easier for him than it was for her. She still didn't have the money even for instate tuition and all the other expenses.

But she was doing everything she could. She was working on setting up a financial aid package. She was trying to avoid loans as much as possible, because that would leave her paying it back for years to come. The finances just weren't coming together the way she wanted them to.

She looked around at her shabby little apartment. It wasn't much, but it was better than living at home.

Of course, she could save more money if she lived at home.

The trouble was, her parents made endless demands on her time there. They wanted her to run errands here, pick up something for them there, buy this or that with her own money. She just couldn't get her schoolwork done at home. And by the time she got back from her errands, Mom and Dad would both be in a stupor in front of the TV.

She sighed a bit sadly. It was too bad her parents didn't understand why she wanted to live on her own. She hated that it hurt their feelings.

The truth was, she really felt sorry for them.

They'd lived in this lousy town all their lives, feeling as isolated in this sea of whiteness as she did. Not that they ever complained about the subtle undercurrent of bigotry here in Angier. But she knew they hated their jobs and probably hated their whole lives. They weren't even happy with each other anymore. They just stayed together out of lack of anything better to do.

Camryn desperately hoped she wouldn't wind up like that. But this whole town felt like a trap that was ready to snap shut on her.

The phone rang again, and this time she looked to see who was calling.

Oh my God! she thought when she saw the name.

It was somebody she wanted to talk to after all.

She picked up the phone carefully without smudging her wet nails.

"Hello," she said in her most mature voice.

"Hello, Camryn. I hope I didn't catch you at a bad time."

"Not at all. This is perfect."

"I've got some information on a scholarship program that I think you've got a good chance for. It calls for a lot of information and an essay, but I think it's ideal for you. I'd like to go over it with you."

Camryn almost let out a yelp of joy. But she managed to keep her voice under control. She didn't want to sound like an overexcited teenager.

"That sounds great," she said. "Could you email me the application?"

"Sure. But before we do that, I'd like to meet with you in person and go over every item together. This is a big one, and you'll have to give it a lot of attention. Then you can take your time filling it out, and I'll be glad to review it for you again."

Camryn's heart lifted. This was just the break she needed, a big financial boost. And if she got it, the prestige would also help.

"When do you want to talk about it?" she asked.

"How about right now?"

Camryn looked at her watch and gulped silently. She only had an hour before she had to be at work. But she didn't even want to mention her crummy job right now.

Besides, which was more important—waitressing or getting a big scholarship?

If she was late for her shift, the other servers would just have to deal with it.

Right now, she didn't much care if she even got fired.

"I'll catch a bus and come right over," she said.

"I'll tell you what, I'm not too far away. I'll come and pick you up."

"Perfect," Camryn said, still trying not to betray her excitement. "Give me just fifteen minutes."

The caller sounded pleased.

"OK. But listen—I know it's tempting to shout this news from the rooftops. But don't jump the gun and tell anybody, not just yet. I want to be sure we know what we're doing and get everything right. And there's a limit on applications from each district. I want to make sure you get first crack at this."

Camryn almost laughed at the idea that she might tell anybody. Who did she know who would even care about it? Besides, she sure didn't want to jinx her chances by bragging about it.

She said thank you, and the call ended.

She hurried to put on nice clothes and comb her hair. She was glad she had done her nails in a muted shade. He was being so helpful, she wanted to look like she was worth all that trouble.

CHAPTER TWENTY

The next morning when she and Jenn drove to visit Holly Struthers's parents, Riley was feeling conflicting emotions.

She didn't know what to expect.

She didn't know what to hope for either.

She knew that Chief Sinard's officers were probably interviewing Trip Crozier right now, trying to make their case against him. It was entirely possible that Crozier's alibi for Katy's murder would fall through and he'd turn out to be guilty.

He also might prove guilty of whatever had happened to Holly Struthers.

On the other hand, there might be no connection at all between Holly's disappearance and Katy's rape and murder.

Whatever the truth turned out to be, Riley was sure of one thing—that she loathed the town of Angier. The town was starting to make her sick to her stomach with its phony facade of wholesomeness and respectability. She couldn't remember the last time she'd had such a negative gut reaction to a town.

Of course, if there was no connection between Holly and Katy, she and Jenn had no more business here.

And that would be fine with Riley. She wanted to get out of here—this morning, if possible.

On the other hand, if there really was a serial killer at large in Angier, she and Jenn had urgent work to do. They had to figure him out before he could strike again.

But then, for all Riley really knew, he had already struck again. The body of another young girl could already be buried somewhere—or even more than one.

A farmer noticing something odd in his tilled field had been a stroke of luck. If George Tully hadn't been out at that spot that morning, the corn planter would have rolled right over the buried body. Then the town would have had two lost girls with no clue to the fate of either one. And a serial killer would have gotten away with it.

As their car approached the Struthers's house, Riley observed that the neighborhood houses were newer than in the area where the Philbins lived. They were also somewhat larger, with wider lawns and two-car garages attached to every home. But these modular houses aped the bungalow designs of an older neighborhood, making them just look superficial as far as Riley was concerned.

This well-cared-for neighborhood was surely what she'd heard real estate people call "high pride of ownership." It probably wasn't the richest part of town, but families would feel good about themselves for settling down here.

Riley could almost smell a certain smugness in the air.

Jenn parked in front of a house with brown siding and beige trim, a broad porch, and a conspicuous garage. It was so neat and dollhouse-like that it looked like it might have been planted here yesterday. Riley half expected to find it inhabited by plastic toy people.

Riley and Jenn walked up onto the porch and knocked on the door. Riley was glad they had called ahead. Perhaps they would cause a little less alarm this way.

A nervous-looking woman answered. Riley guessed that she was in her early forties, although she probably made some effort to look younger.

Riley and Jenn produced their badges and introduced themselves.

"Yes, yes," the woman said in a shaky voice. "I'm Dorothy Struthers. My husband and I have been expecting you."

As she escorted Riley and Jenn into the living room, she called out, "Harold, it's the FBI people."

A trim, ordinary-looking man came trotting down the stairs into the living room. Dorothy invited Riley and Jenn to sit down.

Dorothy's eyes darted back and forth between Riley and Jenn.

"Is there … news about Holly?" she asked.

With his anxious expression, Harold Struthers seemed to be silently asking the same question.

"No, not at this time," Riley said.

She was slightly surprised when the Dorothy let out an audible sigh of relief.

Then Riley realized—she had been worried that she and Jenn had come over to confirm her very worst fears, that her daughter was dead.

Her voice still unsteady, Dorothy said, "Oh, when that girl gets home, she's really going to get it."

Riley was taken aback. The last thing she had meant to do was raise the couple's hopes.

In her current state of denial, Dorothy had taken Riley's words as confirmation that her daughter was probably alive and well. Of course, Riley had said nothing of the sort. Was it going to be even possible for Riley and Jenn to set her straight as to facts?

What facts? Riley thought.

Dorothy continued, laughing nervously.

"She'll never hear the last of it from me ... The nerve of that girl, putting us through this ... She'll be grounded until, I don't know, forever, or when she starts collecting Social Security or something ..."

As Dorothy rambled on nervously, her husband kept gently trying to interrupt her.

"Dorothy ... Dorothy ..."

Finally the woman turned to Harold with an annoyed look.

"What?" she asked.

Harold lowered his head.

"Nothing," he said.

Riley could now tell that Dorothy's husband wasn't in the same state of denial. But he had no more of an idea of what to say to her than Riley did. Dorothy continued her diatribe until Jenn managed to speak.

"Mr. and Mrs. Struthers, we need to ask you some questions."

"About what?" Dorothy said.

She sounded absolutely mystified that there was anything left to discuss.

Jenn asked, "Does your daughter have a history of doing this kind of thing? Running away, I mean?"

Dorothy forced a laugh.

"Oh, yes, more than once. Odd, she was a perfect little girl growing up. But when she hit her teenage years—well, it was like she'd gone completely crazy. She rebelled and lashed out about every little thing. Didn't she, Harold?"

"She sure did," Harold said quietly.

Dorothy said, "She sometimes disappeared for a night or two. Usually she'd sneak away to a friend's house. Once she rented a motel room and holed up there for three nights. Can you imagine? We never called the police before. This time we did it just to make a fuss and embarrass her. If the police picked her up, maybe it would teach her a good lesson."

She sighed.

"Harold and I have no idea what's going on in that little head of hers."

Harold patted his wife's hand.

He said to Riley and Jenn, "Holly just can't commit herself to anything these days. She keeps trying things out and dropping them—cheerleading, soccer, tennis, different kinds of clubs at school."

He pointed to a baby grand piano at the far end of the room.

He said, "Last fall she said she wanted to become a concert pianist. She had some talent, and she seemed so determined, so we were all excited about it and bought that piano. But she lost interest and the piano has just been sitting there ever since."

Riley asked, "Have you contacted all of her friends?"

Harold said, "Yes—at least all the friends we know of. Nobody seems to have any idea where she went this time."

Riley saw that Jenn leaned forward in her chair.

"We need to ask you a few questions about Katy Philbin," Jenn said.

Dorothy tilted her head with curiosity.

"Oh, the girl who was killed. Well, I never knew her. Did you know her, Harold?"

Harold shook his head silently.

Dorothy said, "And I'm sure Holly never knew her. She never mentioned anyone named Katy. I'd remember."

Riley knew that it was a delicate line of questioning that could easily send Dorothy into a full-scale panic.

But Riley soon realized that Jenn was handling things well enough, asking questions that didn't upset either Harold or Dorothy any more than they were upset already.

She's learning, Riley thought.

She decided to let Jenn keep on asking the questions. As she listened, she sat studying the immaculate, middle-class surroundings and made guesses about the family.

Just how dysfunctional were they?

Was anything sinister going on in this household?

Chief Sinard had mentioned that Harold was a chiropractor. Riley suspected that Harold had grown up and studied chiropractic elsewhere, perhaps in a big city. He had come to Angier hoping to really stand out here and make his mark on the community. He'd been financially successful enough to raise his family in comfort, and his wife didn't have to work outside the house.

But Riley doubted whether Harold and his wife were really satisfied with the life they'd carved out for themselves here. They'd surely found that the prominent families of Angier were a closed group that had been here for many generations.

Social climbers with no place to climb, Riley thought.

They didn't seem especially self-aware, so they probably weren't fully conscious of their own lurking resentment.

Their teenage daughter had probably been more aware of it than they were.

Hence Holly's pattern of rebellious behavior.

At least that was one plausible scenario for what was going on here.

Riley heard a clattering of footsteps coming down the stairs. A pimply teenaged boy burst into the room. Riley guessed that he was maybe fifteen or sixteen years old.

He said, "Hey, Dad, we've got to get going. The rocket club event starts in just a few minutes."

Harold introduced the agents to his son, Zach.

The boy's mouth dropped open.

"The FBI!" he said. "Jesus!"

"Language!" his mother said.

Harold said to Zach, "They're here asking questions about Holly."

Zach shook his head.

"Wow. Is that girl in trouble now or what?"

To Riley and Jenn he added, "Well, when you find her, do us all a favor and just keep her. She's a real pain in the ass."

Dorothy let out another exclamation of maternal disapproval, which Zach shrugged off.

Jenn said, "Zach, do you know anyone who might have meant your sister any harm?"

"Aside from me, you mean?" he said with a sneer. "I wouldn't know. I don't ask her any questions about her life, and she doesn't ask me any questions about mine. It works for both of us."

Then he turned to his father and said, "Come on, let's get going."

Riley briefly considered stopping the kid to ask him some more questions. But she had a feeling that he'd really meant what he'd said—that he paid as little attention to his sister as he could. He probably knew next to nothing about what might have happened to her.

Besides, any questions were only going to upset his parents further.

Riley said to Harold and Dorothy, "Thank you both for your time and cooperation. We're sorry to have disturbed you. We'll get in touch if we have any news."

Riley and Jenn left the house and got into the car.

"So what do you think of the kid brother?" Jenn asked.

"Typical teenager, I guess," Riley said. "A classic case of sibling rivalry."

"Do you think there's any reason for us to stay in Angier?"

Riley mulled it over, but couldn't form an opinion one way or the other.

"What do *you* think?" Riley asked.

Jenn thought for a moment.

"I don't know," she said. "So far we don't know of any connection between the Philbin girl and the Struthers girl. And now we know that Holly had a history of rebellion and running away. She might turn up any day, or she might have gotten herself into serious trouble, maybe even killed. So we've got no reason to think that Katy's murder was anything but an isolated event. But even so …"

Jenn's voice trailed off for a moment.

Then she said, "If it's all the same to you, I don't think we should jump on a plane and fly out of here just yet. Holly Struthers went to Lincoln High. Maybe could pay the principal a visit."

"It's Saturday," Riley said. "But let's see if he's at school today anyhow."

Jenn dialed the school number and confirmed that the principal was indeed in his office. When she hung up, she said, "He's willing to talk with us today. He said to press the bell and he'll buzz us in." After a moment she added, "He sounds kind of like a used car salesman."

Riley agreed that seeing the principal was a good idea, and the younger agent started driving toward the high school.

Riley mulled things over as Jenn drove.

Jenn was right. As far as they knew, Holly's disappearance had nothing to do with Katy's murder. In fact, it might even be likely.

But Riley had a bad feeling about Holly all the same. More than a week was a long time for a teenager to deliberately disappear.

Riley couldn't help thinking that something terrible had happened to her.

She reminded herself that she couldn't solve all the problems in a messed-up town like this.

But could she really leave Angier while Holly was still missing?

CHAPTER TWENTY ONE

Lincoln High School looked oddly out of place to Riley. While Wilson High had seemed like some weird throwback to a bygone time, Lincoln looked sparkling and new, all steel and glass. It reminded her of the school that April went to, which was unsettling because it gave a grim reminder that kids weren't safe anywhere anymore.

But something else about the building bothered her.

She realized that she couldn't help thinking of it as phony—a false façade like everything else in this town seemed to be. Riley cautioned herself to double-check her own perceptions. She no longer knew if she was sensing an actual dark underbelly to every part of all this apparent normality, or if she was simply imagining it.

As Jenn rang the buzzer at the front entrance, Riley suppressed a sigh and focused on the job at hand. The door was opened by a nattily dressed man in an expensive-looking shirt, a tie, a sweater vest with diamond patterns, and pleated pants.

"I'm Nigel Pelelo, the principal," he said in a hearty tone. "I believe you're here to speak with me. Right this way."

As Riley and Jenn followed him to his office, Riley looked him over.

He reminded her disagreeably of Carl Walder, except that his face was markedly better looking. He actually had something of the self-confident bearing of a male fashion model.

When they got to his office, the principal invited Riley and Jenn to sit down, then took his place behind his desk.

"Goodness, the FBI!" Pelelo said with a chuckle. "I hope I'm not under investigation."

Riley didn't even try to force a laugh at the lame joke.

"I'm afraid we're here on serious business, Mr. Pelelo," she said. "I'm sure you know that a girl who goes to school here has gone missing."

Pelelo shook his head and clicked his tongue.

"Oh, yes—Holly Struthers," he said. "Very worrisome. I do hope she turns up soon, safe and sound. But why is this a matter for the FBI?"

Jenn said, "I'm sure you're also aware of the rape and murder of Katy Philbin."

Pelelo's eyes widened a little.

"The girl whose body was found yesterday, you mean—the girl who went to Wilson High? But I'd heard that there was a suspect in custody. Good Lord. Surely you don't think that Holly … well, I don't even know how to say it."

Riley said, "At this point, we really don't know if there's any connection. That's why we wanted to talk to you. How well did you know Holly?"

Pelelo swiveled in his chair a bit and steepled his fingers. He struck Riley as practically an encyclopedia of body language—although she didn't yet know how to read his apparently practiced gestures.

Pelelo said, "Well, I'm afraid I'm just now in the process of getting to know all my students. I just became principal here this year." With a grin he added, "You might call me the new kid here at Lincoln. I'm new to Angier, for that matter."

He thought for a moment, then added, "But Holly has made an impression on me, I must say."

Riley felt suddenly queasy. Did she detect a touch of a leer in his voice?

She had a sinking feeling that this wasn't the kind of man who ought to be working around hundreds of teenaged girls.

She also recognized that he was like a lot of administrative-type men she'd known over the years. He was a big-city guy who had managed to dazzle his way into this job in a well-to-do community with charm and good looks and little else.

He'd never be much good at his job, but few parents would notice—and fewer still would care.

Appearances are everything in this town, Riley reminded herself.

And Nigel Pelelo looked picture perfect behind that desk. Parents might even disregard the unsavory way he glanced at female students.

But if his behavior amounted to more than just looking, might they disregard that too?

She was sure that there was a lot of denial in this community.

Pelelo continued, "Holly gets called into my office quite often. For small things mostly—disrupting class, talking back to teachers, rudeness to other students. And she has this little habit of running away from time to time. Never so long before, but she does run away."

Pelelo looked up at the ceiling rather dreamily.

"We've talked and talked and talked," he said.

"About what?" Jenn asked.

Pelelo sounded just a bit defensive now.

"I'm not sure it would be right for me to tell you," he said. "I'm embarrassed to admit it, but I honestly don't know whether there's any kind of confidentiality issue concerning what gets said between a principal and a student."

Riley didn't know either, but she doubted it. Pelelo hadn't been meeting with Holly in the capacity of a professional counselor, after all.

Pelelo leaned forward in his chair.

"But I will tell you that I think she'll be fine when she pulls out of this phase she's going through. And I'm sure she'll come back from wherever she is. She's a good girl, with lots of potential and a great future ahead of her. She's a bright and lovely girl."

Riley's skin was crawling now. She already knew that Holly had been rebelling against her parents. Like so many teenagers, Holly had been convinced that they didn't understand her at all. In fact, Holly may have felt misunderstood, neglected, even mistreated by just about everybody.

Holly was surely vulnerable to the charms of a handsome, charming father figure in a position of authority.

Had Pelelo taken physical advantage of her vulnerability?

Riley hoped not.

But even though she suspected that nothing but talking had occurred in this office, Riley thought that even talking had hardly been appropriate or proper.

This town, she thought yet again. Innocence in Angier seemed to be a hard thing to come by—and an easy thing to lose.

She weighed whether to press Pelelo specifically about his relationship with Holly.

She quickly decided that an indirect approach would be better.

If Pelelo were guilty of anything, maybe he'd give himself away in unintended and even nonverbal ways.

Riley looked at Jenn and gave her a nod, prompting her to ask her own questions.

Jenn took the hint and asked, "Mr. Pelelo, do you know

anybody—students or adults—who might have meant any harm to Holly?"

Pelelo chuckled a little.

"In this school, you mean? The kids here at Lincoln are good kids, and their parents are good parents. As for what happened to Katy Philbin—well, maybe you should be talking to the principal at Wilson High instead of me. Although I doubt that you'll find him at work on a weekend."

Riley caught a hint of school rivalry—and maybe some professional rivalry as well.

But in itself, that seemed hardly surprising or sinister.

Jenn kept asking routine questions, and Riley eyed Pelelo closely. But she reminded herself not to let her suspicions run away with her.

At this point, she had no tangible reason to suspect Pelelo of rape and murder. If she allowed herself to obsess about his creepy relationship with Holly Struthers, she might fail to catch the real killer.

Soon Riley's phone buzzed.

She considered ignoring it. But under the circumstances, it might be something urgent, even life-threatening.

"Excuse me for just a moment," Riley said.

She stepped outside the office and took the call.

"Am I speaking with Special Agent Riley Paige?" the caller asked.

"You are."

"This is Austin Daggett. I'm the mayor of Angier. Chief Sinard gave me your number."

Riley didn't know what to say. What could the mayor want with her?

"Where are you right now?" Mayor Daggett asked.

His voice had a distinctive rasp to it that reminded her of her father.

From years of whiskey and tobacco, Riley guessed.

Riley said, "My partner and I are at Lincoln High. We're talking with Principal Pelelo."

"Well, drop what you're doing and meet me in my office."

Riley was startled. Should she explain that she didn't take orders from him? Right now she was accountable only to Chief Sinard himself, and she actually outranked him on most issues.

"What's this about?" Riley asked.

"I'll tell you when you get here," Mayor Daggett said.

Without waiting for Riley to reply, Daggett gave Riley directions on how to get to Angier's town hall. Then he abruptly ended the call.

Riley stood for a few seconds staring at the phone. She thought the mayor had some nerve giving her orders out of nowhere. She had half a mind to ignore his summons.

But she didn't dare—not if he had some new information pertinent to the case.

She stepped back inside the office and caught a snippet of the exchange between Jenn and Principal Pelelo. The man's smile was looking a little frozen, but it seemed obvious to Riley that all this questioning was getting them nowhere.

She said, "Agent Roston, we've got to go now."

Jenn looked surprised but got out of her chair. Riley managed to force out a polite thank-you to Pelelo for his time and cooperation. Then Jenn and Riley headed back to their car. Riley quickly explained that they were on their way to talk to the mayor.

Jenn shook her head as she got behind the wheel.

"That Pelelo guy gives me the creeps," she said as she started the ignition.

"You and me both," Riley said.

She didn't say so, but she suspected that things were about to get creepier.

CHAPTER TWENTY TWO

During the drive to City Hall, Riley kept flashing back to the image of poor Katy Philbin's body in that cornfield—battered, her mouth full of dirt, with bruises on her thighs …

The girl reminded her of April, of course. That was why Riley kept seeing this awful picture in her mind's eye. Her own daughter had been endangered more than once because of Riley's investigations. She couldn't dismiss the memory of a murdered teenager because it stirred her personal terrors.

Riley tried again to drive the image from her mind, but she couldn't make it go away.

She knew that wasn't good.

She usually managed to keep her personal fears separated from her work. In fact, this one might not even be related to her job. It seemed quite possible that she and Jenn might go back to Quantico without solving Katy's murder. If Holly's disappearance turned out to be truly unconnected to what had happened to Katy, there was no further reason for two FBI agents to stay here.

Riley wondered—would that image keep haunting her even after she got back home?

The thought made her shudder.

She wasn't sure she could make herself leave Angier without catching Katy's killer. She also felt driven to find out what had happened to Holly.

But what if she had no choice?

If there was no sign of a serial killer, how could she stay on this case?

Maybe we'll know more when we talk to the mayor, Riley thought.

But she had a gut feeling that the meeting wasn't going to go well. His phone call hadn't given her any sign that the man might be helpful.

Jenn pulled up in front of Angier's City Hall—a compact but venerable granite-and-brick building that Riley guessed to be about a hundred years old.

The two agents walked inside and made their way through a marble-floored hallway to the mayor's office. Their footsteps echoed through a space that seemed to be largely uninhabited today. But there was a receptionist at a desk inside the doorway labeled "Mayor Austin Daggett." After greeting them with a frown, the receptionist rose from her chair and ushered them directly inside.

Mayor Daggett looked up from his desk with an unfriendly glare, as if Riley and Jenn were unexpected and unwelcome.

He conspicuously did not ask them to sit down, as if he didn't expect them to stay for more than a few minutes.

The man struck Riley as a living relic, a small-town mayor from bygone years. He was a tall man with steel-gray hair who wore a bow tie and suspenders and pants that hitched up above his waist.

There was also a distinct and familiar odor in the office.

Whiskey and cigars, Riley thought.

Her impression of his voice on the phone had been correct. Sure enough, on his desk was a half-full bottle of expensive, eight-year-old bourbon, along with an empty shot glass. There was also an ashtray filled with cigar butts.

The mayor apparently ignored no smoking rules in his personal domain.

She was just as happy that he wasn't smoking right now.

Mayor Daggett said in that raspy voice of his, "There's a guy in the jailhouse who says you two violated his Fourth Amendment rights and beat him up in the process."

Riley suppressed a smirk.

So much for idle chitchat, she thought.

He didn't sound drunk, anyway. Riley remembered how her father had been able to drink almost constantly all day long without showing its effects. Mayor Daggett seemed to have that same capacity.

And now she knew that Trip Crozier had a lawyer, probably a public defender who was hard at work earning as much as he could of taxpayers' money.

Riley said, "The suspect won't be able to make those charges stick."

Mayor Daggett started shuffling papers in his desk, as if to indicate that this conversation was worthy of only part of his concentration.

"I've gotten other complaints about you," he said.

He glanced up from his papers. He seemed to expect Riley and Jenn to explain themselves. Of course, Riley had no idea what he was talking about.

He said, "Barry Teague tells me you made a nuisance of yourselves at the crime scene."

For a moment Riley couldn't place the name.

But then she remembered.

Barry Teague had been the disagreeable medical examiner they had encountered at George Tully's cornfield.

She recalled his palpable resentment that she and Jenn were even there.

"Maybe if you federal folks let me haul the body out of here and do my job ..."

Riley felt herself bristle all over.

She and Jenn seemed to have stepped into a local nest of good old boys who didn't like outsiders.

She said, "My partner and I conducted ourselves in a perfectly professional manner at the crime scene."

"That's not what I hear," Mayor Daggett growled.

Riley took a long, deep breath to keep her temper under control.

"Mayor Daggett, you called Agent Roston and me away from an interview. Perhaps you can tell us why."

Daggett kept idly poking among his papers.

He said, "It's time for you two gals to fly on back to Quantico."

Riley felt her face flush. She could hardly believe her ears.

"How do you figure that?" she asked.

Daggett shrugged without bothering to look at them.

"We've got Katy's killer in custody. And if you haven't made too much of a legal mess out of things, we'll get a conviction. Meanwhile, I don't want you underfoot while my local boys are doing their job."

Jenn spoke up now.

"What about Holly Struthers?"

"The missing girl?" Daggett said. "She'll turn up. She's from a good family."

Riley almost scoffed aloud.

A non sequitur if ever I heard one, she thought.

Jenn said, "Mayor Daggett, there's every possibility that there's a serial killer at large in this town."

"There's not," Daggett said.

"How do you know?" Jenn asked.

"Things like that don't happen in Angier. I've been the mayor here for more than half of my life. I keep a clean town."

Riley didn't know which annoyed her more—the man's arrogance or his naïveté. For the moment, she didn't know what to say.

Daggett added, "I keep a peaceable town, too, with happy people. But yesterday I got lots of calls from folks who are worried and scared. You're the cause of it, as far as I'm concerned. Well, I'm not putting up with it. I want you away from here yesterday, if not sooner."

Riley had had more than enough of him by now.

She said, "Mayor Daggett, we're not here at your request. Which means we're not answerable to your authority. Now if Chief Sinard—"

Daggett interrupted, "Sinard's on board about this."

"What do you mean?"

"He agrees with me. Your presence is no longer needed here. Not that it ever was."

Riley's mouth fell open.

Could Daggett be telling the truth? It was Sinard who had been so anxious that he got a DC relative to call in the FBI in the first place.

Riley had felt sure that Chief Sinard was the only ally in Angier she and Jenn could fully count on.

But then she quickly realized—Daggett truly pulled all the strings in this town.

If Sinard wanted to keep his job, he had to do as Daggett liked. And right now, that meant getting Riley and Jenn out of Angier.

She said, "I'd like to talk this over with Chief Sinard himself."

Daggett shrugged again.

"Be my guest. It's a waste of the government's time, as far as I'm concerned. But then, I guess wasting is all that fed time is really good for."

Riley glanced at Jenn, who looked just as exasperated as she was—and just as ready to get out of this office.

But before they could turn to go, the mayor's desk phone rang.

Daggett picked it up. His face blanched at whatever he heard.

"What?" he said. "Good Lord!"

Riley could tell right away that something awful had happened.

Then her phone rang too.

Before answering her ringing phone, Riley watched the mayor as he listened to whoever had called him. What could the man be hearing that caused him so much alarm? But he wasn't saying anything. He was simply listening with a dumbstruck, horrified expression.

Then Riley answered her own phone. She heard Chief Sinard's voice.

"Agent Paige, where are you right now?"

Riley wondered if maybe Sinard was calling to relay the mayor's message—that she and Jenn were no longer needed or wanted in Angier.

Riley said, "Agent Roston and I are at Mayor Daggett's office."

Sinard groaned aloud. His voice sounded agitated.

"Well, whatever the mayor told you about going back to Quantico, you can ignore it. Another body has been found."

CHAPTER TWENTY THREE

Riley's heart sank. She asked, "Is it Holly Struthers?"

"I don't know yet. I'm going to check on it myself. You'd better come along but it's out in the country. I'll drive by City Hall and pick you up in just a few minutes."

The call ended and Riley looked at Jenn.

Riley said, "It looks like we're still on the case after all."

Meanwhile, the mayor had just hung up his phone. He looked back and forth between Riley and Jenn.

He stammered, "That—that was Marcus Dunning. He runs the landfill outside of town. He says that one of his employees found …"

Daggett's voice faded away. He couldn't seem to finish his thought. But Riley understood what he was leaving unsaid. The body had been found in that landfill.

The mayor seemed at a loss for words. His mouth moved soundlessly.

Riley looked him in the eye and asked, "Do you have a request to make?"

The mayor's head bobbed up and down, nodding yes.

Riley said nothing.

Finally he blurted, "Uh, I'm hereby making an official request for the help of the FBI on this matter."

When Riley still made no answer, the mayor added, "Please."

Riley turned to Jenn and said, "Come on."

Without another word to the mayor, Riley and Jenn went outside to wait for Chief Sinard to arrive and pick them up.

*

The landfill was only a ten-minute drive outside of Angier. Chief Sinard parked his SUV near the edge of the excavation. As soon as they got out of the vehicle, Riley felt her eyes stinging at the stench of the place. She wondered if maybe they ought to be wearing surgical masks.

A burly, middle-aged man wearing overalls came toward them.

He wasn't wearing a mask, so Riley guessed they must be all right without them.

Chief Sinard introduced Riley and Jenn to the man.

"I'm Marcus Dunning," he said. "You'll excuse me if I don't shake hands."

With a slight, self-deprecating chuckle, he added, "I find that visitors generally prefer that I don't—shake hands with them, I mean. I can't imagine why, can you?"

Then his expression abruptly saddened.

"This is terrible. I never thought I'd see the day ..."

Riley felt a pang of sympathy. Marcus Dunning had a hearty, kindly face. He seemed like a warm and caring man, despite the vileness of his work.

Dunning started to lead them around the cratered-out landfill. The smell struck Riley as a combination of strong housecleaning products and rotten eggs.

Dunning seemed to notice his visitors' discomfort.

"Sorry about the smell," he said. "Don't worry, it's nothing toxic, it won't hurt you. It's mostly ammonia and sulfides. You get used to it when you work here long enough."

Riley figured she'd better learn more about this place in order to understand what had happened.

She said to Dunning, "Tell me how this operation works."

As they kept walking, Dunning pointed down to where a bulldozer was pushing garbage against an upright wall of light brown material.

"That's today's load," he explained. "Elliot's driving the 'dozer, shaping the load into what we call a 'cell.' Once we've got it compacted into place, we cover it with woodchips—both over the top and down the side. There are lots and lots of cells beyond this pile, and underneath it too—more cells than you can count, believe me."

They walked on around the excavated portion to where the vast landfill was entirely covered by a horizontal layer of woodchips.

Dunning explained, "I was out here this morning when I noticed an awful smell, like nothing I've ever smelled before."

Riley also could smell it now—a pungent stench that she was much too familiar with, like rotting meat doused in cheap perfume.

Dunning stopped walking and pointed to a spot farther off in the middle of the layer of woodchips. That area had been dug up, with garbage and chips scattered to one side.

"I traced the smell to that spot yonder," he said, his voice shaking a little now. "The woodchips there looked like they'd been disturbed since we put them down. I took a shovel to it, and—"

He choked aloud.

"Oh, Jesus," he said. "I'd rather not look at her again, if you don't mind."

"That's fine," Riley said, patting him on the shoulder. "We're sorry this happened."

Dunning remained standing where he was as Riley, Jenn, and Chief Sinard walked out across the soft, thick, spongy layer of woodchips that covered untold tons of city garbage. When they arrived at the dug-up spot, they found what Dunning had discovered.

The stench was now nearly intolerable, and Riley's eyes were stinging so much that she had a hard time getting them to focus. She knew that surgical masks would have offered no relief for a stench like this.

The first thing to catch her eye was the corpse's face.

It was so swollen and bloated that it hardly looked real—more like some unspeakably hideous Halloween mask. The eyes and tongue were bulging, and the skin was a mottled blend of green and red. Blackish, bloody foam had formed around the nostrils and lips.

Much of the rest of the body was littered with garbage—milk cartons, empty cans and bottles, egg shells, fruit rinds, discarded food, and the like.

As grotesque as the body was, it was recognizably that of a teenage girl who was still wearing what had once been a pretty outfit. The blouse appeared much too tight for her. But Riley knew that was because of the massive bloating.

Riley stooped down for a closer look when she heard a violent choking sound.

She turned and saw that Chief Sinard had buckled over and was vomiting.

She looked at Jenn, who was holding her hand over her nose and mouth, staring wide-eyed at the corpse. Riley had seen corpses in this state of decomposition before, but she reminded herself that Jenn was new to this job.

"Have you ever seen …?" Riley began.

Jenn shook her head. But she pointed to the body's right hand. She said, "I see something—under the girl's fingernail."

Riley crouched beside the body. Jenn was right—there was something purple under a fingernail. In all this clutter, it had taken sharp eyes to spot it.

Riley was impressed at how her younger partner was managing to remain cool, professional, and observant. She knew the younger agent would probably have to face more scenes like this in an FBI career. But she also couldn't blame Chief Sinard for losing his composure, along with his most recent meal.

As usual, Riley had brought along a bag and tweezers to collect samples. But before she had a chance to reach for the purple object, she heard a voice shouting from across the landfill.

"Stay away from that body!"

Riley turned and saw Barry Teague huffing and puffing as he jogged toward them, his enormous belly bouncing all the way. Following right behind the medical examiner were two members of his team. Their official vehicle was parked near where Chief Sinard had parked.

Riley turned toward Chief Sinard to ask whether he had called the ME. But Sinard hadn't stopped vomiting.

Of course he called, Riley realized.

It was the right thing to do, of course.

Not that she was the least bit happy to see Teague—especially not after he had apparently lied to Mayor Daggett about how she and Jenn had conducted themselves back at George Tully's cornfield.

As he got nearer, Teague snarled, "I thought you feds would be gone by now. You don't know when to quit, do you?"

Teague crouched down and looked at the body.

"Hell," he grumbled. "We'll have a devil of a time identifying this one."

Riley couldn't help but relish the opportunity to tell Teague his own business.

"Not so hard," Riley said. "She's in the bloated stage of decomposition, with active decay kicking in. That places her death at a little more than a week ago. Which just happens to be when Holly Struthers disappeared."

Teague looked up at her and emitted a resentful growl.

She pointed at the hand and said, "You might want to check under her fingernail."

Teague peered more closely. With his own tweezers he picked up the little patch of purple.

126

"Some kind of synthetic fabric," he said. "From a carpet, maybe."

He dropped the sample in his own evidence bag.

Riley said, "I'd like to have our FBI lab run tests on that."

The man straightened up and glared up at her. "We can do it here," he snapped.

Riley just held out her hand. She was losing patience with the ill-tempered ME, but she didn't want to get into a physical struggle with him out here on the spongy landfill next to a decaying body.

After a moment, Teague gave in to the power of her glare and handed the little bag over. Without a word, Riley tucked it away to send to Quantico.

Meanwhile, Jenn had walked around to the other side of the body. Still showing remarkable self-control, she stooped down and pointed.

"There's something in her blouse pocket," she said.

Riley walked beside Jenn, stooped down, and used her tweezers to gently pull a sheet of folded paper out of the pocket.

She shook it open and saw that it was a piece of musical staff paper. Some notes were penciled on it, with the title "Holly's Song."

"Do you think that means anything?" Jenn asked, looking over Riley's shoulder.

"It's too soon to tell," Riley said, dropping the paper in her bag. "But I'm pretty sure of one thing. Whoever did this is the same person who killed and buried Katy Philbin."

Jenn nodded in agreement.

"Same careless disposal of the body."

"That's right," Riley said.

Jenn shuddered a little and added, "Which means that this girl was probably raped too."

"Probably," Riley said.

Chief Sinard had gotten to his feet and was wiping off his mouth.

Riley said to him, "You were right to call in the FBI after all. This is definitely looking like you have a serial killer at work here."

Sinard didn't look the least bit comforted by this news.

He asked, "Do you think we've got the right man in custody?"

Riley thought about the sleazy drug dealer called Trip. Although she had arrested him, she didn't feel any sense of certainty that he was also the killer.

"I wish I knew," she said.

She walked back over to where Dunning was still standing.

She asked him, "Do you have any idea how somebody got in here to bury the body?"

Dunning nodded.

"The landfill closes at six," he said. "But there's just a chain across the road and a sign saying closed. Nobody goes poking around here at night. People stay away from this place. It never occurred to me—"

Suddenly a woman's shriek filled the air.

"Where is she? It can't be her! Let me see!"

Riley turned and saw a man and a woman charging toward them across the field of woodchips. She quickly recognized them as Dorothy and Harold Struthers, Holly's parents. Dorothy was screaming and waving her arms as she approached.

Riley gasped.

What are they doing here?

She knew that a horrifying situation was about to get much, much worse.

CHAPTER TWENTY FOUR

As Harold and Dorothy Struthers approached, Jenn rushed away from Riley's side and ran toward them, trying to persuade them not to come any closer. Harold stopped in his tracks and seemed to be trying to restrain his wife. But Dorothy pushed past both him and Jenn.

Riley stepped in front of Dorothy and grabbed her by the shoulders.

"You can't be here," she said. "What are you doing here?"

"The mayor called," Dorothy said, sobbing. "Is it true? What he told me? It can't be true! It can't be her!"

Riley felt a flash of anger.

What did Mayor Daggett think he was doing, calling the girl's parents at this point? Why couldn't he wait at least until the body was in the morgue?

Of course, the answer was quite simple.

He's a damned fool, Riley realized.

Dorothy was struggling free of Riley's grip and it was clear that the only way to restrain the woman would be to tackle her to the ground.

That wasn't an option.

Dorothy pushed past her and scrambled across the landfill. Chief Sinard and Teague and his team all stood back and let her pass.

When she got to the edge of the hole and looked down, Dorothy's face took on an expression of sheer disbelief.

In a croaking voice she gasped, "That's not ... it can't be ..."

Riley understood what was happening. In its current state of decomposition, the corpse's face was unrecognizable, even to a mother.

But in a moment, Dorothy let out a deafening shriek.

"Oh, God! That dress! Her dress!"

Then she rushed back to Riley, beating against her with her fists.

"You said she was all right! You said she'd come home! You

lied!"

Riley grabbed her wrists to restrain her, baffled by her outpouring of accusation.

What does she mean? Riley wondered.

But then she remembered Dorothy's deep state of denial when she and Jenn had been at her house. Neither Riley nor Jenn had said anything to reassure her of Holly's safety. Even so, the mother had taken their every word as confirmation that her daughter would soon be home safe and sound.

Now at last that floodgate of denial had broken, unleashing a torrent of grief.

Dorothy fell to her knees, keening and sobbing uncontrollably.

Riley, Jenn, and Chief Sinard managed to lift her back to her feet and move her to the chief's car, followed by a dazed-looking Harold.

Still crying, Dorothy crouched on the ground while Harold leaned against the vehicle.

Harold's face was pale and his eyes were glazed.

Riley sensed that he was in far too deep a state of shock to cry just yet.

In a dull, stunned voice, he said, "We should have gone out and searched for her ourselves. We should have hired a private detective. Maybe if we'd done more, she wouldn't have …"

His voice trailed off.

"It wouldn't have helped," Riley said.

Harold stared at her and said, "How do you know?"

Riley lowered her eyes. How could she explain it to him? She was all but sure that Holly had been dead and buried here by the time her parents had started to worry in earnest.

But telling Harold that would hardly be any comfort to him.

It was best to keep quiet.

Jenn asked Harold a question of her own.

"Mr. Struthers, please tell us how things were between Holly and your son."

Harold squinted with confusion.

"I don't understand," he said.

Jenn said, "When we met him at your house, he seemed to show a lot of hostility toward her."

Harold still looked perplexed. But Riley understood where Jenn was going with this. She, too, remembered what Zach Struthers had said when Jenn asked her if he knew anyone who might have wanted to harm his sister.

"Aside from me, you mean?"

But Riley hadn't sensed anything murderous about him—just a lot of pent-up sibling rivalry. Besides, he really was just a kid. Riley couldn't imagine that scrawny, nerdish boy carrying out the whole scenario—killing his sister, possibly after raping her, then bringing her out here to bury her. And what about Katy Philbin? How could he have even gotten that kind access to Katy? How would he even know her?

Of course, it wasn't impossible.

But it seemed extremely unlikely.

Riley didn't want to anger Jenn by stepping on her toes again. She now knew that her new partner was sensitive about being undercut. But she didn't want to waste time, either. And she had a question of her own to ask.

She took out the folded piece of musical staff paper they had found in Holly's pocket and showed it to Harold.

"Does this mean anything to you?" she asked.

His expression still dazed, Harold looked at it closely.

"'Holly's Song,'" he said, reading the title on the paper.

He looked at Riley, as if trying to understand what she was getting at.

He said, "So … she was writing a song?"

Dorothy Struthers was getting to her feet. She seemed to be more composed now.

"Let me see that," she said.

Riley held the paper away from her, trying to keep her from grabbing this important piece of evidence away from her. But Dorothy did so anyway.

"My God," she said in a hushed voice. "Music. It hadn't occurred to me, but …"

"But what?" Riley asked.

"The last teacher she had while studying piano … Alec Castle."

Harold let out a slight gasp.

"Mr. Castle? Do you think …?"

"Please explain what you mean," Riley said.

Dorothy thought for a moment.

"A few months back, when Holly thought she wanted to get really serious about her piano studies and we bought her that really nice piano, she also insisted on having a more serious teacher. She said wasn't getting anywhere with the woman she was studying with at school. Mr. Castle had a reputation for really pushing his students. She wanted to study with him."

Dorothy paused to think again.

"We took her to Mr. Castle's house for one lesson. When we came to pick her up when it was over, she was crying."

"What about?" Riley asked. "What had happened?"

"Holly wouldn't say," Dorothy said. "But she said she didn't want to go back there ever again. So she never did. And that was the end of her interest in the piano."

Harold had been listening keenly to his wife.

He said to her, "But if she was trying to write a song … maybe she was having a change of heart. Maybe she wanted to play the piano again."

Dorothy nodded.

She said, "And maybe she went back to Mr. Castle on her own."

Riley's head buzzed with interest.

A piano teacher struck her as a plausible suspect. After all, he might have had all kinds of access to girls Holly's age.

Riley carefully took the paper away from Dorothy and put it back in its bag.

Then she said to Jenn, "I'll be right back."

She hurried over to Chief Sinard, who was still standing near the body. Teague's team was engaged in the delicate process of lifting the decomposed body out of the hole.

She asked him, "What can you tell me about a local piano teacher named Alec Castle?"

The police chief looked surprised at the question.

"Alec Castle … I haven't given him much thought for quite some time. Why do you ask?"

Riley said, "Holly Struthers took one lesson from him. He seemed to have done something to upset her, so she never went back to him again."

Sinard tilted his head thoughtfully.

"So are you thinking he might be a suspect?" he asked.

"I don't know," Riley said. "That's why I'm asking."

Chief Sinard watched Holly's body being taken away while he talked.

"Well, he's a strange guy. He's lived here in Angier all his life, started teaching before I was born. When I was a kid, he was still well respected as a piano teacher. Not exactly *liked*. Nobody I knew ever liked him—quite the opposite, in fact. But he knew what he was doing, and he was strict, and some of his students went on to study music in college. A handful actually became concert pianists."

Chief Sinard scratched his chin.

He said, "I hear that he's kind of semi-retired these days. Probably not altogether by choice. As he got older, he got crankier——and meaner too, I hear. Kids who start studying with him generally don't last long, and parents don't like him either. Kids in Angier generally get their piano lessons at school or from some of the younger private teachers."

Riley's interest was thoroughly piqued now.

She said, "My partner and I need to go talk to him."

*

Chief Sinard drove Riley, Jenn, and Harold and Dorothy Struthers back to Angier in his SUV. He told the Struthers couple that he'd have their own car returned to them. Neither of them was in any emotional condition to drive, and they didn't argue with him. Dorothy was more subdued now, and Harold remained in a quiet state of shock.

After the chief dropped the Struthers couple off at their house, he took Riley and Jenn back to City Hall, where the car they'd been using was still parked, and gave them directions to Alec Castle's house.

Jenn was quiet as she drove. Riley wondered whether she was offended by how she had stopped her from questioning the Struthers.

It couldn't be helped, Riley thought.

She turned her thoughts to the situation at hand.

"Something is bothering me," she said to Jenn. "When we first interviewed Dorothy and Harold, Dorothy only said that Holly had lost interest in piano, the same as how she'd lost interest in lots of other things. She didn't say anything about the teacher."

"Why does that bother you?" Jenn asked in a rather distant voice.

Riley thought for a moment.

"It just seems odd, I guess. Almost as if Dorothy mentioned the piano as …"

Riley's voice trailed off.

133

"As a distraction?" Jenn asked.

"Yeah, I guess that's what I mean."

Jenn shook her head.

"I don't think so," she said. "That woman was in a lot of denial when we first talked to her. She was repressing any thoughts of anything bad that might have happened to Holly. That would include any thoughts about Alec Castle."

Riley was impressed by Jenn's insight. As they fell silent again, Riley realized that Jenn wasn't angry with her after all. Instead, Jenn seemed to be lost in her own thoughts.

Maybe she's got a theory, Riley thought.

Or maybe it was something else—something that Riley wasn't going to like.

She still didn't know whether she could trust her new partner.

CHAPTER TWENTY FIVE

The house at the address they'd been given for Alec Castle wasn't at all what Riley had come to expect in Angier.

"Is this the right place?" she asked when Jenn pulled their car up in front of the place.

"I don't know," Jenn said. "It is the address they gave us."

The house was a brick bungalow much like the one where Katy Philbin's family lived. It was even in the same quiet neighborhood. But this lawn was overgrown with weeds and wild vines climbed up the walls.

At first glance, it looked like no one lived here.

But then Jenn pointed and said, "It does look like that car has been in use."

Tracks worn into the weedy driveway showed that the old car parked there had been going in and out.

Jenn parked their car and they both got out. From closer up, they could see curtains hanging at the windows, drawn nearly shut against the warm and pleasant day.

Riley saw one curtain move slightly, a sign that the house probably was inhabited.

She and Jenn walked along a narrow stone pathway onto the front porch, then knocked on the door.

Almost immediately, a tall, elderly man answered.

"Yes?" he said in a dark, low-pitched voice.

"Are you Alec Castle?" Riley asked.

"I am."

Riley and Jenn introduced themselves. Castle seemed to be only mildly surprised.

"What's your business here?" he asked.

"We'd like to come inside and talk," Jenn said.

Castle didn't speak for a moment. He stared back and forth at Jenn and Riley with piercing blue eyes. He was cadaverously thin, and his thick mane of hair was silvery gray.

Finally, without a word, he turned and walked into the house, leaving the door open.

135

Is he inviting us in? Riley wondered.

She looked at Jenn, who seemed to be wondering the same thing.

Jenn shrugged, and they both went on inside.

They followed Castle into a large, dimly lit living room. The drapes Riley had noticed from outside were dark and heavy. The light that filtered through the narrow opening between them was barely supplemented by the glow from a little table lamp.

Quite unlike the outside, the interior was clean and orderly. But the room struck Riley as strange even so.

White doilies were tidily arranged on the arms and backs of antique furniture. The walls were covered with aged floral wallpaper, the pattern interrupted here and there by old photographs of dour-looking family members. Shelves were filled with decorative china and porcelain figures.

Since she'd come to Angier, Riley had often felt that she'd stepped back in time—but never more so than right now. The room looked and felt as though a hundred years had passed it by.

Something specifically odd about the place was nagging at Riley.

It took her a few moments to bring it into focus.

This isn't a man's house, she realized. This house had been decorated by a woman a long time ago.

And little or nothing had been altered in all the years since.

Two baby grand pianos were positioned back to back at the far end of the room. As if unaware of the agents' presence, Castle sat down at one of the pianos and started to play from memory.

Riley wasn't very familiar with classical music, but the piece sounded familiar—something by Chopin, she guessed. The man's hands appeared to be gnarled with arthritis, but he played skillfully and gracefully even so.

Continuing to play, Castle asked again, "What's your business?"

Standing next to Jenn, Riley felt weirdly stranded. She wished they could sit down, but the nearest furniture was a little too far away for conversation, especially if they had to talk over piano music.

Still standing, she asked, "Did you ever have a student named Holly Struthers?"

He stopped playing at the sound of the name.

"Not really, no," he said.

136

Then he started playing exactly where he'd left off.

Riley said, "Her parents say that you did."

Castle kept on playing. He closed his eyes as if lost in the music.

"She came for one lesson," he said. "It didn't work out. She didn't come back."

Riley hesitated for a moment, then asked, "Are you aware that Holly was murdered?"

Riley knew that the news of the discovery of Holly's body probably hadn't reached him.

All the better to gauge his reaction, she thought.

But Castle didn't stop playing. His expression didn't change.

"No," he said.

A chill went down Riley's spine.

His response struck her as barely human.

She swallowed down her shock and asked, "Did you happen to have a student named Katy Philbin?"

"No."

"Can you tell us where you were on Wednesday night?"

Still playing, Castle said, "Yes, I can. I was at a piano recital. A student of mine was playing at her home for her friends and family. Her name is Avery Dalton. She's not my student anymore, I'm sorry to say. She was the last I had."

"What happened?" Jenn asked.

"She played a few Bach inventions and Beethoven's Pathétique sonata. It was unbearable. I was shocked. Awful phrasing and dynamics, dreadful fingering, sloppy tempos, countless mistakes. She forgot everything she'd been taught, as if she'd never studied with me at all. I found it personally insulting. But her family and friends loved it."

He played a few measures without talking.

"Then she showed off with an encore," he continued. "'The Flight of the Bumblebee,' which I had strictly ordered her *not* to play. Such a banal selection, so vulgar! Girls always want to play it—all those chromatic sixteenth notes played so ridiculously fast, no need for phrasing or nuance. And of course, everybody loved it. Her parents looked so proud."

His face twisted into an ugly sneer.

"Well, I'd had enough by then. I stood up in front of everybody and told them exactly what I thought of the girl's performance. And I told them exactly what I thought of their taste and discernment.

Such philistines!"

Castle came to the end of the piece he was playing.

He said, "But that's nothing new in this town. I've had to deal with it all my life. Imagine growing up in a wretched little town with no culture at all—a sensitive little boy, bullied every single day. And the bullying never stopped. It just took subtler forms—social snubs, smirking disrespect, mockery behind my back."

He shook his head wearily.

"My mother was the only one who ever understood me. And she's gone. Long gone."

He started playing another piece.

Riley's mind was clicking away as she imagined what his life had been like.

This had been Alec Castle's childhood home, and he had lived here with his mother until her death. Riley guessed that his father had abandoned his family at one time or another, probably when he was still a child.

Had he struggled along the way, weighing his devotion to his mother against fantasies of being a renowned pianist?

Riley thought maybe so.

And what was left of him was a bitter shell of a man who hated everyone around him.

He wanted revenge against them all.

Was he capable of murder?

Riley didn't doubt it.

For one thing, she sensed that he was physically much stronger than he looked. He clearly did have a pianist's powerful arms.

She was determined not to leave this house until she knew the truth one way or another.

She still hadn't asked about his whereabouts when Holly had disappeared. She was just opening her mouth to bring that up when Jenn surprised her by speaking up.

"I've studied piano some myself. Do you mind if I ...?"

Jenn gestured to the piano.

Castle stared at her. For a long moment it seemed that he was not going to reply at all.

Then he got up from his piano bench and stood back. Jenn sat in his place.

She immediately started playing. Riley was surprised to hear the same Chopin piece that Castle had just played.

And to Riley's untrained ear, Jenn played it about as well as

138

Castle.

Castle scowled angrily.

In a sharp voice he said, "None of that, girl."

Jenn stopped playing.

Castle picked up a conductor's baton.

"I want scales," he said. "All twelve major scales."

Jenn obediently started playing a series of scales—perfectly accurately at first. During the first couple of scales, Castle simply waved his baton with her beat. But then he started tapping the keyboard with his baton, around her hands. Jenn became distracted and flustered, and she started making mistakes. At every wrong note, Castle struck her hands sharply with his baton.

Jenn finally stopped playing and put her hands in her lap.

Riley thought she saw tears in her eyes.

In a thick voice, Jenn said, "Thank you for your time, Mr. Castle. My partner and I will leave now."

Without another word or glance, Jenn got up from the bench and hurried to the front door.

Riley was flabbergasted. She had a slew of questions she wanted to ask Castle.

But Jenn was on her way out the front door. Riley felt that she had no choice but to rush after her.

What on earth had just happened?

CHAPTER TWENTY SIX

Without a word to the piano teacher, Riley followed Jenn out the door. When she got outside of the house, she saw that the younger agent was hurrying toward the car. Riley broke into a run and caught up with her.

She said, "Jenn, what are you doing? We've got a lot more questions for that man."

"No, we don't," Jenn said, opening the driver's side door.

"Hold it," Riley said.

Jenn froze in place, staring down at the car door.

"You're not driving," Riley said firmly. "Not in your current state of mind."

Without comment, Jenn walked around to the other side of the car and got in on the passenger's side.

Riley looked back at Alec Castle's house. The front door had been closed behind her and the house looked as uninhabited as it had when they'd first driven up. She opened the car door and sat down the wheel, but had no intention of driving anywhere—not yet.

Riley said, "Listen to me. I don't know if Castle's our killer, but he's our most likely suspect so far. Likelier than Trip Crozier, I think. We've got to get back in there. We've got to push him harder."

Jenn drew a deep sigh. "He's got an alibi," she said. "The girl's recital—Avery Dalton, he said her name was. We can check it out."

Riley was growing more flustered by the second.

"Jenn, for all we know right now, he made the whole thing up. Besides, a kid's recital doesn't last all night long. It's not nearly enough of an alibi to prove he didn't kill Holly Struthers. And I didn't even get a chance to ask him where he was when Katy Philbin was murdered."

"It doesn't matter," Jenn said.

"It *does* matter!"

Now Jenn looked directly at Riley. Her voice was suddenly sharp and loud.

"Castle is not our killer, OK?" she said. "He's not a killer at all."

Riley fell into a stunned silence.

Jenn took a long, deep breath.

"Don't laugh when I tell you this," she said. "But when I was a girl, I wanted to be a ballerina."

Riley didn't know what to say.

Why would I laugh? she wondered.

And what did this have to do with Alec Castle?

She waited for Jenn to say more.

"That was why I studied piano," Jenn said. "To get a deeper musical background, to make myself into a better dancer."

Jenn paused for a moment.

"My dance teacher's name was Mr. Katz. Everybody said he was one of the best dance teachers in Richmond. His students often went on to study in New York, and some of them wound up in professional companies."

Jenn swallowed hard.

"I think I was really quite a good dancer. Actually, Mr. Katz told me that I was good—very good. He told me I had real promise, that I could really be a professional dancer someday, maybe even famous. But he also kept telling me how fat I was, telling cruel jokes about my weight. He made me write down every single thing I ate for every meal. No matter how little I ate, he always said it was too much. I was making myself crazy, starving myself. And I couldn't get thin enough. Ever."

Jenn forced a bitter laugh.

"Well, I wasn't fat. I was just big-boned and athletic and muscular—like I am now, I guess. What Mr. Katz wouldn't tell me was that I was just the wrong body type to be a ballerina. Ballerinas have to be thin and willowy. All the dieting in the world couldn't change that. I could never get thin enough."

"I'm sorry," Riley said. "But what does this have to do with—?"

Jenn interrupted, her voice shaking with anger.

"The thing is, he could have just *told* me. I was never going to be a ballerina, and it wasn't my fault or anybody else's, I just got stuck with the wrong genes for it. That didn't mean I couldn't keep on dancing and really enjoy it. Maybe I could even take up choreography or teaching."

Jenn let out a growl of quiet fury.

"But he just kept *lying* to me about it, saying if only I weren't so grotesquely fat, I could take the dance world by storm. And the only reason he treated me like that was …"

She fell quiet.

Riley finished her sentence.

"Sheer cruelty."

Jenn nodded.

"That's right. It took me a long time to realize it wasn't just me he treated like that. He had it in for girls especially. If a girl wasn't a natural-born star, he did everything he could to make her life miserable, all the while building up her hopes. Girls who studied with him got injuries left and right, working themselves too hard, starving themselves for no good reason. He didn't care. It was all a game to him."

Jenn lifted her head and looked at Riley.

"He was a misogynist—and a sadist. And I learned a lot from him about misogynists and sadists, and still more while training for the BAU. I learned that there are two kinds of sadists—the kind who torture and rape and kill, and the kind who are just petty and mean. And believe me, there's a big difference. Mr. Katz wouldn't kill anybody. He was too much of a coward for that. And he enjoyed the torture too much to ever end it. He kept his victims going as long as he could get them to study with him."

Jenn shook herself, as if trying to throw off her anger.

"I was testing Alex Castle just now by asking if I could play for him. I knew he'd show his true character. I could tell as soon as he started hitting me with that baton—not even hard enough to hurt really bad physically, just enough to make me feel thoroughly humiliated. That was all he really wanted—to make me cry if he possibly could. That's what he does. That's why Holly was crying after the one lesson she took from him."

Jenn swallowed hard and wiped her eyes.

"But he's not a killer, and not a rapist either. Believe me, Riley, I really know what I'm talking about."

Riley's mouth had dropped open at what Jenn had been telling her.

She had no idea what to say.

And at the moment, she didn't know what to think, either.

Was Jenn right about Alec Castle?

She looked at the house and again caught the slight motion of the heavy drapes in one window. She could picture the cadaverous man standing there peeking through the opening to see what they were doing.

Jenn's words began to make sense to her. Castle would keep his students struggling to develop a skill most of them could never be good at. He would urge parents to buy expensive instruments and to keep paying for lessons. He would hold painful recitals and make parents feel they should appreciate his efforts. Ultimately, he would humiliate them all.

She thought that it was to Holly Struthers's credit that she didn't fall into this trap. When the music teacher had first humiliated her, she hadn't returned for more pain. But that was not likely what led to her death.

It was clear that Castle took his revenge for his own miserable life out on his students. But not by murdering them.

Riley started the car.

She said, "We'd better check in with Chief Sinard at the police station."

As she drove, Riley thought about the music teacher's alibi. Of course they would have someone check it out. They would always take the correct procedural steps. The alibi would hold up. It might still leave questions and they would check those out too. But in the long run none of that would matter.

They hadn't found the killer they were looking for. At least Jenn had prevented them from wasting more time on the wrong man.

Riley felt strangely impressed by what her new partner had just done.

Like Riley herself, Jenn seemed to possess keen powers of intuition. But Jenn's methods were startlingly different from Riley's—perhaps even more unconventional. She was perfectly willing to make herself emotionally vulnerable in order to find out whatever she needed to know.

But was that a good thing or a bad thing?

Riley didn't know, and the question worried her. She still had a lot to learn about her new partner.

And she suspected that some of what she was going to learn would be very disturbing.

143

CHAPTER TWENTY SEVEN

As she drove toward the police station, Riley realized that she was getting increasingly unsettled by the town of Angier. She had the uneasy feeling that evil encroached on her from all sides of these perfectly ordinary-looking streets. She kept telling herself that was just because of the interview with the sadistic piano teacher.

Earlier she'd gotten used to thinking of Angier as a small rural community. But as she and Jenn drove past blocks and blocks of similar houses, she reminded herself that it wasn't as small as it seemed. With a population of about 25,000, it was as large as Fredericksburg, where Riley lived. But this town had an overall sameness of style. It didn't include well-preserved historic districts or modern malls. The only unkempt area she had seen was the music teacher's yard.

It does have a lot of potential suspects, she reminded herself.

It didn't help that so many people she met here seemed to be guilty of something, if only petty cruelty.

And she and Jenn couldn't exactly go door-to-door interviewing everybody.

They had to narrow down their possible suspects.

After Riley parked at the police station, she and Jenn walked toward the imposing brick building. Like the nearby City Hall where she and Jenn had met with the mayor, it had columns on each side of the doorway. From her last visit for the questioning of the sleazy little drug dealer, she knew that Chief Sinard ran a surprisingly large and sophisticated operation with plenty of high-tech equipment. This wasn't a stereotypical little sitcom small-town police station.

Once inside, she and Jenn headed straight for the chief's office. Sinard looked up and leaned back in his desk chair, apparently eager to see them.

He asked, "Did you check out the piano teacher?"

Jenn said, "We talked to him. We don't think he's our killer. He's got an alibi we can check out."

Riley didn't contradict her. By now, she felt pretty sure that

Jenn's instincts had been correct.

Chief Sinard shook his head wearily.

He said, "We've been looking into Trip Crozier's alibi, and it seems to hold up. We tracked down the motel in Des Moines he had a receipt for, and we faxed his picture to the manager. A desk clerk there recognized him right away. He was definitely in Des Moines when Katy Philbin was killed. We've got him cold on drugs, though. At least he'll be off the streets."

Riley suppressed a sigh. They were now back at square one as far as suspects were concerned.

Jenn asked, "What about the girls' laptops or cell phones?"

Sinard replied, "Nothing. Neither of their cell phones have been found. Our techs have gone over everything else, two laptops, and Holly Struthers also had a tablet. They found nothing useful. They're still going through the emails but they haven't come across anything useful so far."

Sinard gestured toward a couple of chairs.

"Make yourselves comfortable," he said.

Riley and Jenn sat down in front of his desk.

Sinard leaned on his elbows toward them.

He said, "Look, I'm new to this whole serial killer thing. I'm going to need input. And I hope you don't mind if I ask a lot of questions. What kind of killer do you think we're dealing with?"

Riley said, "Well, due to the state of decomposition of Holly Struthers's body, it's going to be hard to determine whether she was sexually assaulted. But we know that Katy Philbin was raped, so Holly probably was too."

Sinard asked, "So how typical is this case, as far as sexual killers go?"

Riley knew that Jenn had a good command of this information. She glanced at her, cluing her to fill Sinard in.

Jenn shook her head.

"I'm afraid it's not very typical. Most victims of serial sexual killers are prostitutes. That's clearly not the case here. We've got to consider other identifiers."

"Such as?" Sinard asked.

Jenn thought for a moment.

"Well, I can give you some general information. They're usually white males between the ages of twenty-four and forty-three. Most have jobs and education beyond high school."

Sinard drummed his fingers on his desk.

He asked, "Do you think maybe these murders were the work of some drifter—a guy who came through town for a week or so, killed twice, and went away?"

"It's always possible," Jenn said. "Sexually motivated serial killers generally use a ruse or a con to get to their victims and a clever stranger could do that. But BAU has found that in most cases the victim and the killer already knew each other. So the con played on some prior relationship—a level of trust or friendship. These killers usually contact victims in familiar places, often in their own homes."

Riley spoke up.

"We'll keep asking whether anyone has noticed strangers hanging about. But what would really help is if we could find any connection between Katy and Holly, especially someone that both of them knew. But we haven't been able to find anything. They went to separate schools, and Holly's parents don't think they even met."

Sinard shook his head.

"How are we ever going to home in on a suspect?" he asked.

Jenn said, "I can think of one way. Most of the type of killer we're looking for have prior records, criminal histories. I suggest that we look over reports covering, say, a hundred miles during the last ten years."

Sinard nodded and got up from his desk.

"Come on," he said. "I'll take you to our records room."

*

Later that evening, Riley and Jenn were eating hamburgers in a cheap restaurant within walking distance of the motel where they were staying. They were both discouraged after a long, tedious day of poring over records.

"Do you think we got anything useful done today?" Jenn asked.

Riley finished chewing a bite of her hamburger and took a sip of beer.

She said, "Well, we confirmed Alec Castle's alibi, so we can eliminate him. We've got the names of a couple of registered sex offenders we can run down tomorrow. Maybe we'll get lucky."

She doubted it, and judging from Jenn's silence, Riley guessed that she doubted it as well.

Riley thought a bit more and added, "We know that Katy's

friends last saw her at a place called the Burger Shanty. We should find out whether Holly ever went there as well."

Jenn was jotting down some notes.

"Let's check that out," Jenn said. "And let's get pictures of both girls out to the public, see if anybody ever saw them together."

"That's a good idea," Riley said.

Jenn put down her pencil and said, "I don't know how you do it, Riley. I mean, this job is tough enough all by itself. But you're raising—what?—three kids these days. How do you do this and have a family and any kind of a personal life?"

Riley chuckled dourly.

She said, "When I figure that out, I'll let you know."

Jenn put down her hamburger and yawned.

"I'm too worn out to finish eating," she said. "I need to turn in for the night."

"Go on back," Riley said. "I just want to sit here and snack for a little while."

Jenn left the restaurant, and Riley sat there finishing her meal. She found herself wondering about Jenn's future, and what kind of example she might be setting for her younger partner. After watching Riley struggle with her conflicting priorities, would Jenn avoid relationship commitments altogether?

Riley hated to think that she might have that effect on Jenn.

But she reminded herself that what Jenn did with her own life was up to her in the long run. She had already seemed completely dedicated to her job when they first met.

Riley finished up her burger, paid the restaurant bill, and left. On her way back to the motel, she walked by a liquor store. She paused, then went inside and bought a bottle of bourbon. She took the bottle back to her room, took a hot shower, and got ready for bed.

Then she poured herself a glass of bourbon and sat down on her bed.

She hesitated before starting to drink. This was a familiar point in her investigations. Too familiar, and usually nonproductive.

She was feeling discouraged, and knew that one drink would be followed by another.

Was she going to give in to that temptation tonight?

Just then her cell phone rang. She smiled when she saw that she had a text message from April.

Hey Mom, how're U doing?

Riley typed back …

OK I guess. Miss you. Is everything OK there?

April replied …

We're fine. How close are U to solving the case?

Riley sighed and typed …

I wish I knew. I'll let U know when I do. Give my love to everybody.

April replied …

I'll do that. Love U, Mom.

Riley felt better as she put down her cell phone. She sat up against her bed pillows and sipped her bourbon, which felt good going down her throat. But the temptation to down one glass after another had disappeared.

Not surprisingly, though, she found herself thinking about Shane Hatcher and the threat he had made against her family.

How seriously had he meant it?

She knew he had been angry at the time. Maybe his anger had faded and he had simply wandered off somewhere. He was wealthy, after all. Wouldn't he want to enjoy his freedom somewhere comfortable? Why would he risk everything just to get back at Riley?

The truth was, Riley didn't know.

She could only be sure of one thing—that he was out there somewhere.

And she remembered the last message she had gotten from him.

You're a long way from home.

She sighed. She certainly felt a long way from home—too far away to look out for her family. But she reminded herself that her house was well guarded by agents of the FBI.

It was a comforting thought.

It was also comforting to have heard from April just now. For the moment, Riley knew that her loved ones were all safe and sound.

She finished the glass of bourbon, feeling much more relaxed and ready to sleep.

*

Riley found herself roaming through a wax museum full of grizzly exhibits.

Here were the rooms where Lizzy Borden's parents lay, brutally axed to death.

Then came a small Victorian room with a disemboweled woman—one of Jack the Ripper's victims.

After that came a torn-up floor revealing corpses wrapped in plastic bags—boys raped and killed by John Wayne Gacy.

Then came a partially devoured corpse—a victim of Jeffrey Dahmer.

Riley's skin crawled.

She hated these fake settings and wax effigies even more than she did real murder scenes.

She wasn't sure just why.

Next came an outdoor scene with a naked woman stiffly posed and made up to look like a doll ...

... followed by a woman's corpse hanging by chains from a lamp post ...

... followed by a man lying dead with a cup of tea overturned beside him ...

... followed by an emaciated woman's corpse whose arms were pointed in weird directions ...

... followed by a dead soldier slouched next to a barracks with a single bullet hole in his forehead.

It took Riley only a moment to realize that the scenes were all images from her own cases, the acts of murderers she had hunted down herself.

Her heart jumped up in her throat when she came to the last exhibit.

In a large, darkened room lay a young woman with a bleeding chest wound.

It was Lucy Vargas, Riley's brilliant partner who had been killed much too young.

Riley was suddenly filled with terrible sorrow. The loss of Lucy was almost more than she could bear.

She tried to remind herself ...

It's not real. It's just a wax exhibit.

But suddenly, Lucy's lips moved and she gasped aloud.

"Help me!"

Lucy wasn't wax anymore. She was real—and still barely alive.

Riley wanted to rush toward her and try to stop the bleeding. But then she heard a chorus of voices behind her crying out ...

"Help me!"

She turned and gasped with horror at what she saw.

The victims she'd just passed by were all alive and on their feet, stretching their arms toward her in desperate appeal, all of them calling out in unison ...

"Help me!"

Riley's eyes snapped open; she was shaking all over from her nightmare.

She sat up in the motel bed and groaned aloud.

Nightmares like this weren't new to her. Her subconscious mind seemed to have some terrible need to make her feel guilty about people she hadn't been able to save from vicious monsters.

But this was the first nightmare in which Lucy had appeared.

Was Lucy going to keep haunting her nightmares from now on? The thought filled Riley with dread.

As she sat rubbing her eyes, she heard her cell phone ring.

She picked it up and saw that it was a message from Bill.

She read it with a shudder of horror.

Just so you know. Been sitting here with a gun in my mouth.

CHAPTER TWENTY EIGHT

Riley stared at the message in stunned horror.

Sitting here with a gun in my mouth.

Was Bill about to shoot himself?

Had he done it already?

She was fully awake now, shock surging through her body. She punched Bill's number into the cell phone.

The phone rang for a moment, then went to Bill's voice mail.

Under the circumstances, the outgoing message sounded bizarrely cheerful.

Riley screamed into the phone at the sound of the beep.

"Bill! Pick up, damn it! This is Riley! Don't play games with me! Pick up now!"

No one answered.

Riley's hands were shaking so much that she could barely hold onto the phone.

Her mind raged with the image of Bill sitting alone with a loaded gun, thinking about swallowing a bullet.

Has he done it already?

She punched in the number again.

This time Bill answered. His voice sounded low and muted.

"Hey, Riley. What's up?"

Riley couldn't stop screaming.

"What's up? What do you *think* is up? I got your message. What the hell is going on, Bill?"

Bill let out a forced, awkward chuckle.

"Oh, yeah, that. Pretty embarrassing, huh? I didn't mean to send that. Really, I didn't. I was just half-asleep and fooling around, hit 'send' by mistake. I didn't mean to alarm you."

Riley was shocked at how lamely Bill was trying to disguise his action. She was on her feet now.

"Well, I *am* alarmed. Where is your gun?"

Bill didn't answer for a moment.

"Where is your gun?" she repeated.

"In a safe place," Bill muttered.

She knew he was lying.

"Where is it, Bill?"

A silence fell.

Then Bill said, "Right here on the kitchen table in front of me."

Riley's heart was beating so hard she could hear it between her ears.

"Is it loaded?" Riley asked.

"Don't worry about it, Riley."

"Is it loaded?"

Bill let out a groan of despair.

"Yeah, it's loaded."

Riley took a long, slow breath, but it didn't make her feel any calmer.

She said, "I want you to unload it. Right now."

There was another silence.

"I'd rather not do that," he said.

"Why not?"

Bill only made a strange choking sound.

"Why not?" she insisted.

"I'm having these nightmares, Riley. Somebody's after me. I don't know who it is. But it's got something to do with Lucy. And the kid I shot. It's somebody who wants … justice, I guess."

Riley felt a pang of sympathy. She knew what it was like to have nightmares like that.

She'd just woken up from one herself.

She said, "It's just a dream, Bill."

"Yeah, I know it's just a dream. But it scares the hell out of me. And having a loaded gun nearby makes me feel safer, I guess."

Riley sat down on the edge of the bed, trying to gather her wits.

"Well, you're not safer, Bill. Have you been drinking?"

"No."

Something in the flatness of how Bill said that word convinced Riley that he wasn't lying.

She said, "You just texted me that you'd had the gun in your mouth. Is that true?"

Bill didn't reply at all.

"Empty the damn gun, Bill."

There was still no reply.

"Let me talk you through this," Riley said. "Take the magazine out of your gun. I want to hear you do it."

Riley heard a flurry of movement, followed by the familiar

152

rattle of a magazine being ejected from the pistol's handgrip.

"Now empty the magazine."

"Oh, Riley—"

"Do it. I want to hear it."

Riley could hear the sounds of bullets rattling on the table. She tried to count them. She thought she heard each of the fifteen rounds that Bill's Glock could hold, but she wasn't sure.

"Check the chamber," she said. "Make sure it's empty."

She heard Bill pull the slide back.

"It's empty," he said.

Riley was breathing a little easier now. But she wasn't sure what to tell him to do next. She wished she could separate those bullets from him. Get them out of his reach. But how? He couldn't exactly throw live ammunition in the trash, much less out the window.

Besides, she knew that Bill had plenty more ammo in his house.

Finally she said, "Pick up the bullets and put them wherever you keep the rest of your ammo. And stay on the phone while you do it."

Riley heard a grunt of irritation. It was followed by the clatter of bullets as Bill gathered them together in his hand. Then came the sound of his footsteps as he padded through his apartment. Riley heard a drawer open and the bullets falling in. Then she heard the drawer shut again.

"It's done," Bill said.

"Good," Riley said. "Now sit down somewhere. Keep me on the line."

Again she heard him moving around. She guessed that he was heading back to his kitchen table.

"I'm here," Bill said.

"Talk to me. What set you off?"

Bill's breathing heaved some, as if he were trying to keep from crying.

"I heard from Maggie earlier today. Our divorce is going through in the next couple of days. I knew that already. What I didn't know is that Maggie hasn't been wasting any time. She's already in another relationship—with a dentist, his name is Sebastian I think. They're getting married right away, then moving out to St. Louis. Early next month, she said."

Riley immediately understood Bill's despair.

"Is she taking your boys?" she asked.

Bill let out a bitter, angry laugh.

"What do you think, they're going to stay here with me?"

Riley was about to ask him whether Maggie was now going to insist on full custody. But she quickly realized …

That's a dumb question.

After all, how much time was Bill going to get with his boys if his ex-wife took them to St. Louis? She probably wouldn't even battle him for custody unless he challenged her right to move them away. But if they did get into a court fight, he'd be likely to lose.

She said, "Bill, I'm so terribly sorry. I know you've been afraid you'd lose contact with them."

"I was right to worry," he muttered.

"But you can't let yourself fall apart like this."

"Why not? What else am I good for? I'm no kind of an agent anymore—not after letting Lucy die and shooting that kid."

"It wasn't your fault," Riley said.

"The hell it wasn't. And now just listen to me. Do I sound like the kind of man who will ever be able to get back on the job?"

Judging from Bill's current state, Riley couldn't help but wonder. But she didn't dare say so. She found herself on the verge of tears now.

"Bill, you can't do this—*to me.* I need you in my life. You're my partner. My best friend. Don't you dare bail on me now."

A long silence fell.

"Stay on the phone," Riley said. "I'm going to do something."

"What?" Bill said.

Riley suppressed a sigh of despair. The truth was, she had no idea.

But she had to think of something.

Riley sat on her bed holding onto the cell phone for dear life, scared that Bill might hang up at any second. If she couldn't hold on to him now, she could lose him forever.

Slowly, a desperate plan began to form in her mind.

"I know what I'm going to do," she said. "Don't hang up. Whatever you do, don't hang up on me."

"What are you going to do?" Bill asked.

Riley knew better than to tell him her plan.

He wouldn't like it.

In fact, he'd refuse to go along with it.

"Just trust me," Riley said.

Another silence on the other end.

"Bill," Riley said sharply. "Do you trust me?"

She heard a heavy sigh, then he said, "You know I do."

"Then just stay with me."

Still holding the phone, she dashed out of her motel room. She realized that it was dark outside—the wee hours of the morning. She knocked on the neighboring door, where Jenn was staying.

She kept knocking fiercely until Jenn groggily opened the door.

"Jesus, Riley," Jenn said, rubbing her eyes. "What's going on?"

"Get dressed," Riley said. "You're driving me to Des Moines."

"Why? What's this all about? What are we doing?"

Riley thought …

Probably ending my FBI career.

But she didn't say so aloud.

"Just get ready," she said.

She ran straight back to her room.

CHAPTER TWENTY NINE

Riley sat back down on her bed, mentally juggling all that she needed to do during the next few minutes.

It was all she could do to keep her panic from overwhelming her.

She said, "Bill, I'm making another call on the motel phone. But stay on the line. Don't hang up."

"What are you doing?" Bill asked.

"Just trust me," Riley said again.

She put her cell phone down on the bed. Then she picked up the motel phone and dialed Mike Nevins's personal number. She'd reached the forensic psychiatrist for emergencies at this number in the past at some pretty crazy hours, so she hoped she wouldn't have to leave a message.

She was relieved when he answered.

She tried to speak softly enough so that Bill couldn't hear.

"Mike, I need your help. It's about Bill."

"What about him?"

"He's suicidal."

"What? I can't believe that! I saw him again yesterday. He seemed to be doing much better. We have another appointment tomorrow."

Riley was almost hyperventilating now.

"Things have happened since then," she said. "I don't have time to tell you now. But you've got to believe me, he's in really bad shape."

She paused to put her thoughts together.

"I'm in Iowa right now," she said. "I'm calling you on my motel phone, and I've still got him on my cell phone. What can you do from where you are?"

"I can get an ambulance there with medics right away."

"Do that. Please. I'm keeping Bill on the phone till then."

She hung up the motel phone and put Bill on speakerphone. She started talking to him as she changed her clothes and got ready to leave.

"Are you still there, Bill?"

"Yeah."

"Good. Just keep talking to me."

"What about?"

"Anything. I don't care."

A silence fell.

Then Bill said, "Well, how have you been lately?"

He laughed a little at the absurd triteness of his question, and Riley did too.

Riley said in a mock-casual voice, "Oh, you know. The same old same old. Feeling guilty. Having nightmares."

Bill chuckled sadly.

"Yeah, I know what it's like. How is the new case going?"

Riley was relieved that Bill was showing interest in something other than his own crisis. As she kept getting ready, she filled him in on how the case was going—which of course wasn't well at all.

"Just remember," Bill said when she was finished. "Every case seems impossible at some point."

"Yeah, well. This one might actually *be* impossible."

"Come on, Riley. You've got to keep a positive attitude." He let out a snort of self-mockery. "Not that I'm setting much of an example. What do you think of your new partner?"

Riley was almost ready to leave now.

"OK, I guess. Sometimes not so OK. It's kind of touch and go. She takes some getting used to. But then, I'm sure I also take some getting used to."

Riley paused, then added, "I miss you, Bill. I miss working with you."

She almost added that she also missed Lucy. But she quickly remembered how guilty Bill felt about Lucy's death.

She said, "Promise me we'll work together again soon."

Bill didn't reply. His silence worried her.

Then she heard the sound of a siren over the phone.

"Is that an ambulance?" Riley asked.

She heard Bill get up and walk to his window.

"Yeah. Something bad must have happened to somebody in the building."

"The ambulance is for you, Bill."

Bill said nothing for a moment. The siren ended as the vehicle came to a stop outside.

Bill finally said, "What do you mean, it's for me?"

"I called Mike Nevins. I told him what was going on with you. He sent an ambulance."

"What? Where do they think they are going to take me?"

Bill was starting to sound angry.

"I don't know," Riley said. "That's Mike Nevins's call. But I'm getting the next flight I can out of Des Moines. I'll be with you as soon as I can."

"Like hell you will. You're on a case. You could get yourself fired."

"Yeah, well, I've gotten myself fired before."

"Don't come down here, Riley. I mean it."

Riley didn't have time to argue with him.

She said, "Just get in the ambulance, Bill."

She ended the call. A split second later she wished she hadn't. What if Bill wouldn't cooperate with the medics? What if he tried to fight them off?

She heard a knock on the door and ran to open it.

It was Lucy, all dressed and ready to go.

Riley grabbed her go bag and headed out to the car with her. Jenn started the car and pulled out the motel parking lot.

"You said we're going to Des Moines, right?" Jenn said.

"That's right," Riley said. "To the airport."

Riley took out her cell phone and started looking for flights out of Des Moines to any of the major Washington airports.

"Do you mind telling me what this is all about?" Jenn said.

Riley stifled a groan of despair.

How was she going to explain that she was not only about to jeopardize her own career, but she was going to leave Jenn on her own to handle a murder investigation?

It seemed so crazy that Riley had to wonder …

Am I really going to go through with this?

Before she could think of what to say, her cell phone buzzed. The call was from Mike Nevins.

Mike said, "I just talked to a medic in the ambulance. The team picked up Bill."

Riley breathed a huge sigh of relief that Bill hadn't refused to go with the team.

"How is he?" she asked.

"Not in great shape. But the medic says he doesn't seem to be of any immediate danger to himself."

"Where are they taking him?"

"I told them to take him to my clinic. I'll head over there right now. I'll see him in just a few minutes."

Riley was flooded with gratitude. Mike had done this before, working any day and any hour to help someone out. She had no idea how to put her feeling into words.

So she simply said, "Thank you, Mike."

"Don't mention it."

"I'll meet you both at your clinic as soon as I can get there."

Riley heard a slight gasp.

"I thought you were in Iowa. Aren't you on a case?"

Riley sighed.

"Mike, don't argue with me, please. Bill's my best friend. He needs me right now."

Mike fell silent for a moment.

"I'll see you in a while," he said, with a note of disapproval in his voice.

They ended the call. Riley found herself breathing easier, knowing Bill was in safe hands.

Jenn said, "This has got something to do with your partner, doesn't it?"

For an instant, Riley wondered how Jenn knew. She was pretty sure she hadn't mentioned Bill's name during the short phone call.

But then she reminded herself …

She's got great instincts.

Riley simply nodded. She knew that she still had explaining to do, and she didn't know where to start.

Jenn said, "I heard that Agent Jeffreys is on leave. It sounds like he's taking Agent Vargas's death pretty hard. I guess things just got a lot worse with him."

Riley was relieved that Jenn was able to figure out so much on her own.

"Yeah, he's in really bad shape," Riley said. "I think I just stopped him from …"

She was on the verge of saying she'd stopped Bill from shooting himself. She realized that might not be wise.

"You don't have to tell me," Jenn said.

Riley was surprised by the matter-of-fact tone of Jenn's voice.

She really did owe Jenn as full an explanation as she could give her.

"Jenn, I'm sorry to leave you everything. I don't think I'll be gone long. I just need to …"

In exactly the same tone as before, Jenn repeated, "You don't have to tell me."

Riley sat staring at Jenn, not knowing what to say.

Finally Jenn said, "What's happening right now isn't happening at all. I'm not driving you anywhere. Tomorrow we'll both be back on the job. Maybe we'll have to split up, follow different leads, so nobody will see us together. But you'll be right here in Angier."

Riley was quietly stunned.

Jenn was assuring Riley that she'd cover for her, even if she had to lie about it.

Jenn was putting her own job in jeopardy for Riley's sake.

Riley was both grateful and uncomfortable.

It was the sort of assurance that she might expect from Bill—a friend and partner of many years' standing.

But it was the last thing she expected from someone she wasn't yet sure she could even trust.

Riley wondered if she was making some kind of implicit, involuntary bargain with Jenn—a bargain she might eventually come to regret.

Would Jenn someday call in some darker favor in return?

All Riley knew at the moment was that she was in no position to argue.

She almost said "thank you" aloud.

But she reminded herself that the less she and Jenn said to each other right now, the better.

She picked up her cell phone and resumed looking for flights. She found a flight out of Des Moines to Reagan International Airport scheduled to leave in a little more than an hour.

With just a little luck, Riley figured she could catch it.

*

The morning sun was shining by the time Riley sat looking out the airplane window as Des Moines disappeared below. The upcoming two-hour flight already felt purgatorial to her. She couldn't communicate with anyone, so she couldn't find out how Bill was faring under Mike's emergency care.

There wasn't much she could do at all except ask herself troubling questions.

Why am I even doing this? she wondered.

In a way, it seemed like the story of her life.

She'd broken rules left and right for as far back as she could remember, even before she'd become an FBI agent. As a school kid, she'd spent countless hours in detention or principal's offices.

She'd even found it impossible to color inside the lines in coloring books.

Conformity and compliance had never been her style.

And what if she lost her job because of what she was doing right now?

Well, it was like she'd told Bill on the phone …

"I've gotten myself fired before."

Her FBI career had been marked by successes and commendations, but also by plenty of reprimands and suspensions.

But what if this time she got kicked out for good? Sooner or later, it seemed inevitable. But whenever it happened, what would be left for her in life?

She looked outside and saw white clouds beneath the airplane wing.

It was a soothing, calming sight.

She tilted her chair back and closed her eyes and asked herself …

What will I do if I can't be an FBI agent?

Little by little, a tentative answer started to form in her mind.

What I'm doing right now.

What I always do.

Whatever it might mean to her career, she was on her way to DC for a good purpose—perhaps even a noble one.

She was going to help a dear friend in a time of need.

As she looked back over her life, she realized that her priority had almost always been to take care of people.

She smiled at the thought.

A caregiver.

It was a word she'd never connected with herself somehow.

And yet, wasn't caregiving at the root of even her detective work? How many lives had she saved because of the criminals she stopped?

She'd been a protector and helper of people in need all along.

It seemed to come naturally to her—so naturally that she'd never really thought about it before.

It was an instinct that had kicked in when she found Jilly in that parking lot and decided to take care of her.

It had kicked in again when Liam needed to get away from his abusive father.

And it was kicking in right now, urging her to hurry to a friend's aid, heedless of the consequences to herself.

She almost laughed as a thought dawned on her.

Taking care of people.

Wasn't that what women were expected to do?

She'd never thought of herself as fitting any kind of conventional image. But then, she was hardly a stereotypical docile female.

She had her own style of caregiving—one that often involved being as hard as nails and kicking serious ass.

She realized she was tired, and started to drift off to sleep.

It's a pretty good life, she thought drowsily.

And maybe it could even be a pretty good life if she lost her job.

But as she fell asleep, a dark thought occurred to her.

She was still bound to one nemesis, one threat that could destroy everything and everyone she loved.

That nemesis was Shane Hatcher.

CHAPTER THIRTY

Riley awakened when the plane landed at Reagan International Airport. She shook her head to clear her mind of dark dreams she couldn't quite remember. She was sure she had dreamed something about Hatcher, but he wasn't what really concerned her right now.

She rented a car and drove straight to Mike Nevins's office and clinic in DC. She hurried into the building, but when she walked into Mike's office, the reception room was empty and silent.

She was hit by a moment of panic.

Has something happened? she wondered. *Did Bill even get here?*

Then she remembered—it was Sunday. Mike's receptionist and most of the staff wouldn't be working. Mike himself wouldn't usually be here on Sunday. The building was just open for the minimal clinic activity that would normally go on today.

Nervously, she knocked on Mike's office door.

Mike opened the door. Riley was relieved to see that Bill was sitting on his office couch.

Mike looked his usual self—a dapper, rather fussy man wearing an expensive shirt with a vest. Riley found it hard to believe that she'd awakened him in the wee hours of the morning and that he'd come straight here from home. But she knew that Mike was like that—perfectly groomed no matter what the circumstances.

By contrast, Bill looked like a wreck. He hadn't shaved and was wearing an undershirt and tattered jeans—the same clothes he must have been wearing when Riley had talked to him on the phone. Not surprisingly, the medics who had picked him up had given him no time to change.

Mike sat back down in his chair without saying a word to her. She couldn't tell from his expression whether or not he was glad to see her.

She had a feeling that Mike wasn't sure either.

There was no such mystery about Bill's reaction. He looked up at her and grumbled, "What the hell are you doing here, Riley?"

"Shut up, Bill," Riley said in a gentle voice.

She sat down on the couch with him and patted his hand.

"You could lose your job," Bill said.

"I don't care," Riley said.

Bill took hold of her hand and swallowed hard with emotion.

"How are you doing?" Riley asked him.

"I don't know," Bill said. "Ask the doctor."

Riley looked over at Mike, who was smiling ever so slightly.

Mike said, "We're working through some issues. He'll pull through this."

Riley didn't know how to delicately ask the question she wanted to ask.

She said tentatively to Mike, "Does he … have to …?"

Mike's eyes twinkled. He seemed to understand Riley's question.

"I don't think he needs to be hospitalized or anything like that," he said. "I just want to keep working with him for a while. Then he can go home."

The three of them sat in awkward silence for a few moments.

Riley wished she could have just a few minutes alone with Bill.

Seeming to realize this, Mike stood up and nodded silently. He walked out the door.

A single sob rose up in Bill's throat.

"Riley, I'm sorry. I'm so, so sorry."

Despite her own surge of emotion, Riley told herself not to cry. Bill didn't need her to fall apart right now.

"It's OK," she said, squeezing his hand. "You're in good hands with Mike."

Bill shook his head.

"Mike keeps saying I'll get through this. But I just feel so overwhelmed. The whole thing with Maggie and the kids … it just hit me out of nowhere. I mean, on top of how I feel about Lucy and the kid I shot … it just seems like too much."

Riley found herself remembering dark days of her own, when she'd been put on leave after being held captive in a cage by a murderous psychopath. She, too, had wondered if she would ever be able to go back to work.

Mike and Bill had both helped her pull through that awful time.

Now it was her turn to do the same for Bill.

"It's *not* too much," she said quietly. "Not for you, Bill. You're one of the strongest people I've ever known."

Bill's voice dropped to a whisper.

"The worst of it is … I let you down."

Riley knew right away what he was talking about. Riley had asked him to watch out for her family now that Shane Hatcher was at large. And Bill had made a promise …

"I'll keep an eye on things. I need to do something useful."

But here he was, not doing what he'd said he was going to do.

Riley knew better than to gloss over his failure. That would be dishonest, and she mustn't be dishonest with Bill—not if she could possibly help it.

A little toughness was needed.

"You're right—you did let me down. That's one reason you've got to pull out of this. I've got to be able to count on you."

Bill gazed at her with deep concern.

"How is your family?" he asked. "Is everybody safe?"

Riley hastily tried to remember—when had she last communicated with anybody at home?

Then she remembered the messages she had exchanged with April last night. She hoped nothing had changed since then.

"Everybody's fine, Bill," she said. "And with agents like Craig Huang and Bud Wigton on the lookout, I shouldn't have to worry. But I worry anyway. I'm going to have to fly back to Des Moines ASAP, and it will be out of my hands again. That's why I need for you to keep checking in."

Bill nodded.

"I'll do that," he said. "As soon as I get out of here, I'll do that."

Riley and Bill fell silent. The silence felt oddly comforting, reminiscent of how easy their relationship had long since become.

Then the text Bill had sent her in the wee hours of the morning flashed through Riley's mind again.

"Sitting here with a gun in my mouth."

Riley spoke haltingly.

"Bill, when you … sent me that text, you … you have no idea how …"

Bill sighed.

"You were scared. I know. I'm sorry. That was awful of me. But …"

He paused, as if trying to find the right words for what he wanted to say.

"I talked with Mike about that text. I asked him why the hell

I'd ever do something like that. He pointed out something really important. If I'd really *meant* to … you know, shoot myself, I'd never have sent you that message. Just by reaching out to you, I was telling myself that suicide wasn't an option."

Bill paused again.

Then he said, "You're my lifeline, Riley. As long as you're there, I'll never take that option. As much as anything or anyone else in my life, you keep me rooted in the world, in my life."

Riley felt a tear trickle down her cheek. She hastily brushed it away.

She felt truly overwhelmed now—overwhelmed both by the staggering responsibility of what she meant to Bill, and how wonderful it felt to be so needed.

For a fleeting moment, she felt as though her life made complete sense.

She truly mattered in the world—not just to Bill, but to everyone she loved and cared for.

She let go of Bill's hand and patted it again.

She said, "I'd better go and let you and Mike get back to work."

Bill smiled.

"Yeah, I guess so," he said. "Thanks for everything."

Riley walked out of the office. Mike stood waiting in his front room with his hands in his pockets.

He smiled and said, "He's going to be all right, Riley."

Riley simply nodded.

Then Mike said, "Thanks for coming."

Riley was surprised. She had doubted that Mike really approved of her coming here.

She shrugged and said, "I wasn't able to do much."

"You did more than you know," Mike said. "He needed to see you. The only reason I didn't ask you to come when you called was … well, I knew you were working on a case. I didn't want to get you into trouble."

Riley chuckled a little.

She said, "Trouble's my middle name, I guess. I'm pretty much used to it."

Mike looked worried now.

"Riley, if anybody at the FBI asks me if you showed up here …"

His voice trailed off. Riley understood what he wanted to ask.

"Don't lie about it, Mike. Not for my sake. I'll deal with the consequences if I have to."

She thanked Mike again and went out to her car. She knew she had to fly back to Des Moines as soon as she could. But first she wanted to check things at home. She had her return ticket and knew the plane schedule. She had time to drive home, say hello, give everyone a hug, and drive back to the airport again. She hoped to slip back into Angier, Iowa, before anybody except Jenn realized that she'd been gone.

*

As Riley neared her house, she was seized by a wave of panic.

When she'd last been here, an FBI vehicle with two crack agents and high-tech equipment had been parked on the street. They'd been staked out here in the expectation of catching Shane Hatcher, and that had also provided her family with real protection.

Now the van wasn't anywhere in sight. In its place she saw a modest sedan.

Riley could tell by its license plates, antenna clusters, and tinted windows that it was an unmarked police car.

Where is the van? she asked herself. Where is the FBI?

And what about the second van that had been parked in the alley behind her house?

Had something terrible happened?

Riley pulled into her driveway, jumped out of the car, and ran to her front door. As soon as she unlocked it and rushed inside she heard a scream,

"Help me! Why won't you help me!"

It's Jilly! she thought. *And she's in trouble!*

CHAPTER THIRTY ONE

Riley heard Jilly scream again …

"I said help me!"

Now Riley could tell where the voice was coming from.

Riley put her hand on her gun, then rushed frantically through the house and yanked open the door to the family room.

She froze in her tracks at what she saw.

Jilly, April, and Liam were all in there, looking perfectly safe and sound.

Liam was sitting in a beanbag chair wearing headphones and reading a book.

April seemed to be trying to read a textbook of her own, but Jilly was pacing back and forth in front of her waving her arms.

"What kind of big sister are you?" Jilly yelled.

April grumbled, "I've got homework of my own. I can't do yours too."

"I'm not asking you to *do* my homework!" Jilly said. "I'm just asking for some help! It's not like I ever ask you for all that much."

"You're always asking for something," April said. "Do your own homework."

Riley let out a gasp of exasperated relief.

"You kids scared me half to death," she said.

Still listening to his headphones, Liam seemed to be oblivious that anything was happening.

The girls looked at Riley with wide-eyed alarm.

"Mom!" April said.

"Are you going to shoot us or what?" Jilly asked.

It took Riley a moment to realize that she still had her hand on her gun.

She let her hand drop to her side and slumped into the nearest chair, trying to catch her breath.

"I heard screaming," she said. "I thought something was wrong."

Jilly was still quite agitated.

"Well, there *is* something wrong! April won't help me with my math!"

Riley let out a groan of irritation.

Teenagers! she thought.

Liam had finally noticed that Riley was here. He took off his headphones.

"Hey, what are you doing home?" he asked.

Riley didn't feel like explaining what had happened with Bill. Besides, she was worried about the van that had disappeared.

Just then Gabriela hurried into the room.

"*Señora* Riley! We hadn't expected you home so soon!"

Riley asked Gabriela, "What happened to the van out front? Is the one in the alley gone too?"

"*Sí*, they both left, just this morning. Now there are two nice policemen out in front. They came in to introduce themselves. They didn't say why the vans went away. They just told us all they'd be right outside and there was no need to worry."

Riley suppressed a sigh.

No need to worry!

Something had happened, and she didn't know what it was. Had they pulled off the vans because Hatcher was in custody?

But of course not, she realized, *because then they wouldn't have put a car out there.*

"Mom!" Jilly demanded her attention. She was standing there with crossed arms, tapping one foot.

Riley looked back at her younger daughter.

"Mom, would you please tell April to help me with my homework?"

"Huh-uh," April said. "I always end up doing all the work."

Riley felt overwhelmed. She didn't know why the vans were gone, and she had a plane to catch in just a little while. And now her two girls were arguing over homework.

It was enough to make her want to scream.

But now was no time to make even more of a scene out of this situation.

She turned to Liam and said, "Do you think you can help straighten this thing out between April and Jilly?"

"Straighten what out?" he asked. "I'm sorry, I wasn't really paying attention."

Riley said, "Jilly says she needs help with math, and April doesn't want to help her."

Liam grinned, obviously pleased to be called upon to help.

169

"Gladly," he said. Then he said to Jilly, "Bring your homework over here. Let's see what we can do."

Jilly stuck out her tongue at April, who made a face back at her. Then Jilly crouched down beside Liam and showed him the problem that was giving her trouble.

Riley drew a breath of relief as Liam started explaining the problem.

Gabriela asked Riley, "Will you be here for dinner?"

Riley shook her head.

"I'm sorry, and I know this sounds crazy, but I've got to fly right back to Des Moines."

Gabriela looked puzzled, but she headed back to the kitchen without asking any questions.

Riley checked her watch. Time was getting tight, and she didn't have much time to find out what had happened to the vans. She went outside and walked over to the sedan that was parked there. The two uniformed cops sitting inside smiled at her and rolled down the window.

Just a couple of patrol cops, Riley realized. *Not even full detectives.*

They certainly didn't inspire her with any confidence.

"Hey, guys," she said. "I'm Riley Paige, and I live here."

The cop in the passenger street said, "Yeah, we recognized you from the picture the FBI gave us. I'm Officer Maddox, and this is my partner Officer Carney."

Carney waved at Riley from the driver's side.

"We're surprised to see you," he said. "We'd heard you were in Iowa working on a case."

Riley reminded herself that she wasn't supposed to be here. So what should she say?

She almost smiled when she realized …

Why not the truth?

She said, "Yeah, something came up here. I'm headed right back to Iowa, though. Nobody's supposed to know I'm here, so … keep this quiet, OK?"

The officers nodded, obviously thinking that Riley was back on some official secret business.

She said, "When I left here, there were vans in front and back of the house with FBI agents and equipment. What happened?"

The officers glanced at each other.

Then Maddox said, "The guys in the vans went down to

Norfolk."

Riley felt a twinge of surprise.

"Norfolk?" she asked.

"Yeah," Carney said. "Shane Hatcher was sighted there just this morning. They think he's holed up in an apartment building."

Riley almost gasped.

"Hatcher's in Norfolk?" she asked. "Are they sure?"

"Positive," Maddox said. "A local cop spotted him, identified him from an FBI bulletin. He even got a good picture of him."

Maddox brought up a photo on his cell phone and showed it to Riley.

Riley felt a tingle of excitement as she studied the face for a moment. It showed Shane Hatcher walking down a street, apparently oblivious to the fact that he had been spotted.

There was no question in Riley's mind that it was really him.

That face, his expression, the way he carried himself—it was all imprinted on her mind.

She could never confuse him with anybody else.

Maddox explained, "The cop called the FBI right away, and the teams in the vans drove straight to the area where he'd been spotted. You know, they've got a load of high-tech equipment to help pin him down."

Carney added, "They're pretty sure they've tracked him to an upscale apartment building near where he was sighted. They think he's probably got some associates in there. The vans are posted nearby, and the teams are conducting surveillance to find out what kind of danger he and his people might present. They don't want to charge right in and put innocent people in danger."

Maddox said, "One way or the other, they'll catch him for sure."

Riley could hardly believe her ears. It seemed almost too good to be true.

Carney said, "The feds stationed us here to keep an eye on your place. You know, just in case some of Hatcher's accomplices show up here. Sounds pretty unlikely, if you ask me."

It sounded pretty unlikely to Riley as well.

And if what the guys were saying was true, a couple of cops in an unmarked car ought to be more than enough to watch over her house now that Shane Hatcher was elsewhere.

Riley thanked the cops and walked back toward her house. She looked at her watch again and figured she had enough time to clean up a bit and put on some fresh clothes.

On her way back inside, she tried to get her head around what seemed to be going on.

Now that she thought about it, it made more and more sense.

She went upstairs and opened her closet to pick out a fresh blouse. But then she noticed a small box on the closet shelf.

It looked all too familiar.

And it shouldn't have been there.

She reached up and took hold of the box. It was too heavy to be empty. She took the box down and stared at it for a moment.

Then she opened it.

Inside was a bulky envelope with her name written on it. She took hold of the envelope and let the box fall to the floor.

Now she realized she was breathing fast.

She opened the envelope, and there it was, folded in a sheet of paper …

… a chain-link bracelet made of gold, with a fancy clasp.

Riley felt dizzy now.

This is impossible, she thought.

She wondered if she was dreaming.

The chain had been a gift from Shane Hatcher—a symbol of her bond with him.

He wore one just like it.

She'd worn this one, too, when she'd been fully under Hatcher's grim thrall.

But she knew for a fact that she'd thrown it away not long ago—thrown it into the trash.

Its presence here again could only mean one thing.

Hatcher had been watching her closely. And he had been here in the short time since she'd gone to Iowa—right here in her house in spite of the FBI vans outside.

CHAPTER THIRTY TWO

As she held the gold chain in her hand, Riley felt her knees become wobbly. Sheer terror surged through her body. She staggered over to her bed and sat down.

As the sensation of fear ebbed, she recognized the feeling of violation she'd experienced before when her home had been invaded. She'd thought that it couldn't happen this time.

She'd been wrong.

But how on earth had Hatcher made it past the crack teams in the two vans and actually had gotten into her house?

She reminded herself that she mustn't underestimate him. He had brilliant and uncanny skills in every area of criminality. He was as well-equipped as any military assassin.

She should have realized that he would be able to creep through a respectable neighborhood unnoticed despite the FBI's high-tech precautions.

Then a horrible new realization crept over her.

Not only had Hatcher come here to put the chain in the box in the closet—but he had *known* that she used to keep it in that very box in that very place.

He'd been here before in the past—perhaps many times.

Had he even stood watching over her when she'd been sleeping?

What about the other people in the house—the kids and Gabriela? Had he spied on them?

Riley shuddered at the very idea.

Should she officially report what had happened? Riley let out a groan of despair.

And tell them what? she asked herself.

The bracelet was a relic of a forbidden and illegal relationship. She'd never told a single soul about it, and knew that she never could.

Besides, she wasn't even supposed to be here in Fredericksburg. She was supposed to be back in Iowa doing her job.

She studied the chain for a moment and saw a familiar tiny

inscription on one of its links.

"face8ecaf"

She'd long since solved the riddle of that inscription. It meant "face to face," and it was suggestive of a mirror—the mirror that Hatcher considered himself to be toward Riley, a personification of her darkest impulses.

The inscription was also a video address she'd used in the past to get in touch with Hatcher.

Could she reach him now?

Should she even try?

She didn't stop to think about it.

She moved over to her desk chair and turned on her computer. She opened the video chat program, and typed in the characters.

She let the call ring for quite some time, but nobody answered.

She wasn't surprised. She knew from experience that Hatcher couldn't be reached if he didn't want to be reached.

Then she looked at the piece of paper that had been folded around the chain. She carefully flattened it out on her desk.

On it was written …

Au revoir, Riley Paige

Like most of Hatcher's messages, it was surely a riddle of some sort.

What did this one mean?

She knew that *au revoir* was a way of saying goodbye in French.

The meaning seemed obvious—perhaps even too obvious.

He was returning the chain to her as a sort of farewell gift.

He's going away, Riley thought.

But where and how?

Things were starting to make sense to her. Hatcher had gone to Norfolk, which had multiple highways, bus lines, and Amtrak. It had a large naval base with miles of waterfront. It was also a commercial shipping port and had an international airport.

Norfolk offered a vast range of possibilities for getting away—even for leaving the country.

And that must be what Hatcher intended to do.

Or at least that had been his intention until he'd been spotted in Norfolk.

But now what was going to happen? She reminded herself

again that it was out of her hands.

Riley's phone suddenly buzzed. She saw that Jenn was calling.

When she answered, Jenn's voice sounded agitated.

"Riley, I just got a call from Chief Sinard. He says another girl has gone missing. I'm headed right down to the station to meet him."

Riley heard Jenn emit a discouraged sigh.

"I'm sorry, Riley, but I don't see how I can keep covering for you. I told Chief Sinard that you were over in a town called Hammett interviewing a registered sex offender. But he's expecting you back soon. What do you want me to tell him?"

Riley was still so shaken by her discovery that it took a moment for her to grasp what Jenn was saying. Once she did, she felt guilty that Jenn had had to lie for her.

But what was she going to do now that she knew Hatcher had been in her house?

Could she really leave at a time like this?

She reminded herself that Hatcher was in Norfolk right now, and he would surely be arrested at any moment.

Her family was safer from him than they'd been for a while now.

Finally Riley said, "Tell Sinard I'll be there as soon as I can get there. For what it's worth, that's actually true. I'm on my way to an airport to catch a flight back to Des Moines."

"I wish I could pick you up at the airport but—"

Riley interrupted.

"It's all right, I know you can't get away. I'll rent a car at the airport and drive back to Angier. I'll call you when I get there so you can tell me where I should meet you."

They ended the call.

Riley got up from her chair and looked around the room, again seized by the sickening awareness that Hatcher had intruded here.

She shook herself all over, trying to throw off that feeling.

But it wasn't easy to do.

Hatcher had more than proved his stealth and cunning by getting into her house.

Mightn't he slip out of the trap the FBI had set for him in Norfolk?

She looked again at the message he had written for her.

Au revoir, Riley Paige

And she reminded herself that he was planning to go away.

Even if he escaped from the FBI, he'd soon be gone.

She tossed the bracelet and the note back into the shoebox, put it into a desk drawer, and locked it.

As she did, so she murmured aloud …

"*Au revoir,* Shane Hatcher."

Then she headed downstairs to tell her family that she was leaving again.

CHAPTER THIRTY THREE

As soon as Riley got off the plane in Des Moines, her phone buzzed. Her heart quickened when she saw that the call was from Bill. She answered the phone as she walked toward the car rental booths.

Bill sounded worried.

"Riley, something's wrong. When I left Mike's clinic, the first thing I did was head over to your house. I'm here right now. The FBI vans are gone. There's just this unmarked police car parked out front—"

"It's OK, Bill. Craig Huang and the rest of the team took the vans down to Norfolk. They've got Shane Hatcher cornered in an apartment building there."

She heard Bill gasp a little.

"Are they sure?" he asked.

"Yeah, they're sure. And there's no way for him to get away. For all I know, they've got him in custody already."

Bill fell silent for a moment.

Finally he said, "Shane Hatcher—captured at last. It's hard to believe."

"I know," Riley said. "I feel that way too."

She walked a few feet without saying anything. She wondered—should she tell Bill that Hatcher had been in her house?

No, there didn't seem to be any point in that.

Even so …

She added cautiously, "Bill, could you keep driving by my place and checking on things from time to time? I don't know why, but it would make me feel better. And would you also check in to see how the stakeout is going in Norfolk?"

"Of course. It's the least I can do. Any news on the case in Iowa?"

"Yeah, but it's nothing good. Another girl has disappeared. That's all I know right now. I should find out more soon."

Riley hesitated, then added, "Bill, I wish you were here. This case is getting to me in a way I can't put my finger on. For one thing, this little town gives me the creeps."

Bill said, "Don't tell me—everything's just too perfect."

"Yeah, everything's all picket fences, nice lawns, perfect houses. But as soon as Jenn and I peek behind the façade, we find rot everywhere—predatory drug dealers, creepy school principals, sadistic piano teachers. Practically everybody seems like a suspect. We don't know where to begin."

"Follow your gut, Riley. Your instincts won't steer you wrong."

Riley let out a snort of discouraged laughter.

"My instincts aren't exactly clicking this time around."

"They will. Just remember—whatever *seems* too perfect usually is. Keep looking behind those façades. You'll find what you're looking for."

Riley felt a lump in her throat.

She knew that Bill was telling her exactly what she needed to hear.

She said, "Bill, thank you for …"

She couldn't find the words for all that she felt grateful for.

"Just everything," she said.

Bill didn't reply right away. When he did, his voice sounded huskier.

"Riley, after all that you've done for me in the last few days—"

Riley interrupted.

"Don't give it another thought, Bill. Just get better so we can work together again. I miss you."

"I miss you too."

They ended the call just as Riley arrived at the car rental booth. She rented a car, and when she got into it she punched in Jenn's number on her cell phone. She put the call on speakerphone, and she and Jenn talked as she drove away from the airport.

Jenn filled her in on the new missing girl.

"Her name is Camryn Mays, and she's older than the others—twenty-one years old. She's in her second year at the local community college."

"Does she live with her family?" Riley asked.

"No, she's got an apartment of her own, not even a roommate. So nobody noticed she was missing right away. She works at a local restaurant, Vern's Café. That's where I am right now, with Chief Sinard and his people. We've been interviewing everybody here. She missed her shift yesterday, but nobody thought anything of it.

When she didn't show up today, her boss started to get worried."

Riley mulled over what she was hearing.

It was, of course, possible that Camryn Mays had wandered off for reasons of her own. But after what had happened to Katy Philbin and Holly Struthers, Riley knew better than to make that assumption.

She just hoped they could get to Camryn while she was still alive.

Riley asked Jenn, "Do you want me to join you at the restaurant?"

"No, we'll wrap things up here pretty soon. In a little while we're headed to the girl's apartment. That's where you should probably meet us. I'll give you the address."

After Jenn read Riley the address, Riley said, "Jenn, I'm really sorry … for putting you on the spot like I did."

Jenn was quiet for a moment.

Then she said, "Just get here as soon as you can, OK?"

"I'm driving right now," Riley said.

When they ended the call, Riley wondered whether Jenn now had regrets about agreeing to cover for her. She hoped not. But she knew she couldn't blame Jenn if she did.

*

Riley followed GPS directions to Camryn Mays's apartment building. When she parked outside, she saw that the car that she and Jenn had been driving was already there, and so was Chief Sinard's official SUV.

The red brick apartment building had a sign and a name— Monterrey Apartments. Riley knew better than to assume the name suggested quality or class. After all, she knew that the girl worked in a restaurant and didn't have a roommate.

During Riley's own college days, she'd lived in a similar building called the Devonshire, but her apartment had been anything but large or glamorous. She knew that some landlords had a peculiar way of giving apartment buildings pretentious names for no good reason.

In fact, as she approached the place, she saw that it was in something of a state of disrepair. The sidewalk was badly cracked, and the lawn wasn't especially well kept. She peeked through a tall wooden fence and saw an empty swimming pool full of leaves and rubbish.

Riley went into the building and found the right apartment on the second floor. She knocked on the door, and Chief Sinard let her in.

"Did you have any luck in Hammett?" Sinard asked.

Riley was puzzled for a moment.

Then she remembered—Jenn had told the chief that Riley was interviewing a registered sex offender in a town called Hammett.

"I'm afraid not," she said, walking on inside.

She hoped Sinard wouldn't ask for details.

Jenn was already here, as Riley had expected. So were Laird and Doty, the local cops who had met Riley and Jenn at the airport. Everybody was hard at work, poring over the place carefully. Jenn glanced up from her own task, visibly relieved that Riley was finally here.

Riley glanced around. There wasn't much to see. With five people in it, the tiny place was pretty crowded. The apartment was startlingly like the no-frills place she remembered from her own college days. A small front room doubled as a living area and a kitchen, with some cheap furniture and a stove and refrigerator. There was an open door to one side. Riley saw that it led into a tiny bedroom with an adjoining bathroom.

But it was different from Riley's old apartment in one significant way.

Like many college students, Riley had been a slob, leaving clothes and kitchen utensils and empty wrappers all over the place, and never doing any cleaning to speak of. The young woman who lived here was anything but a slob.

Everything was neat, clean, organized, and sparse. There was a laptop computer on a Formica-topped table. Some textbooks were carefully lined up between bookends on a small table. But despite all the neatness, there were no decorations anywhere—no framed pictures or trinkets of any kind. There wasn't even a TV.

Riley breathed slowly, taking in a vaguely familiar smell. It was partly the decay of a rather poorly maintained apartment.

But there was also a feeling in the air that she dimly recognized. She couldn't quite put her finger on what it was—at least not yet.

She turned to Sinard and said, "Tell me about the missing girl."

Sinard pulled up the young woman's photo on his cell phone. She was a smiling, eager-looking young African-American.

Sinard said, "Camryn Mays has been finishing up her second year at Angier Community College. She graduated two years ago from Wilson High."

Riley nodded and said, "The same school that Katy Philbin went to. Do we know of any connections between the two girls?"

"Not yet," Sinard said. "Since they were two years apart, they may not have known each other well, or even at all. And right now we don't have any reason to think that Camryn knew Holly Struthers either."

Riley kept looking around, her head full of unanswered questions. For example,

since Camryn was a local girl, why she wasn't living with her family? She must have moved into this apartment for a reason.

"Who reported her missing?" Riley asked Sinard.

"Her parents," Sinard said. "She'd missed work at a restaurant for a couple of days. When the manager couldn't reach her by her cell phone, he called her parents to ask what was wrong. They got worried, and so they called me."

Officer Laird had opened the girl's laptop computer.

He said to the others, "Her computer's locked. Since we don't know the password, we'll have to turn it over to our tech guys."

"Let's do that," Chief Sinard said. "Not that it will probably do any good. We didn't find anything suspicious in the other girls' emails or social messaging. My guess is that we won't be able to track down her cell phone either. The other girls' phones seemed to have disappeared—maybe destroyed by their captor."

Chief Sinard sighed.

He said, "Of course, we don't know for sure that Camryn Mays is in any danger, but …"

His voice trailed off doubtfully.

Riley wished she had something reassuring to say to him.

As she stood looking around the room, that vague, familiar feeling of hers started to become clearer.

At last she was able to put a name to it.

Freedom.

Yes, that was what Riley had felt all those years ago when she had gotten away from home and moved into an apartment of her own.

It had been wonderful and intoxicating to be on her own for the first time in her life.

The girl who lived here had felt the same thing—a giddy sense of freedom, of a whole future full of possibilities.

She was also full of hope.

Or at least she had been until …

Riley tried not to imagine that Camryn Mays had met the same fate as Katy and Holly.

But the hope that Riley sensed in the air here was hardly contagious.

She'd seen too much of the world's evil and darkness to get her own hopes up.

Anyway, she felt sure that she and her colleagues weren't going to find any clues here.

She said to Chief Sinard, "Let's go talk to the girl's parents."

CHAPTER THIRTY FOUR

As she drove, Jenn was wondering why Camryn's disappearance especially troubled her. She was following behind Chief Sinard's vehicle to the Mays family home. In the passenger's seat beside her, Riley was quiet, obviously considering questions of her own.

Of course, they hadn't yet determined whether Camryn Mays was even a victim. It was still entirely possible that she'd simply wandered off and might show up at any time.

So why was this girl's disappearance pushing her buttons?

Could it be because Camryn was African-American, like her?

Jenn hated to think that might be a reason. All victims ought to be equal and alike as far as she was concerned. It was her job to see things that way.

And if the worst had happened, like it had with Katy and Holly, it obviously wouldn't have had anything to do with race.

Jenn remembered something that Riley had said about Angier.

"Towns like this give me the creeps."

Jenn had been feeling much the same way, although perhaps for different reasons. Even now as she drove, she didn't spot a single driver or pedestrian of color. Angier seemed almost eerie in its lack of diversity.

And she couldn't deny that she'd felt an especially painful twinge back at Camryn's apartment.

Jenn had sensed something disturbing in the air—a palpable feeling of isolation.

The poor girl must feel so alone in this town, Jenn thought.

That's what bothered her when she thought about Camryn, not race specifically but the loneliness it must have caused her. Even though Jenn had grown up in much more diverse environments, she knew that feeling well from personal experience.

Jenn sternly told herself to put these feelings aside. After all, they had nothing to do with the matter at hand.

Jenn parked their car behind Chief Sinard's vehicle in front of the Mays residence in a modest, working-class neighborhood. At first glance, everything looked similar to the neighborhood where Katy Philbin had lived—the same streets with large trees, well-kept bungalows, perfect lawns.

And yet everything struck Jenn as so …

What was the word she was looking for?

Little, she realized.

This area was the same as the rest of the town, but in miniature—almost like a model or a toy. This working-class neighborhood was markedly less prosperous than other parts of Angier. But even so, its residents made the most of what little they had. And they were obviously proud of what they had accomplished in life.

Jenn and Riley met Chief Sinard as they walked toward the house. Sinard knocked on the door, where they were greeted by an African-American woman wearing a white blouse and a nametag that said LYLA MAYS. The woman looked worried—although from the deep lines on her face, Jenn guessed that worry was chronic, an inescapable part of her everyday life.

Chief Sinard introduced himself and Riley and Jenn. Lyla nervously invited them inside and introduced them to her husband, Trent, who was wearing a blue-gray jumpsuit.

The couple invited their visitors to sit down in a small but cozy living room. Jenn noticed that Chief Sinard chose the chair that was farthest away. She guessed that he wanted to leave Riley and her free to ask questions.

As Riley explained who they were and why they were here with Chief Sinard, Jenn looked around the living room. On the walls, she saw plenty of family pictures that had been taken over many years. There were images of Camryn at many different ages, and also an older boy—Camryn's brother, Jenn was pretty sure.

She observed that Trent Mays kept looking at his watch. He seemed very anxious about the time. She wondered what could possibly preoccupy him more than his own daughter's disappearance.

Jenn asked the couple, "May I ask what the two of you do for a living?"

Trent said, "I work as a janitor over in City Hall."

"I'm a clerk at the supermarket," Lyla said. "Been working there for twenty years."

Lyla sounded proud of her job.

Trent looked at his watch again, and Jenn was finally able to guess why.

Judging from their clothes, both Lyla and Trent had come home hurriedly from work. She thought it likely that Trent's employers had frowned upon his leaving in the middle of his shift. Maybe both of them were under pressure to get back to work.

It was clear that life wasn't easy for the Mays family. But at least Trent and Lyla were together, and from what she could tell, they were devoted parents.

Jenn found herself flashing back to her own broken childhood—a depressive, alcoholic mother who'd disappeared when she was little, a father who'd wandered off to start another family, leaving Jenn to spend much of her youth in foster homes. When she'd tried to escape into the world of ballet, her dreams had gone sour.

By comparison, Camryn seemed to have lived a perfect life.

So lucky, she thought.

But had this girl's luck had run out in the most terrible way imaginable?

Riley said, "We'd like to ask you a few questions, if we may. When was the last time you saw your daughter?"

Lyla and Trent exchanged a sad look.

Trent said, "Quite some time, I'm afraid. A couple weeks or more."

Riley looked surprised. She said, "But she lives right here in the same town."

Jenn couldn't help but cringe a little. Riley's comment struck her as slightly insensitive. Even back at Camryn's apartment, Jenn had sensed that the girl was somewhat distant from her family— although probably not outright estranged. Camryn had gone to considerable trouble to carve out a separate life for herself, if only in another part of the same town.

Lyla shrugged a little.

"She's just got so much to do, I guess," she said. "With work and school and such, she just doesn't have any time for ..."

Lyla stopped herself from finishing her sentence. Trent patted her hand sympathetically.

Jenn detected sadness in Lyla's tone—and also a bit of resentment. She sensed that Trent felt the same way.

The family's story was becoming clearer to Jenn. This couple had worked hard at menial jobs all their lives in a town where they scarcely fit in, raising children with dreams and hopes they themselves couldn't imagine. Those children's dreams couldn't be realized under this roof with these two humble people.

Judging from the pictures, Jenn guessed that Camryn's older brother had moved away some years back. And now, one way or the other, Trent and Lyla were losing their daughter as well.

Lyla shook her head.

She said, "I just don't know what it is she wants to do with her life. Can't she do anything she likes right here with us? I guess she doesn't think so. She keeps telling us she has dreams, but she never says what they are."

Jenn could hear that resentment spilling out of Lyla Mays now. And Jenn suddenly didn't like her tone.

Why couldn't Lyla and her husband wish their daughter a happier, more prosperous life than they had lived themselves?

Lyla's worry seemed to be mounting. She sat wringing her hands.

She said, "Oh, please, please tell us that Camryn's going to be all right."

"That's what we're trying to find out," Riley said.

Lyla shook her head anxiously.

"We told her not to go to that community college," she said. "Colleges are such violent places, so many girls get raped there these days. It's just not safe for them to go to college anymore."

Jenn winced again at her words. Could the woman have said anything more defeatist? Anything more likely to keep Camryn from achieving more than they had?

The poor girl, Jenn thought.

Jenn was tempted to explain that it was only a myth that more women were raped on campus than were nonstudents of the same age. The truth was actually the other way around. Of course, Jenn knew that campus rape was certainly a huge issue these days. But that was because women students were more aware and empowered than nonstudents. They understood what was going on, and they were determined to do something about it.

But now was no time to set the couple straight as to facts. Jenn realized that her own feelings were starting to interfere with her judgment.

She sat listening as Riley asked all the sensible questions. Did the parents know of any connection between Camryn and the other girls? Did she ever complain of anything being amiss at school or at work? Did they know of anyone who might have threatened her or made her uncomfortable?

Trent and Lyla simply didn't know any answers.

Worse still, Jenn sensed that they were becoming more and more upset with every passing question.

The direness of what might have happened to their daughter was becoming all too real to them. By the time Riley finished asking questions, Lyla was in tears, and Trent was begging them to find their daughter safe and sound.

Jenn felt sick in her heart that neither she nor Riley could make any such promises.

*

Riley headed for the driver's seat of their car as they left the Mays house, but she realized she didn't know where to go next.

She turned to Chief Sinard. He stopped by his own car and said, "It's getting late. I'm going to quit for the day. You should too."

Riley looked at Jenn. The younger agent agreed, "I don't know what else we can actually do today."

Riley realized she didn't know either. She also couldn't think of anything else they could do, and she was tired after a long day that had included hours on an airplane. Tomorrow morning they could start afresh, perhaps by interviewing people with some connection to Camryn.

Riley had noticed Jenn's silence during most of the interview. She was still being very quiet as Riley drove. Something seemed to be troubling her.

Cautiously Riley asked, "Jenn, is something wrong?"

Jenn was peering out into the darkness.

"Why do you ask?" she replied.

Riley shrugged a little.

"I don't know. I just wondered."

A silence fell.

Well, I guess she doesn't want to tell me, Riley thought.

After a while, Jenn said, "Riley, do you think Camryn … I mean, do you think the same thing happened to her that happened to …?"

Jenn's voice trailed off.

"What do *you* think?" Riley asked.

Jenn's voice sounded distant and wistful.

"I don't know. It's just that … well, does she fit the profile? She's so different from the others. Older, different school, a whole different kind of life. And African-American."

Riley said, "The truth is, we really don't have a victim profile to speak of—or a suspect profile, for that matter."

Jenn fell silent again.

Finally she said, "Riley, I—I want her to be OK."

Riley's throat caught a little. She knew the feeling all too well.

Jenn added, "Do you ever get used to … well, this job?"

A good question, Riley thought. And like most questions, it didn't have an easy answer, much less a comforting one.

Riley resisted the answer that came to mind:

Not used to it exactly.

But numb.

At least some of the time, to some of it.

The numbness comes and goes.

Instead, Riley said, "Do you *want* to get used to it?"

After all, that was surely the more important question for a promising young agent to be asking herself at the beginning of her career.

Jenn didn't reply, and Riley kept on driving. She wished she could say something to make Jenn feel better. She especially wished she could tell her that Camryn Mays was still likely to turn up safe and sound.

But something in Riley's gut said otherwise.

She had the terrible feeling that it was too late to save Camryn.

The best they could do now was to catch the monster, to make sure that no other girls were raped and killed.

But Riley didn't say so out loud.

Keep your thoughts to yourself, Riley decided.

Besides, she could still be wrong. She had to hope she was wrong.

They drove the rest of the way to the motel in silence.

CHAPTER THIRTY FIVE

Later that night in her motel room, Riley's phone buzzed just as she had stretched out on her bed to go to sleep.

Her nerves quickened with apprehension when she saw that the call was from Bill.

She answered quickly.

"Bill! Has something happened at home?"

"Relax," Bill said. "I've been by your place, and everything looks fine."

Riley breathed a bit easier.

She asked, "Any news from Norfolk? Have they caught Hatcher yet?"

"No, but don't let that worry you. They're still tracking him."

Riley felt puzzled.

"Tracking him? I thought they had him cornered in that apartment building."

"No, it turns out that he's at large in Norfolk. I don't know any details, but Huang and Wigton and their team are following his every movement. He's been meeting with a lot of criminal cronies in town. Huang's really excited about it. It looks like they're going to catch a lot of high-level bad guys in the same net as Hatcher. They're taking their time, though. They want to make the most of their opportunity."

Riley thanked Bill and ended the call. She closed her eyes and realized how tired she was. A good night's sleep would certainly be welcome right now.

But she couldn't help but feel a pang of uneasiness.

She knew she'd sleep a lot easier once she knew Shane Hatcher had been captured.

*

Early the next morning Riley awoke from restless dreams to the sound of her phone buzzing again.

She let out a groan of despair.

This isn't good news, she thought.

She picked up the phone and heard Chief Sinard's voice.

"Agent Paige …"

She heard Sinard gulp audibly.

"I just got a call," Sinard said. "Camryn Mays … has been found."

Riley could tell from Sinard's voice that there was no need to ask whether the girl was alive or dead.

That gut feeling she'd had yesterday had proved all too correct.

Riley suppressed a sigh. Sometimes she wished her gut could be wrong more often.

"Where is she?" she asked the chief.

"Cruikshank Park," Sinard said. "I'm there right now."

"We'll drive right over," Riley said.

The call ended, and Riley shook herself awake. She went to the bathroom and splashed water on her face, hurried to the adjoining door to Jenn's room, and knocked loudly.

Jenn came to the door looking bleary-eyed.

Riley said, "Sorry to wake you so early. But we've got to go right now."

"What's going on?" Jenn asked.

Riley simply shook her head.

Jenn's eyes widened. She seemed to grasp what Riley wasn't saying aloud.

"Oh," she said in a hushed voice. "I'll be ready in a minute."

Jenn ducked back into her room, and Riley rushed to get herself dressed and ready to go.

*

Just a few minutes later, Riley and Jenn were in their car following GPS directions to Cruikshank Park. As soon as they pulled into the parking lot, Riley was struck by how unusual the park looked.

It seemed to be arranged like some kind of compact golf course, except with concrete patches here and there and basket-shaped objects on upright steel pipes.

"What kind of park is this?" Riley asked as she and Jenn got out of the car.

"Looks like a disc golf course," Jenn said.

"Disc golf?"

"Yeah. I've heard of the game, but I've never actually seen a course. Instead of golf balls, you try to throw Frisbee-like discs into those baskets."

"And it's called golf?" Riley asked.

"You can see that it's got all the usual golf course stuff—water hazards, roughs, and everything."

Riley felt an oddly discombobulated. The very idea of the game sounded silly to her—and silliness was a jarring feature at a homicide scene.

Jenn said, "There they are."

Sinard's SUV and the medical examiner's van were both parked on a road next to a stand of trees. Several people were gathered there, including Sinard and Barry Teague, the medical examiner.

Riley and Jenn broke into a trot and joined them.

The men were gathered by a drainage ditch next to the trees. The girl's body had been uncovered. Riley recognized her as Camryn Mays immediately. At a glance, she could also tell that the body hadn't been here very long—probably a little less time than Katy's had been buried in George Tully's field. The stench of decomposition was just starting to set in.

Riley felt her heart sink as she stared at the body. Three girls had been lost. If she had stayed in Angier, could she have saved this one?

But she realized that the answer was *no*. Camryn Mays had been dead by the time they were notified that she was missing. The same was true of the others.

He had murdered them before anyone had even raised an alarm.

Jenn asked Sinard, "How was she found?"

Sinard said, "A guy was out here a little while ago for an early morning jog. He noticed some loose dirt and leaves piled up kind of carelessly down there. I guess he probably wouldn't have thought anything about it if it weren't for the other murdered girls. It's a good thing he got in touch with me. My boys uncovered the body."

Riley could see the dirt and leaves that had been pushed aside. Someone had simply dumped the body here and carelessly covered it with debris from among the trees. The killer had barely tried to bury the corpse at all.

Barry Teague, the obese county ME, was crouched next to the

body. Riley crouched down next to him.

"What have you found so far?" she said.

Teague pointed to bruises on the young woman's thighs.

"She was raped, that's for sure," he said. "Same as Katy Philbin. It was harder to tell about Holly Struthers, because her body was more decomposed, but my postmortem showed that she'd been raped as well."

Then she said, "I assume you've sent semen specimens off to have the DNA analyzed."

Teague looked up at her and squinted.

"We didn't find any semen in the other girls. Traces like that can get to be hard to find after a corpse has been lying around for a while. Oh, sometimes you can get lucky and find semen days or even months after death. Maybe we'll do better with this one."

Riley got back to her feet.

Sinard asked her, "What do you think is going on here?"

Riley didn't reply. She looked down at the body again. Like the other three corpses, Camryn's had been carelessly disposed of. In fact, her body was almost certain to be discovered sooner or later.

Riley found the whole thing puzzling.

A killer who concealed a body usually did so precisely to keep anybody from finding out that a murder had been committed.

Was this one conflicted about that? At some subconscious level, did he want to be caught?

Sinard shook his head sadly.

"I guess I'd better go notify Camryn's parents," he said.

Riley's heart went out to him. She briefly wondered whether she and Jenn should go with him.

But they had to get back to the investigation. They had already interviewed the girl's parents. They had seen her apartment and Jenn had been to her workplace. Like the others, no cell phone had been found with this body. Sinard's techs would have to work on pulling any relevant electronic information together.

Riley fought back a wave of futility. Where could they pick up a new lead?

The deadly kidnappings were coming closer together now, and they knew that he killed soon after he took them.

They had to stop this killer before another girl was lost.

CHAPTER THIRTY SIX

As Teague's ME team loaded the girl's body onto a gurney, Riley and Jenn headed back to their car. Riley's thoughts churned as the reality of this new murder overwhelmed her.

"What do we do now?" Jenn asked.

Riley didn't answer right away. What *could* they do now? she wondered. Somehow they had to get ahead of this killer.

She had seldom felt so desperate for leads at this point in an investigation.

Connections, she thought. *We've got to find connections.*

They hadn't yet found any common links among the three dead girls.

Either they had something in common or the killer was just taking girls randomly. But Riley had tracked random killers before, and she had no sense of that kind of mind at work here. She had a strong feeling that the killer was someone the girls knew and trusted. Someone who had a seemingly legitimate reason to be in contact with them.

So they had to have something in common.

And somebody somewhere had to know what that connection might be.

Thinking out loud, she said, "We know that Katy Philbin went to Wilson High, and we also know that Camryn Mays graduated from there a couple of years ago."

Riley looked at her watch.

"The school day hasn't started yet," she said. "Let's head on over to Wilson High."

"We've already talked to girls on the soccer team there," Jenn said.

Her voice sounded a bit doubtful.

"Yeah, but we haven't talked to everybody there," Riley said.

The truth was, Riley didn't feel especially confident either.

As Jenn drove them to the school, Riley mentally outlined their visit. They hadn't yet met the principal at Wilson High. First they could talk to him, ask what he might remember about Camryn Mays. Then they could find out what teachers Katy and Camryn had in common. They could talk to them as well.

Riley could think of plenty of questions to ask them. For example:

Even though the two girls had been two years apart in school, did they have any friends in common? Did they belong to any of the same clubs? What about sports or other extracurricular activities?

Riley tried to convince herself that they were about to make some progress.

Instead, she couldn't help but feel as though she and Jenn were grasping at straws.

Holly Struthers had gone to a different high school from Katy and Camry, after all.

What were the chances of finding a connection among all three girls at Wilson High?

It didn't seem likely. But Riley didn't know where else to start.

The school grounds were bustling and cheerful as they pulled into the parking lot. Parents were dropping students off at the curb, and kids were everywhere—some heading on inside, others milling around laughing and talking.

When Riley and Jenn got out of the car and walked toward the school, they heard a voice call out.

"Agent Paige! Agent Roston!"

Riley turned and saw a man sitting at an outdoor table waving at them. She recognized his bearlike form right away. It was the school's soccer coach, Judd Griggs. Sitting across from him was a woman with a wide, welcoming smile. A couple of teenaged girls were hovering around the table talking to them.

Griggs waved at Riley and Jenn.

"Come on over! Sit down!"

Riley and Jenn walked over to the table, and the teenagers went on their own way. As they sat down, Griggs gestured toward the woman sitting across from him.

"Agent Paige, Agent Roston—I'd like you to meet my wife, Renee. Renee, these are the two FBI agents I told you about."

Renee Griggs was serving hot scrambled eggs and sausage out of a warming dish onto paper plates. Renee and her husband were sipping coffee that had been poured out of a steaming thermos.

"Oh, Judd is so glad you're here," she said. "So am I. Would you like a bite to eat?"

Then with a light chuckle, she added, "I fixed too much, as usual."

Riley hesitated. She was anxious to get inside and find the principal. But neither she nor Jenn had had coffee or breakfast. Maybe a little nutrition was exactly what she and Jenn needed before they tended to matters at hand.

Besides, she could ask the coach some of the same questions she planned to ask others. She glanced at Jenn, who seemed to be thinking the same thing.

"Thank you," Riley said to Renee. "That would be lovely."

Renee chattered away as she dished out servings and poured coffee for Riley and Jenn.

"Breakfast here has gotten to be kind of a ritual for Judd and me. He's always so eager to get to school and see the kids, I couldn't get him to sit down and eat breakfast at home."

Judd added with a laugh, "So she took to chasing me down with sausage and eggs."

Renee waved her finger at him in a mock-scolding manner.

"Now Judd, that's not true and you know it."

Before she could say more, another couple of girls came up to the table to say good morning and chat for a moment with Judd. Riley recognized them from the soccer team's locker room. The girls kept glancing at Riley and Jenn a bit uneasily. Obviously they wondered why the agents had come back.

As the girls kept talking with Judd, Renee leaned across the table toward Riley and Jenn.

"Do you see what happens?" she said in a playful whisper. "The girls can't stay away from him, and he spends all his time with them. I have to do whatever I can to squeeze in a minute edgewise with him. Otherwise, they'd get him all to themselves."

Riley was enjoying the woman's cheerfully noisy prattle. Renee spoke in a slightly raspy but chronically happy voice that reminded Riley of other middle-aged Midwestern women she had met over the years. Renee appeared to be about her husband's age—maybe a few years older than Riley. They both seemed to have put on weight over the years, but they had aged gracefully and were still attractive in their way.

Renee's eyes sparkled at Riley and Jenn as she kept right on talking.

"I'm president of the local PTA, so I'm here at the school a lot, almost as much as Judd is. This is just a lovely way for us to start off our mornings—at least when the weather is nice. We never miss this little ongoing date of ours when we can possibly help it."

The girls who had been talking to Judd waved and hurried on their way.

Now no students were nearby. Riley was trying to think how to tell them that another girl was dead when Judd asked, "So what brings you around here? Good news, I hope."

Riley took a long breath and said, "I'm sorry, but I'm afraid not. Another girl has been killed. We found her body just this morning."

Judd's mouth dropped open, and the coffee cup shook in his hand.

"Oh, dear God. Not another girl on my team, I hope."

"No. She's an older girl who graduated from here a couple of years ago. Her name was Camryn Mays. Did you happen to know her?"

Judd knitted his brow.

"The name is familiar. But no, I … I don't think I knew her personally, at least not very well. But even so … it's just such a terrible …"

He choked a little, and his voice faded away with emotion.

His wife patted his hand comfortingly.

She said quietly to Riley and Jenn, "I can't tell you how hard Katy's death has been on poor Judd. He liked her so much, and she had such promise. And then there was the other girl, the one who went to Lincoln, and now this new one today."

She looked down and shook her head sadly.

"Oh, please, please," she said to Riley and Jenn. "Make this stop. Make sure it doesn't happen again. I don't think Judd can take much more of this. I'm not sure I can either."

Riley felt a deep pang of sympathy for both of them, especially Judd. She hated to bring anybody such terrible news. It was a part of her job that she could never get used to.

A silence fell as Renee put her arms around Judd, who seemed to be fighting back his tears.

So unfair, Riley thought.

Since she and Jenn had first come to Angier, she'd met very few people whom she'd liked. Too many of them had seemed guilty of something—the piano teacher, the principal at Lincoln High, the predatory drug dealer, even the mayor.

Of all the people she'd met here, Judd and Renee Griggs

seemed the most decent, the most caring and compassionate.

Which of course made them all the more vulnerable to grief and pain—which was what struck Riley as unfair.

At the same time, Riley felt a pang of envy for them.

They'd obviously had such a beautiful relationship for many years, and everything about them seemed to be so …

It took a moment for Riley think of the right word.

Perfect.

The thought of that word hit her in a strange, discordant way.

She wasn't sure at first just why.

Then she remembered what Bill had told her over the phone.

"Just remember—whatever seems *too perfect usually is."*

CHAPTER THIRTY SEVEN

Riley sat there staring at Judd and Renee Griggs in a state of silent shock.

So perfect, she kept thinking.

Renee kept her arms around her husband's shoulders, whispering comforting words in his ear while he struggled to keep his composure.

It just didn't seem possible that Judd's grief and horror weren't perfectly sincere.

It also didn't seem possible that as good a woman as Renee could possibly devote her life to anyone other than a fine and decent man.

And yet …

Too perfect, she thought to herself.

Riley heard Jenn say, "We're sorry to trouble you, but we'd like to ask you some questions …"

Yes, questions, Riley thought.

Riley's head was exploding with questions, but surely not the ones Jenn intended to ask. For example—where was Judd Griggs last Wednesday night, when Katy Philbin had been raped and killed?

But she kept her mouth shut as Jenn kept talking, gently trying to coax Judd into remembering whatever he could about Camry Mays.

It was a struggle to keep her alarm from showing. She noticed that she was trembling a little. Had her face grown pale? What would happen if Judd noticed her inner turmoil?

She felt she had to get away from here—right now.

She pretended that she felt her phone vibrating in her pocket, then took it out and looked at it.

"Oh, my," she said. "Something has come up. Agent Roston, we've got to go right now."

Jenn sat staring at Riley in disbelief as she got up from the table.

Riley said to Judd and Renee, "I'm so sorry to rush off after you offered us such a lovely breakfast. But this is terribly important. And urgent. Believe me, my partner and I are sorry that we had to bring you such terrible news."

Judd looked up at her and nodded.

"I understand," he said. "Go, do what you have to do."

His wife nodded as well.

"God bless you for trying to make things right," she said. "We'll pray that you succeed."

Riley strode away from the table toward the car, and Jenn trotted along beside her.

"Riley—what the hell is going on?" Jenn whispered.

Riley shushed her.

They got into the car, and Riley started to drive.

Jenn seemed quite agitated now.

"I'm not stupid, Riley. I know you didn't get any kind of a message. You just made that up. You just wanted to get away. Why?"

Riley didn't reply.

Jenn gasped.

"Oh, my God," she said. "Surely you don't think …"

Again, Riley said nothing.

Jenn said, "Riley, do you have a single rational reason for suspecting …?"

"No," Riley admitted. "I don't."

"Then what are you thinking? Have you lost your mind?"

Riley shuddered a little.

She half-wondered whether she *had* lost her mind.

"Where are we going now?" Jenn asked.

It was a good question, and Riley didn't know the answer.

She knew that she couldn't pursue her awful hunch without finding some kind of evidence. Should they head over to the police station, make use of the considerable high-tech equipment that was available there?

She'd have to explain her reasons to Chief Sinard.

So what would she tell him?

That she suspected a beloved girls' soccer coach of rape and murder, for no rational reason at all?

That would surely be a disaster.

Riley said to Jenn, "Let's stop someplace for coffee."

They drove downtown and found a corner café. Riley parked the car by the curb, and the two of them went inside and sat down in a booth together.

While Jenn ordered coffee for both of them, Riley set her laptop on the table. She ran a search for the coach's name …

"Judd Griggs."

She got a list of results, and quickly discovered that his full name was Judd Colton Griggs. Many of the listings were news articles, all of them full of glowing praise for the coach. He'd led his team to plenty of championships, but those seemed to be the least of his accomplishments as far as the town of Angier was concerned. He'd received honors and awards for all kinds of services to the community, especially young people.

He'd been more than a teacher or a coach.

He'd been a mentor and a guide.

Just last year, a banquet had been held in his honor. Former students had come to personally thank Judd Griggs for how he had inspired and motivated them to achieve remarkable success in life.

Riley also found many fulsome references to Renee Griggs, whose work with the PTA had helped Wilson High achieve heights of academic excellence.

Jenn came around to Riley's side of the table and sat down next to her. She looked at the information on the screen.

"This is crazy," she said. "There's nothing wrong with this guy, and everything that's right. Surely you can see that."

Riley couldn't very well argue.

But as she viewed more and more praise for the coach, that knot of suspicion in her chest grew tighter and tighter.

Too perfect, she kept thinking.

She scrolled through the news articles, tracing them back through the years.

Finally, she found one from twenty years ago, announcing that Wilson High had hired a new gym teacher and girls' soccer coach named Judd Griggs.

Just then Riley noticed something odd.

She pointed to the screen and said to Jenn, "That's the earliest reference to Judd Griggs I can find. There doesn't seem to be any other mention of him in the whole Internet."

"So?" Jenn asked.

"So—didn't he have any kind of life before he came to Angier?"

"Maybe not," Jenn said. "This seems to be where things really started for him."

"No, that can't be right," Riley said. "A guy this remarkable couldn't have come from out of nowhere. He must have impressed people much earlier, in college or even high school. But I see no sign of that here."

Jenn let out a groan of disapproval.

"Riley, you're reaching. You're looking for evidence that's just not there."

Maybe, Riley thought.

But she doubted that more and more.

And she knew someone who might be able to help her sort this out.

She took out her cell phone and punched in Sam Flores's extension at the BAU. When she got the crack lab technician on the line, he sounded glad to hear from her.

"Hey, Agent Paige—what's up?"

Riley's brain cranked away as she tried to put her thoughts together.

"Sam, I'm looking for information on a gym teacher and soccer coach here in Angier. His name is Judd Colton Griggs. I've run a search, and I can't find anything about him before he came to work here twenty years ago."

"Say no more," Sam said. "I'll see if I can access some official records."

She heard Sam's fingers clattering on his computer keys.

Then she heard him gasp a little.

"Uh, this is interesting," he said. "I've found a record of his birth, forty-six years ago. There's nothing to speak off after that. He seems to have been pretty much a complete nonentity until twenty-six years later."

"What happened then?" Riley asked.

Sam fell silent for a moment, then said …

"He died."

CHAPTER THIRTY EIGHT

Riley's pulse was pounding at the words Sam Flores had just spoken.

Judd Griggs—dead!

What could that possibly mean?

"How did it happen?" Riley asked.

"I found his official death certificate. He drove off an embankment and crashed his car—a one-vehicle accident. His neck was broken, and he was presumed to have died instantly. The certificate doesn't say anything more about the circumstances of his death."

Jenn was staring at Riley wide-eyed, obviously wondering what was being said. Riley wished she could put the call on speakerphone so Jenn could join in.

But she couldn't do that—not in a public place like this café.

In fact, she shouldn't be holding this conversation here at all.

Nobody was nearby, and she didn't think she was being overheard.

Even so, Judd Griggs was well-known in this town, and she could unleash a whole world of weird rumors if anybody heard her talking about his death.

Riley said, "Sam, hold on a minute. We've got to get somewhere where we can talk freely."

Riley hastily scooped up her things, including her laptop. She put enough money on the table to pay for their coffees, plus more than enough for a tip.

"Come on," she said to Jenn.

She got up from the table, and she and Jenn left the café and headed for their car.

"What's going on?" Jenn asked.

Riley said, "It seems that Judd Griggs died quite a few years ago."

Jenn gasped. "What? I don't understand!"

"I don't either. Maybe we both will in a minute."

Riley and Jenn climbed into the front seat of the car. Riley opened her laptop again and put the call on speakerphone.

Riley said to Sam, "Agent Roston is listening too."

"OK," Sam said. "But I've got some catching up to do. Why are you so interested in this guy?"

Riley said, "There's a Judd Griggs coaching at a local high school—and he's definitely alive and well."

"And you consider him a suspect?"

Riley hesitated, then said, "Yes."

Jenn asked, "Where did it happen? Where did Judd Griggs die?"

"Way up in northeast Iowa," Sam said. "A little town called Barrows, in McGrath County."

Riley heard Sam clicking away at his keyboard again.

Soon he said, "I found an obituary in the local paper. It's even less informative—no picture, not even a cause of death. Nobody seems to have cared very much that he'd died. It's not like he made a big mark on the world. But he was born in Barrows and spent his whole life there."

"Any other official documents?" Riley asked.

After a few seconds of typing, Sam said, "I've found a driver's license with his photo on it. I'll email it to you right now."

In a few moments, Riley received the email on her laptop.

The image wasn't very good, and it was hard to make out the man's face very well. Nevertheless, the man *could* be the same man they'd talked to at the school just a little while ago, Riley thought. After all, a lot of years had passed since then.

She thought for a moment, "Is this really all you can find out about him? Prior to when he supposedly moved to Angier, I mean?"

Sam clattered away some more.

"Not a thing," Sam said. "What do you want me to do now?"

Riley felt stymied and baffled. She looked at Jenn, and could tell that she felt the same way.

But as the seconds passed, a hunch began to take shape in Riley's mind.

She remembered how they had already run a search of criminal records for one hundred miles around Angier during the last ten years.

They hadn't turned up anything especially useful, but …

Finally Riley said to Sam, "I want you to run a search of registered sex offenders."

"What kind of parameters?"

Riley thought for a second.

"Try within two or three years of when Judd Griggs died. Search right there in the same town—Barrows, Iowa."

Riley heard Sam's fingers at work again.

As he typed, he said, "Barrows is a really little town—just over a thousand people. Something like that really ought to stand out like a…"

Then he fell silent.

Finally he said, "Yeah, I've got somebody. A guy named Dillon Connor Crandall. He was charged with possession of child pornography, about a month after Judd Griggs died."

Riley could barely keep pace with her own thoughts now. But she knew she was on the verge of finding out something vital.

She hastily ran a search on her own computer.

Dillon Connor Crandall … child pornography … Barrows, Iowa …

She added the year in question.

Sure enough, a newspaper article appeared on her screen, bearing the headline …

Local Gym Teacher Charged With Child Porn Possession

Even more startling than the headline was a photo of the arrested man.

He, too, looked like a younger version of the local coach. But the resemblance was much stronger than it had been with the driver's license photo of Judd Griggs.

Riley and Jenn stared at each other with amazement.

Then Riley said, "Sam, I'm sending you a link."

She immediately emailed Sam a link to the article.

"Holy cow," Sam said.

As Riley read the article, her amazement increased. It described a young man who had been born and bred in Barrows, and was well-liked and respected there. He'd been an Eagle Scout, an excellent student, and a high school football champion. After going away to college to get a teaching degree, he'd come back to Barrows to teach at the local high school and coach athletics there.

According to the article, the closely knit community was in a state of shock about the charge of possessing child pornography. Lifelong friends said they simply couldn't believe it. The school principal, the mayor, and other high-ranking citizens expressed their disappointment and sorrow. His parents refused to make any kind of statement.

Jenn nodded and said to Riley, "This is it. This is our guy."

Maybe so, Riley thought.

But she didn't dare let herself feel sure of it yet.

She said, "Sam, can you find any court records of that case?"

Sam typed, then said, "It looks like he pleaded no contest to the possession charge. He wasn't charged with any kind of assault. There's no mandatory minimum sentence for possessing child pornography in and of itself. So he didn't do any prison time. But he did have to register as a sex offender. And he got fired from that school."

Riley thought hard and fast.

She said to Sam, "What can you find about Crandall after this happened—his sentencing and firing?"

Sam searched for a little longer this time.

"Not a thing," he said. "It's as if he disappeared off the face of the earth."

Riley felt her face flush with excitement.

But she knew that they still had important dots to connect before they could take any action.

Jenn was staring at Riley's laptop.

"So what you're saying is … when Judd Griggs died in a car wreck, the disgraced Dillon Connor Crandall assumed his identity."

Riley nodded excitedly.

"And the man who then called himself Judd Griggs eventually moved to Angier to start a new life."

"Sure looks like he did," Sam replied.

Jenn asked, "Do you think we can nail him with this?"

"Not with this, yet," Riley said. "We have nothing to actually connect him with the murders. So far we can't even connect him with all three victims."

"Katy Philbin played soccer," Jenn said. "Camryn Mays also went to Wilson High, so it's likely that she at least knew the coach." She hesitated and then added, "But we haven't found any possible connection with Holly Struthers."

Sam Flores pitched in, "Maybe I can help you with that."

"Take a look at the school records for Holly Struthers. We know she went to Lincoln High. Was she ever on the soccer team?"

A few moments later, Sam said, "She's not listed on any sports team at all. Not even sports-related clubs."

"Did she ever go to Wilson High? Even for just a short time?"

After another wait, Sam told them, "There's no sign at all of her at Wilson. Not even with any kind of organization. Sorry."

"Thanks anyhow, Sam. You've been a great help. You've given us a whole lot more than we had to work with before."

Riley ended the phone call. She and Jenn stared at each other for a moment.

"What do we do now?" Jenn asked.

Riley said, "We've got to convince Chief Sinard that Judd Griggs is our killer."

Jenn shook her head and said, "You're going to tell him that one of Angier's most beloved citizens is a rapist and murderer? That's going to be a hard sell, Riley."

Riley suppressed a discouraged sigh.

Jenn was right.

It was definitely going to be a hard sell.

CHAPTER THIRTY NINE

Sitting in Chief Sinard's office just a little while later, Riley tried to be patient. What could happen next was up to Sinard.

She and Jenn had showed him the information they'd put together. By that time, Sam had sent them still more evidence, including a stolen Social Security number, forged teaching credentials, and hard proof that the two men had been cousins.

Sinard stared at the documents on Riley's open laptop, pale with shock.

"This is impossible," he kept saying over and over. "I don't believe it."

Jenn looked at Riley doubtfully, as if to say …

"We're never going to convince him."

But Riley sensed that Sinard was wavering inside.

I've just got to get through to him, she thought.

After all, they had no time to lose. The murders were happening closer together now.

They couldn't allow another one.

Riley pointed to the documents on the screen and said, "Chief Sinard, it's all here in black and white. The man you know as Judd Griggs used to be Dillon Crandall, a registered sex offender in Barrows, Iowa. I don't see how you can come to any other conclusion."

Chief Sinard shuddered a little.

He said, "OK, some twenty years ago, it looks like Griggs got in trouble for possessing child pornography. It wasn't a violent offense, and he didn't even have to do time with it. But he moved on under an assumed name and made a new life here. What does that have to do with the life he's lived ever since? Doesn't he have a right to put his past behind him?"

Sinard got up from his desk and started to pace.

He said, "And what about Holly Struthers? She didn't even go to the same school as the other girls. We have no reason to think Griggs even knew her."

Riley didn't reply. That was the flaw that nagged at her. But she still felt sure it would make sense once they had all the facts. And if they couldn't find the connection with all three girls, they would just have to find a more direct link to the murders.

Riley stepped in front of him and held his gaze carefully.

"Chief Sinard, be honest with yourself. This man has been in your midst all this time, teaching with forged credentials, keeping this guilty secret. Do you really think it doesn't have anything to do with what happened to Katy and Holly and Camryn? Coach Griggs is the first viable suspect we've come across. And it sure looks to me like he's guilty as hell."

Sinard broke eye contact with her and shuddered.

"My God," he said.

He fell silent for a few moments.

Then he said, "What do you think we should do?"

Riley looked at her watch. It was still early in the school day. Judd Griggs was still at school, and it was likely that his wife was as well.

She asked Sinard, "How long would it take to get a warrant to search Griggs's house? We need to look specifically for evidence of the murders."

"What?" Chief Sinard said with a gasp.

"Can we get one by this afternoon?" Riley asked. "Is there a judge available?"

Sinard stared at her with disbelief.

"Agent Paige, this is crazy. What if we're wrong? You have no idea how liked and respected Judd Griggs is in Angier. I can't even imagine what kind of hell there will be to pay if—"

Riley interrupted him sternly.

"I asked a question, Chief Sinard."

Sinard nodded slowly.

"I could write out an affidavit, fax it to Judge Finn along with all this other evidence. He's usually available this time of day. I can talk him through it if he has doubts—and I'm pretty sure he will."

"Then you'd better get started," Riley said. "My partner and I will leave you to it."

Riley and Jenn left the police station. It was a pleasant day, so they sat down on a bench on the lawn.

"The chief is scared," Jenn said.

Riley nodded.

"He's got good reason to be. One way or the other, things are going to get very ugly very soon in this town."

They sat in silence for a moment. There was a pleasant breeze, and the shade was nice. Riley wished she was in the state of mind to enjoy it.

Finally Jenn said, "Riley, I'm sorry I doubted you."

Riley looked at her. For a moment, she didn't understand what Jenn meant.

Jenn said, "After we talked to the coach, I mean. I refused to believe he could possibly be guilty. I'd never have investigated him if I'd had my way."

Riley was surprised.

"Jenn, *of course* you doubted me," she said with a slight laugh. "I hit you with a half-assed and unbelievable theory, and I had no evidence at all for it. It's your job to question judgments like that. Bill would have done the same thing."

Jenn shook her head.

"Yeah, but … Riley, how do you do it? It's like you pulled the coach's guilt out of thin air. Your intuitions are just uncanny. I can't imagine being able to do what you do."

Riley felt warmer inside. She'd never known Jenn to show such humility and respect toward her.

In a gentle, kindly voice, she said, "Jenn, give yourself time. I didn't develop these skills overnight. When I look at you, I see myself at your age. But …"

Riley paused for a moment.

"I'm not sure I had your promise. I think you're the most amazing new agent I've worked with except …"

Her voice trailed off.

Jenn smiled and finished her thought.

"Except for Lucy Vargas."

Riley felt a lump of emotion in her throat. She nodded silently.

Jenn took in a long, slow breath.

Then she said, "Well, I just want you to know it's an honor to work with you. I hope I can live up to your expectations. And another thing …"

Jenn fell silent, then said, "I'm not going to push you about the Shane Hatcher thing anymore. You had your reasons for whatever kind of relationship you had—or have. I respect that. I understand that. I've had my own questionable contacts and advisors."

Riley felt slightly unsettled. She'd suspected as much about Jenn for a long time.

"You don't have to tell me," Riley said.

"No, you deserve it. I'll tell you—when I'm ready."

They didn't say anything for a minute or so.

Then Riley said, "You know, every time we've sat down to coffee or something to eat, we've been interrupted. Let's go get something to eat."

CHAPTER FORTY

Judd Griggs stared at Riley in stunned amazement.

"Under arrest?" he gasped. "For what? This is crazy!"

Riley glanced at Jenn, who looked startled. Nevertheless, Jenn took her cue and got out her handcuffs.

Fortunately, Griggs seemed too badly shaken to put up any resistance.

As Jenn pulled Griggs's arms behind him and put on the handcuffs, Riley said …

"You are under arrest for identity theft."

"What?"

"I think you heard me. Agent Roston, read him his rights."

Jenn read him his rights as she maneuvered him into the chief's SUV.

Renee Griggs was jabbering and weeping and pacing back and forth.

"What's going on? This is crazy! Why are you doing this?"

Chief Sinard tugged Riley away from the others.

He whispered angrily, "Agent Paige, what in the hell is this all about?"

"I thought I was pretty clear," Riley said.

Sinard just stared at her, dumbfounded.

"Let's get him down to the station," Riley said.

Sinard shook his head and climbed into the SUV behind the wheel.

Riley joined the rest of the team in back with Griggs.

The door slid shut, and Sinard backed the vehicle out of the driveway.

Renee Griggs was pounding on the side of the SUV screaming at the top of her lungs.

"You're making a terrible mistake! I'm calling our lawyer! You'll be sorry you did this!"

As they pulled out into the street and left the woman behind, Riley realized that she *did* feel sorry.

She felt sorry for poor Renee Griggs, who clearly had no idea that she was married to a monster.

She's in for an ugly awakening, Riley thought.

*

A short while later, Riley, Jenn, and Chief Sinard escorted Judd Griggs into the station's interview room and seated him at the gray table. Before they could start asking him any questions, a heavyset man burst into the room, looking highly agitated.

He said, "I'm Hunter Grunewald, Mr. Griggs's attorney. And I demand to know why you have arrested my client."

Riley looked the man in the eye.

She said, "He's under arrest for violation of the Identity Theft and Assumption Deterrence Act."

"The *what*?" the lawyer said.

Riley said, "It's a law that was passed in 1998. Violation carries a maximum term of fifteen years imprisonment."

"Yeah, I'm familiar with that law," the attorney said. "But what the hell does it have to do with my client?"

Riley set her laptop computer on the table and opened it. She laid out all the evidence they had against Griggs—birth and death certificates, newspaper articles, forged credentials, and assorted documents.

Through it all, the lawyer stared at the computer screen in astonished silence.

But as Riley laid out more and more information, Griggs started to weep quietly.

He kept saying over and over again …

"Oh, God …Oh, God … Oh, God."

When Riley finished, the lawyer struggled to gather his wits.

"I don't care what he did all those years ago," he blustered. "You're still making a mistake. The 1998 law doesn't say that identity theft is illegal, per se. It has to be carried out with intent to aid or abet some other unlawful activity."

Riley was a bit taken aback.

In her haste to act, she hadn't thought through all those details.

But now that she did …

"He *did* have illegal intent," she said. "Remember, he forged teaching credentials. He's been using his stolen identity for fraudulent purposes for twenty years. He's got no business teaching in a classroom or coaching a soccer team. We've got him dead to

212

rights. And before long, we'll have him for first-degree murder as well."

The lawyer's mouth dropped open.

"Murder? What murder?"

Riley said, "The rapes and murders of Katy Philbin, Holly Struthers, and Camryn Mays."

Grunewald turned pale.

Then he said to his client, "I order you not to say anything at all. Don't answer any questions."

Griggs was shaking all over now.

"No, no," he sobbed. "I've been carrying this around too long. I'm tired of running away from it."

Riley exhaled sharply.

Was he about to confess to everything?

"It's true," Griggs said. "About the pornography, I mean. I was young and stupid and … not mentally well. And after I was caught, I was so ashamed, so disgraced. I lost my job, lost all my friends, lost everything, and I deserved it, but …"

He choked on a sob.

"But I'd learned my lesson. I wanted to turn my life around. Around that time, Judd Griggs died, and nobody thought much of him. He flunked out of school, and he couldn't hold onto a job or a relationship, and he drank much too much. He was drunk when he crashed his car. And after that happened, I …"

He seemed to be struggling to put his thoughts into words.

"I had … some idea … that I could find some kind of redemption … for us both."

Griggs's eyes darted around the people in the room.

"I thought … maybe if I just took his name and started over … I could make everything right after all."

He shook his head miserably.

"But over the years, I've realized … a lie is a lie. I've tried to be the best man I could be. But I was still living a lie. And it's been eating me up inside for all this time. And I can't begin to tell you … what a relief it is … to finally just come out and say …"

He was seized by a spasm of sobs.

"But I never physically harmed a single human soul. Not back then, not ever since. I swear to God I didn't."

Chief Sinard hadn't said anything so far.

Finally he said, "How does your wife figure into this whole story?"

Griggs's lawyer touched him on the shoulder.

"That's enough," he said. "Not another word."

Judd Griggs nodded mutely, his tears falling on the table.

Riley could tell that he had said all he was going to say—for the time being, at least.

The lawyer said to the others present, "That's all the time you get with my client. I demand some time alone with him."

Riley, Jenn, and Sinard had no choice but to leave the interrogation room. As they walked down the hall, a tall, angry man came striding toward them.

Riley recognized him right away.

It was Mayor Daggett.

In a sharp, raspy voice, he said, "I just got a call from Judge Finn, then another from Hunter Grunewald. What in the name of God do you people think you're doing?"

Chief Sinard stepped toward him and said, "We've arrested Judd Griggs."

Riley sensed that Sinard was cowed by the mayor's arrival but was trying to sound and look more assertive than he felt.

"What on earth for?" the mayor asked.

Sinard said, "We're going to charge him for identity theft. And we're holding him on suspicion of murder."

The mayor's eyes bulged with disbelief.

"Murder?" he said to Sinard. "The three girls, you mean? You're crazy. I've known Judd for years, ever since he came to Angier. He's no murderer. He's the finest man I know."

Then he turned to Riley and Jenn.

"This is all your doing," he told them. "You two feds have been nothing but trouble since you came here. You've got no respect for the Constitution, conducting illegal searches and beating up suspects, and the county ME says you made a nuisance of yourselves at another crime scene."

He wagged his finger at them.

"And you've got no idea the trouble you're in now, arresting a man as decent and good as Judd Griggs. This whole town is going to explode right in your face. Your superiors are going to hear about it, believe me. And you'll lose your badges if I've got anything to say about it."

Riley felt a surge of anger. She moved directly into the mayor's personal space.

"Mr. Mayor, the last time we met, you told us there was no

214

serial killer. Things like that don't happen in Angier, you said. It's such a peaceable town with happy people, you said."

Riley leaned closer to his face and spoke even more sharply.

"Well, it's not so peaceable, and not so happy. We've got three corpses to account for now—three raped and murdered women. You'd better hope we've got the right man, or else there will be others."

Riley pushed past him and continued on her way down the hall, joined by Jenn and Chief Sinard.

Sinard murmured to her quietly, "I've got a very bad feeling about this."

Riley said nothing in reply. There was nothing to say—and nothing more for her and Jenn to do. She knew they might as well head back to their motel.

As she and Jenn walked back to their car, something started nagging her.

Could they have gotten the wrong man?

But no, that was impossible. In the heat of the arrest, she was letting herself get irrational.

Still, she sensed that her doubts weren't going to go away. She would have to find out the truth.

CHAPTER FORTY ONE

Riley and Jenn got into the car, and Riley started driving back to the motel. It was early evening now. Riley's head was still spinning from all that had happened this afternoon.

And that nagging feeling of doubt wouldn't go away.

Was it possible—just dimly possible—that the coach wasn't the killer?

"So what now?" Jenn said as Riley drove.

Riley glanced toward her and shrugged.

"Well, you know the procedure. The district attorney has to review the evidence and decide about charges. Chief Sinard is probably in touch with him right now, getting that ball rolling. It probably won't get done today, though. Tomorrow the suspect will appear before a judge and there will be talk about bail, but considering the murder charge …"

Jenn interrupted her with a chuckle.

"I know all that. I mean what about us? We've closed the case, there's no need for us hang around. The locals can take it from here. So we'll be flying back home tomorrow, I guess. I'll sure be glad to get out of this town. I'm sure you feel the same way."

"Yeah," Riley said quietly. "I do feel the same way."

She decided not to mention the vague and shapeless doubts that were floating around in her mind.

After all, they didn't make sense—not even to her.

Gazing out the window, Jenn said, "I've never worked a case like this one before. I expect a real crash will kick in soon, huh? I'm already starting to feel myself falling into a state of collapse. Even so, I still feel high from it—how we pulled it off, I mean, worked together as a team. I can't wait for the next case."

Jenn fell quiet for a moment.

Finally she said, "I can't tell you what a great experience this has been for me. It's been such an honor working with you."

Riley felt momentarily tongue-tied. She knew that she ought to return the compliment. Regardless of her own lurking doubts, Jenn had earned a pat on the back.

"You've done great work, Jenn," she finally said.

It sounded lame, and Riley knew that Jenn deserved better. She really had done superb work. But Riley couldn't think of anything better to say. She was too distracted.

She kept thinking about Judd Griggs, and his tearful confession.

He had seemed so utterly, painfully sincere. And maybe he had put all that delinquent behavior behind him.

Of course, that didn't mean much.

Riley knew from long experience that murderers could feign sincerity quite brilliantly.

But her mind was still in turmoil. How certain were they, really, that he was the murderer?

Wasn't it possible that Griggs was simply a good but flawed man desperately trying to put his shameful past behind him?

If so, what business did they have destroying everything he had done to redeem himself, humiliating him all over again among a whole community of people who had come to admire and love him?

Stop it, Riley thought. *Don't do this to yourself.*

After all, her gut had told her that Griggs was their man.

And her gut was very seldom wrong.

*

With nothing else demanding their attention, Riley and Jenn went to Riley's room, ordered a pizza and some beer, and started watching a movie. Riley remained distracted and had trouble paying attention to the story, but Jenn kept chattering about what was going on in it, at least for an hour or so.

Then Jenn got quieter and started to yawn from time to time.

"Wow, I really am starting to crash," she finally said, stretching her arms and letting out a huge yawn. "I had no idea how tired I was. I don't think I can even stay awake for the rest of this."

"That's OK," Riley said. "Go get a good night's sleep. You deserve it."

Jenn headed back to her own room, leaving Riley alone.

Riley stared at the TV screen until the rest of the movie finished. She had no idea what was going on in it, and she didn't really care. When it was over, Riley turned off the TV. She realized that she had already forgotten how the plot had unfolded.

She fetched the bottle of bourbon she'd bought a couple of

days ago and poured herself a glass, reminding herself to go easy with it. She was feeling strangely gloomy already, and getting drunk wouldn't make her feel any better.

As she sat sipping her drink, she realized she hadn't communicated with her family since she'd left home yesterday.

She picked up her cell phone and punched in the house number, and April answered.

"Hey, Mom! Have you cracked the case yet?"

Riley suppressed a sigh.

"I think so. Maybe."

April laughed a little.

"You don't sound exactly enthused."

Riley forced a chuckle.

"It's been a long day, I guess. Is everything OK there?"

"Just fine. We miss you."

"I miss you too."

"When will you be coming home?"

Riley hesitated, then said, "Tomorrow, I think."

"Great! We'll see you then! Love you, Mom."

"I love you too," Riley said.

They ended the call, and Riley suddenly realized how relieved she was that everyone at home was safe and sound.

She sent a text to Blaine.

Miss you. Hope to be back soon.

There was just one more thing she wanted to check on.
She sent a text to Bill.

Any news about Hatcher?

The message was marked "delivered," then "read," and then came Bill's reply.

Things are just the same. I'll let you know what happens. Don't worry.

Riley frowned.
Don't worry. Fat chance of that.
But she typed back …

I won't. Thanks for everything.

Bill replied.

Glad to help.

Riley finished her drink, took a shower, and climbed into bed.

She was tired, but for some reason she didn't feel ready to sleep yet. Slowly, it began to dawn on her what she was missing.

Whenever she was working on a murder case, there typically came at least one moment when she felt a strong connection with the killer, managed to get under his skin and into his very psyche.

That hadn't happened on this case. She'd had only vaguest of impressions about this killer.

Maybe it was overdue. Could she make it happen now?

She stretched out under the covers, breathed slowly and deeply, closed her eyes, and started to imagine and visualize climbing into the killer's very body.

First she chose the time and setting.

It was mid-afternoon, and he was sitting in the stands watching the girls practice soccer.

His eyes lighted on young Katy Philbin.

Such a star, *he thought with fatherly admiration.*

So much promise.

But as he watched her, his thoughts darkened.

He felt familiar surge of ugly lust welling up inside him.

No, *he told himself with dread.*

Not this time.

Not her.

Not Katy.

After what he'd done to the other girl, he'd promised himself ...

Never again.

He tried to fight it down, but that feeling kept getting stronger.

Finally, he gave up fighting it, surrendered to it, let the lust sweep through him.

His lust mingled with another terrible emotion—implacable, inexplicable hatred.

It was an exhilarating feeling, intoxicating, addicting.

It was an irresistible call to evil.

A quiet snarl curled up inside his throat.

His face twisted itself into an ugly, vicious sneer ...

Riley's eyes snapped open.

She realized that she'd snarled aloud, and she could still feel the shape of that hateful emotion on her own face.

But something felt wrong.

She pictured Judd Griggs in her mind. She tried to imagine that same expression on his face.

She couldn't do it.

Why not? she wondered.

The scenario she'd imagined was wrong somehow.

But how?

Riley heaved a deep sigh.

She ought to have known this wouldn't work—not here in her motel bed. She had usually summoned those uncanny moments of connection in the very locations where a crime had been committed. Or at least somewhere connected to the murder.

No, it wasn't going to work here.

But at least she was feeling more tired now.

She closed her eyes and went fast asleep.

*

Riley heard her phone buzzing on the bed stand.

She opened her eyes and saw sunlight through the window. The clock said it was eight o'clock.

Riley was surprised that she'd slept so late.

But after all, yesterday had been a long, tiring day.

She grabbed the phone and answered it.

"Agent Paige, this is Chief Sinard. I thought you should know that we just now released Judd Griggs."

Riley sat bolt upright in bed.

"What?" she said with a gasp.

"The DA was wavering about bringing charges against him even yesterday. But today he's sure that Griggs isn't guilty—and so am I."

Riley rubbed her eyes.

"What do you mean?"

"Another girl has gone missing," Sinard said. "It happened while Griggs was in custody."

CHAPTER FORTY TWO

Riley's mind reeled at what Chief Sinard had just said. She actually felt dizzy.

Another girl—missing! she thought.

"I don't believe it," she said aloud into the phone.

But the truth was, part of her did believe it. After all, she'd been struggling with doubt since yesterday evening.

Sinard sounded bitter and angry.

"You don't have to believe it. Frankly, I want you to stay out of this from now on. You've failed to catch the killer, and you've destroyed a good man's reputation. I want you and your partner to fly back to Quantico immediately. Call for the BAU plane, and I'll send Officer Laird to pick you up and drive you to the airport. You can leave my car in the motel parking lot. I'll have someone pick it up later."

Riley said nothing.

"Did you hear me?"

"I hear you," Riley said.

She abruptly ended the call.

Then she sat on the bed trying to gather her chaotic thoughts.

Sinard's words kept echoing through her brain.

"I want you and your partner to fly back to Quantico immediately."

She knew it was his prerogative to send them back. They were here at his official request, after all. He could change his mind at any time.

And yet …

There's a killer loose in Angier, she thought. *He's more dangerous than ever.*

Did she really think the local police were capable of stopping him?

She decided to wake Jenn up right away.

They needed to get the police station as soon as they could.

*

221

During the short drive to the police station, Riley told Jenn what had just happened.

Jenn seemed to be even more shaken by the news than Riley had been.

"I don't understand," Jenn said. "I just don't understand."

"That makes two of us," Riley said. "But don't expect Chief Sinard to give us a cozy welcome. He won't be glad to see us."

"Um, Riley," Jenn said, pointing. "I don't think he's the only who won't be glad to see us."

Riley was just then pulling up in front of the police station. As she parked, she saw a crowd of people clustered around the front steps. Standing at the top of the steps were Judd Griggs, his wife, and their lawyer. They were flanked by a couple of uniformed policemen.

"Oh, no," Riley murmured.

She and Jenn got out of the car and approached the crowd.

Judd Griggs was still speaking to the crowd, smiling broadly.

He said, "A night in jail was a new experience, I can tell you that. Not one that I ever want to repeat, though."

There was a burst of laughter among the crowd.

The coach had obviously been talking for a little while now, charming the crowd and winning their sympathy.

He continued, "Folks, you're going to hear some bad things about me during the next few days—maybe even sooner. Some of those things might not be true, but I'm afraid others might be. If it's true, I'll admit it. I won't pretend that I've lived a perfect life. But I think you know that I'm a man who owns up to his mistakes. And I put those mistakes behind me many years ago."

He hugged his wife, who was also smiling.

"Renee came into my life at a very bad time. She saw something in me that I didn't even see in myself. She turned my life around, made me a better man. I owe everything I have to her."

A man's voice called out from the crowd.

"What are you going to do now, Coach? Sue the city?"

Griggs's lawyers took a step forward. He looked eager to answer the question with a resounding "yes." But Griggs waved him back.

"That's not our first priority, believe me," Griggs said. "Right now Renee and I are going right back to everything exactly as usual."

He still had his arm around Renee. She called out to the crowd.

"Meanwhile, there's a real killer loose in this town. Chief Sinard just told us another girl is missing! The FBI sent agents here from all the way out east to solve it, but what did they wind up doing? They accused my husband! I don't know about you, but that makes me mad! And scared!"

The crowd yelled out in rowdy agreement.

Then Renee pointed to Riley and Jenn.

"And there they are! They've got the nerve to show up here! Agents Paige and Roston, I think you owe my husband and the good people of Angier an apology. And you'd better be able to tell us what you're doing at long last to keep our children safe!"

Riley and Jenn were suddenly engulfed by angry people, pushing and shoving at them and calling them liars and demanding an apology. Riley grabbed Jenn by the arm and pulled her toward the police station through the crowd. She was worried that things might get violent—not on account of what might happen to her and Jenn, but because of what they might have to do to defend themselves.

The last thing she wanted right now was for anyone to get hurt.

She and Jenn pushed their way among the jostling people. When they got to the door, even the two uniformed cops stood with their arms crossed, making a show of being unhelpful to them.

Riley pulled the door open, and she and Jenn got inside.

"What do we do now?" Jenn said, breathless from their tussle with the crowd.

"We've got to talk to Chief Sinard," Riley said. "Whether he likes it or not."

They headed straight to the chief's office. Not surprisingly, he greeted them with a grim expression and didn't get up from his chair.

"I thought I told you that your work here is over," he said, shuffling papers on his desk.

Riley stood at the edge of desk looking down at him.

"The least you can do is tell us what happened," she said. "Who is this missing girl? Why are you so sure she *is* missing?"

Sinard's eyes darted back and forth between Riley and Jenn, as if trying to decide whether to bother offering them an explanation.

Finally he spoke in a tight, angry voice.

"Her name is Amelia Stack. She's a junior at Wilson. She was last seen yesterday afternoon at play practice after school, which finished at about four-thirty. I don't need to tell you that that was *after* you apprehended the coach."

He paused for a moment.

"She and her cast mates were supposed to meet for snacks after rehearsal. She didn't show up, and her friends said that wasn't like her. She didn't go home for dinner either, so her parents started to worry. She'd told them she planned to go over to a friend's house later that evening to study. They called the friend's parents—she never showed up there. They called all of Amelia's friends, and nobody had any idea where she was."

Sinard drummed his fingers on his desk.

"The parents were beside themselves. Amelia's a good and reliable girl, and they knew she wouldn't just wander off for no reason. They called me. My men and I spent the whole night looking for her and couldn't find her."

Sinard got up from his desk and started to pace.

"Well, I called the DA early this morning. He'd already had his doubts about bringing charges against Coach Griggs, but this was the last straw. He ordered me to release him a little while ago."

He waved his finger and Riley and Jenn angrily.

"I told you I wanted you gone, and I meant it. If I feel like we need BAU help, I'll call in someone else—agents who *might* have some idea of what they're doing. Meanwhile, I want you out of this town, do you hear me?"

Riley locked eyes with him for a silent moment.

"Was Amelia Stack on the soccer team?" she asked.

Sinard glared at her. "I don't know," he snapped. "That doesn't really matter now."

Then Riley turned around and said to Jenn, "Let's go."

As Jenn followed her out of the office, Sinard yelled after them.

"Did you hear what I said. I want you gone!"

Riley and Jenn headed down the hallway toward the front door.

"We've still got work to do," Riley said.

"How?" Jenn said. "I don't understand."

Riley wasn't sure herself—not just yet.

But another girl was missing, and she might be dead already.

They had no time to lose.

Fortunately, the crowd had dispersed by the time they left the building, and there was no sign of Coach Griggs and his wife anywhere. They got into the chief's car, and Riley started to drive.

"Where are we going?" Jenn said.

A frantic plan was brewing in Riley's mind.

"I'm going to drop you off at Wilson High," she said. "You can ask whether or not Amelia Stack was on the soccer team. She must have had some connection to the coach. See what you can find out about that."

Jenn sat in the passenger seat gaping at Riley with disbelief.

"Are you kidding?" she said. "*That's* what you want me to do? Do you really think I'm going to learn anything there fast enough to save—"

Riley interrupted her in a sharp voice.

"That's an order, Agent Roston."

It was the first time Riley had called her that in several days.

Jenn looked like she'd been slapped.

She said with a bitter tone, "And what about you—*Agent Paige*? What are you going to do while I'm asking questions at Wilson High School?"

Riley's jaw clenched.

"That's my own business," she said.

Jenn let out a growl of anger and frustration.

"If you say so," she said.

They drove the rest of the way to school in silence.

Riley hated having to talk like that to Jenn. But she knew it was for Jenn's own good.

Taking Jenn to Wilson High served no purpose except keeping her away from Riley.

Riley was about to do something desperate, something that would probably end her own career.

There's no reason to ruin Jenn's career too, she thought.

CHAPTER FORTY THREE

Bill had been making this same short trip almost every day since Riley had gone to Iowa. His regular drive-by checks of Riley's house had only been interrupted by his emotional collapse on Sunday.

He knew that PTSD could happen to anyone. He'd even helped see Riley through a terrible bout with it. But it still embarrassed him that he had fallen apart and drawn Riley away from her assignment.

Now that Riley was back to her job, Bill felt good to be back to his unofficial duty.

But then he noticed something unsettling.

The unmarked police car parked in front of the house appeared to be empty.

What the hell? he thought.

Bill parked his own car nearby, got out, and looked inside the other vehicle.

Sure enough, nobody was in the car.

He felt a rush of anger.

During the last couple of days, he'd talked to both pairs of cops who had been taking turns watching Riley's house. He knew that Maddox and Carney were supposed to be here on the day shift. They'd struck him as OK guys, but not especially bright. Still, Bill had figured they were up to the job of watching a house where nothing was likely to happen.

After all, the last he'd heard, the FBI team was still tracking Shane Hatcher down in Norfolk.

Bill grumbled aloud …

"What are those clowns doing? Taking a stroll for a doughnut?"

He shook his head with frustration, then decided he'd better check Riley's house for himself. He walked up to the front door and rang the doorbell.

No one answered. He knew that the kids were in school, but where was Gabriela?

Then Bill noticed something that alarmed him.

226

The door wasn't completely closed.

He pushed the door, which swung open. Had Gabriela accidentally left the door ajar? No, that didn't sound like Gabriela at all.

Bill took a deep breath to cool his nerves. Then he drew his weapon and walked on into the house.

In the middle of the living room, he saw Officer Maddox lying in a pool of blood.

He hurried over to the body, knelt down, and felt for a pulse.

There wasn't any.

Maddox was dead.

And next to his body was a bloody chain.

Shane the Chain! Bill thought with a shudder.

It was Hatcher's legendary calling card, and his preferred method of murder—to bludgeon his opponents to death with a chain. Bill knew that Riley believed Hatcher to have put such vicious acts behind him.

He obviously hadn't.

He'd reverted to the heartless killer who had always lurked beneath his educated surface.

Bill saw that Maddox's eyes were wide open in an expression of sheer terror.

Bill gulped hard.

It must have been a nasty way to die.

But Bill didn't have time to dwell on that. It seemed entirely possible that Shane Hatcher was still in the house. If so, where was the second cop? And what might have happened to Gabriela?

His gun still ready, Bill moved slowly through the house, looking through all the doorways. He heard no sounds at all except for his own breathing and cautious footsteps.

When he got to the back of the house, Bill found that the door to the back deck was also ajar.

Bill remembered that Gabriela lived in the downstairs apartment, so he made his way down the stairs. He found the door partly open.

When he stepped into the apartment, he saw Carney's body.

Carney had died a different death—his throat slit wide open with a bloody knife that still lay on the floor nearby.

Like Maddox, Carney appeared to have been dead for about an hour.

Bill's heart was pounding now.

Where was Gabriela? Was Shane Hatcher still in the house?

Bill dashed up the stairs and continued on up to the second floor. He frantically searched through all the rooms and closets. There was no sign of Hatcher anywhere—or of Gabriela.

Bill felt dizzy with confusion. He walked back downstairs, trying to gather his thoughts, to figure out just what had happened. Little by little, things started to make some sense.

Hatcher had slipped through the BAU's fingers down in Norfolk. He'd left false trails all over the place to keep them busy. He'd only gone there in the first place as a ruse, to free him up to come here without anybody's knowledge.

Hatcher must have broken in through the back door, then disarmed the security system. Even so, something must have alerted Maddox and Carney that something was wrong in the house—possibly something as simple as a shadow moving past a window.

The two cops had stormed inside and separated to search the place. Carney had been the first to encounter Hatcher down in Gabriela's apartment. Hatcher had killed him swiftly, ruthlessly, and silently. Then Hatcher had crept upstairs, taken Maddox by surprise, and viciously bludgeoned him to death.

But where was Hatcher right now?

And what had happened to Gabriela?

Fortunately, Bill had Gabriela's cell phone number. He punched in the numbers and breathed a sigh of relief when the Guatemalan woman answered.

"Gabriela, this is Bill Jeffreys. Where are you right now?"

"Out shopping for groceries. Is something wrong?"

"Are the kids in school?"

"*Sí*, of course. What is the matter? You are scaring me."

Bill tried to sound calmer than he felt. There was no point in telling Gabriela about the two dead cops.

He said, "Gabriela, whatever you do, don't come home."

"Why not?"

"Just trust me."

"But where should I go instead?"

Bill thought for a moment.

He remembered that charming guy whom Riley seemed to be dating these days.

He said, "Can you get over to Blaine Hildreth's house?"

"*Sí*, I am very near there right now."

"How long will it take for you to get there?"

"Just a few minutes."

"Go there right now. I'll call him and tell him you're coming. Stay with him until I get in touch with you."

Bill ended the call, then quickly found Blaine's number and punched it in.

When Blaine answered, Bill told him who was calling.

"Where are you now?" Bill asked.

"At home. I was just getting ready to go to my restaurant."

"Don't," Bill said. "Stay right where you are. Riley's housekeeper, Gabriela, is on her way to your house. You've got to keep her there."

"What's going on?"

Bill struggled with what to say next. He'd avoided telling Gabriela about the grisly scene he'd discovered. He didn't like alarming civilians if he didn't have to. But he was putting Blaine in the middle of this situation. Blaine deserved to know.

He said, "The cops who've been watching over Riley's house have been killed, right here in Riley's house. Shane Hatcher was here. He did it. Now he's on the loose, and it looks like he's on some kind of murderous rampage."

"Jesus," Blaine murmured.

Bill hoped Blaine wasn't about to panic.

But Blaine sounded clear-headed as he spoke.

"So Gabriela's coming over to my place. What about Riley's kids? Are they safe?"

"They're in school."

"That's not what I asked. Are they safe?"

Bill felt a jolt of alarm.

That's a damn good question, he thought. After all, Hatcher surely knew that they were in school.

Was that where Hatcher might strike next?

It was a mind-boggling, horrifying possibility.

Bill thought hard and fast.

He quickly remembered something that Riley had casually mentioned at one time or another. Because Riley was away so often, she'd given Gabriela a lot of her own parental prerogatives and authority.

Bill said, "Gabriela's going to be there any minute now. Drive her to the school, and she can pull Riley's kids out of school. Take them all to your house. Then none of you go anywhere. Have you got that?"

229

"Yeah," Blaine said. "Bill …"

Bill could hear hesitation in Blaine's voice.

"What is it?" Bill said.

"I've got a gun," Blaine said.

Bill shuddered slightly. He knew that Blaine was trying to reassure him that he could keep everybody safe. But from long experience, Bill found the idea of a civilian trying to play the hero to be anything but reassuring.

"You won't be needing it," Bill said.

He ended the call, hoping he was right.

Meanwhile, there was plenty that he needed to do right here and now. He had to get in touch with the Fredericksburg police and also the FBI.

He decided to call the FBI first.

They needed to know that their stakeout had ended in a tragedy and that Hatcher was at large, probably in Fredericksburg.

He punched the FBI number into his cell phone.

CHAPTER FORTY FOUR

Riley's instincts were telling her loud and clear that she needed to search the coach's house. With a girl missing and in danger, she knew she had no choice but to follow her gut. There wasn't time for anything else.

She parked her car in the driveway, walked up to the house, and rang the doorbell.

She didn't know whether the coach and his wife would be at home. She hoped not. But if either Renee or Judd came to the door, she knew exactly what to say.

She'd apologize abjectly for the trauma she'd put them through, and promise that nothing like that would ever happen again.

It would be humiliating, of course, and it would leave Riley's purpose unfulfilled.

She breathed a little easier when nobody answered the door.

She took out her lock-picking kit and opened the front door.

As soon as she stepped inside, she saw something amiss.

One of the big living room chairs had been moved.

Riley walked across the carpeted floor. On the other side of the dislocated chair was a gaping square hole in the floor.

It was an open trapdoor, its lid folded back. She could see stairs leading downward.

A basement! Riley thought.

When she and Jenn had searched the place yesterday with Sinard and the others, they'd all believed that the house had no basement. There were no signs of one.

But now she knew better.

Standing above the entrance, staring into the dim light below, Riley couldn't see much except for a concrete floor with rugs scattered on it.

But as she listened carefully, she heard something.

Something or someone was moving about down there. She also heard what sounded like a girl's voice, muffled and moaning.

Amelia's down there! she thought.

And so, Riley was sure, was the coach.

And the coach must know that Riley was here.

He couldn't have missed the sound footsteps on the floor above him.

What should she do now?

She considered calling down, identifying herself and announcing that he was under arrest.

But what if he used the girl as a hostage? Perhaps he was already holding her with a gun to her head.

Riley made a decision. She drew her own weapon and charged down the stairs.

At the bottom was girl lying on a rug on the floor. She was tied up, her mouth was taped shut, and her face was badly bruised.

And standing over her, smiling that charming smile of his, was the coach.

She aimed her gun at him, and said, "Judd Griggs, you already know who I am. You are under arrest for …"

Riley was interrupted by a sharp blow to the back of the head.

She fell dizzily to her knees, and her head whirled round as she still clutched her gun.

Before she could put her thoughts together, her head took another blow.

This time the gun flew from her hands and the world became dim and blurry.

*

Blaine and Gabriela hurriedly went through the process of picking up kids from two schools. During the drive back to his house, his passengers bombarded him with frantic questions. He said as little as possible. He made a point of not mentioning Shane Hatcher. They were all scared enough as it was.

Besides, his head was buzzing with questions of his own—and he had no one to answer them.

The direst question was …

How safe will they all be in my house?

All he knew about Shane Hatcher was what Riley had told him.

And what Riley had told him was both terrifying and awe-inspiring.

It had sounded to Blaine as if Shane Hatcher had the mind of a brilliant chess player, always thinking several moves ahead, anticipating his opponent's every move.

Would Hatcher guess that Riley's family might seek safety in Blaine's house?

It seemed like a distinct possibility.

As soon as Blaine arrived at home and got everyone inside, he shepherded them all through the door that led down to his furnished basement.

"Go down there and stay put," he said. "I've got to go get something. I'll join you in a minute."

April was looking at him, wide-eyed with fear and perplexity.

"But why, Blaine?" April asked. "What's going on?"

"I'll explain everything later," Blaine said.

Jilly crossed her arms and frowned indignantly.

She said, "I'm not going anywhere until you tell us what's going on."

Blaine felt a surge of impatience—and also a surge of authority that took even him by surprise.

He grabbed Jilly firmly by the arm.

"You *are* going down there, young lady," he snapped. "And so are all the rest of you. I'm in charge right now. You'll do exactly as I say. And I don't want to hear any more out of you."

The group stared at him with their mouths hanging open. Then they silently nodded and moved almost herd-like down the stairs.

Blaine shut the basement door and locked it.

He dashed upstairs to his bedroom closet and fetched the locked box where he kept his gun. He took out the gun, snapped open the cylinder, and loaded it with six bullets.

He shuddered a little as he did so.

He'd never fired this gun anywhere except at the firing range.

He'd never even loaded it here in his own house.

His actions felt weird and dreamlike.

Is this really happening? he wondered.

The gun felt strange and foreign in his hand, as if he'd never handled it before in his life.

He left his bedroom with the gun and dashed down the stairs.

Then he heard the violent sound of breaking glass.

He whirled and saw that the sliding doors leading to his back yard had been shattered, its shards scattered in all directions.

Wading through the glass and looking straight at him with an evil smile was a large African-American man. He was swinging a heavy chain at his side—the chain he must have used to break the

233

glass.

Blaine had never seen him before, but he immediately knew who it was.

Shane Hatcher.

Like a consummate chess player, Hatcher had indeed anticipated that Riley's family would seek safety here.

In fact, he'd probably anticipated it before Blaine had known it himself.

Struggling against fear, Blaine backed up toward the wall, pointing the gun at Hatcher. He was holding the weapon properly, just as Riley had taught him. Even so, it was all he could do to keep his arms from shaking.

Hatcher stepped slowly toward him, swinging the chain in a threateningly casual manner.

Hatcher said, "Blaine Hildreth, I presume. Riley's new beau. Odd, I pictured you as … well, more formidable, I suppose. Riley's taste in men is rather a mystery to me."

Hatcher seemed amused by the sight of the gun in Blaine's hand.

"Have you ever killed a man, Blaine?" he said. "I've found it very easy to do—quite enjoyable, actually. But other people tell me that it's not so easy. In fact, many people can't bring themselves to do it at all."

He moved closer to Blaine, swinging the heavy chain in full circles now. The end of the thing was now whirling just a couple of feet from Blaine's face. If Hatcher took another two steps it would strike him.

"My guess is you are one of those people who can't do it."

Hatcher's words echoed in Blaine's ears. It truly did feel terrible and unnerving to point a gun at another human being.

No, he couldn't imagine himself pulling this trigger.

Despite the impending danger, he just couldn't.

But there's another way, Blaine realized.

He shut his eyes and imagined he was at the shooting range.

He's a target, he told himself. *Just a paper target.*

Sure enough, he could see the target clearly in his mind's eye.

He felt the familiar kick of the weapon as he blindly fired one shot … then another … then another.

*

234

Riley struggled against losing all consciousness.

I can't, she told herself. *I can't.*

She'd surely wind up dead if she passed out.

Painfully, she lifted her head. As her eyes began to focus again, she could see her assailant standing over her holding a wooden board.

It was Renee, the coach's wife.

Impossible, Riley thought.

Was she hallucinating?

But no—that horrible expression on the woman's face was all too real.

And for some mysterious reason, it was all too familiar.

Riley asked herself …

Why did she recognize that expression?

From where and when?

Then she flashed back to last night, when she had tried to get into the mind of the killer.

She'd felt her own face take that shape—an expression of murderous hatred.

But even so …

It doesn't make sense, Riley thought.

As she tried to pull herself to her feet, Renee gave her a swift kick in the belly, knocking her back again.

Riley lay gasping for air. Her consciousness was wavering again.

Renee Griggs knelt down beside Riley, peering closely into her eyes, her expression twisting with pure evil.

"Why, look here, Judd!" she said in a purring voice. "Look at the little gift that just dropped into our hands!"

She gripped Riley's chin in her hand, turning her face back and forth as if examining it.

Renee said, "You know, little lady, when I met you yesterday, I didn't take you for my husband's type, you were too old and too strong. But now that you're here … so weak and helpless and all … well, I'm looking forward to seeing what he's going to do to you. I'll sure enjoy finishing you off afterwards."

At last, the horrible truth finally came clear to Riley.

Judd Griggs was the rapist, but he'd only been acting at Renee's bidding.

Renee was the true killer.

She'd abducted this girl while Judd was in jail, confident that he'd soon be free.

Riley summoned her strength and tried to shove Renee away.

Renee grabbed her by the hair and slammed her head against the floor.

To Riley, the room seemed to spin around her.

Then she heard a familiar voice behind her.

"Drop that board! Drop it or I'll shoot!"

It's Jenn, Riley realized.

But the woman still hovered over her, raising the board as if to slam it against Riley's head with a final, fatal blow.

A shot rang out, and the board clattered to the floor. With a yelp of pain, Renee collapsed onto Riley.

Ignoring the pain in her head, Riley struggled out from under the thrashing woman.

She scrambled toward her gun.

In another instant, Riley was standing and pointing the gun at the woman who lay at her feet.

Renee was moaning and clutching her thigh, which had been grazed by the gunshot.

Riley glanced over her shoulder and saw that Jenn was already putting the coach into handcuffs.

"Good shot," Riley said. "Thanks for not hitting me."

Jenn smiled back at her.

"Glad to oblige," she said.

She felt wobbly but completely in control now. She stooped and deftly handcuffed Renee Griggs.

Then she hurried over to the Amelia Stack, who lay moaning desperately. Riley untied her and removed the tape from her mouth as gently as she could.

The girl let out a wail of horror mingled with relief.

Riley held her close as she began to weep more quietly.

"It's all over," Riley told her. "You're safe now."

As Riley rocked the girl in her arms, she heard Jenn talking on the phone.

"Chief Sinard? I need an ambulance at Coach Griggs's house. We also need your prisoner transport van. That's right, we're making arrests … two of them."

Riley could hear a note of deep satisfaction in Jenn's voice.

Riley smiled.

She felt exactly the same way.

CHAPTER FORTY FIVE

Bill drove as fast as he could manipulate his car through traffic. After the local cops had arrived at Riley's home, he'd tried to call Blaine several times but had gotten no answer. He figured that even without the siren and lights of an official car, he could reach Blaine's house as fast as a 911 call would get someone there to check things out.

What the hell's going on? Bill wondered.

When Bill pulled up in front of Blaine's house, it didn't look like anything was amiss, at least not from outside.

He parked his car and ran to the front entrance. But ringing the doorbell and pounding on the door didn't get an answer either. And the door was locked.

Bill's heart was pounding now, and he was seized by massive waves of guilt and self-doubt.

Had he made a fatal mistake by asking Blaine to pick up Gabriela and Riley's kids?

Had he sent them right into a trap?

He drew his weapon and dashed around the house to the back entrance. There he saw a shattered glass sliding door. A trail of blood led out of the house and across the back deck.

Bill scrambled up onto the deck and ran through scattered shards of glass into the house.

Blaine was sitting slumped over and motionless in a chair.

Is he dead? Bill wondered.

But as Bill approached, he saw that Blaine was shivering all over.

Blaine was holding a gun in his hand and he was in an apparent state of shock.

Bill put his own gun away and gently removed the weapon from Blaine's hand.

"What happened here?" Bill asked. "Where are Gabriela and the kids?"

Blaine slowly lifted his head, looking dazedly surprised to see Bill.

"They're downstairs," he said. "They're safe. I …"

He fell silent, as if trying to remember exactly what had happened.

Finally Blaine said, "It was Hatcher. He came here. I shot him … I think. The next thing I knew he was gone."

Bill glanced back at the trail of blood that led out back.

He said, "Yeah, you shot him, all right. Any idea how many times?"

Blaine shook his head.

"I fired three shots. I didn't see …"

His voice trailed off again.

Bill patted him on the shoulder.

"You did good," Bill said.

Blaine looked into Bill's eyes.

"I didn't know if I … I didn't think I …"

Then Blaine smiled a little.

"But I did it," he said. "I did what I had to do."

Bill felt strangely moved. It only took him a moment to realize why. Bill had experienced exactly the same feeling the first time he had used deadly force out of necessity. It wasn't pride exactly—it never felt good to shoot anyone. Even so, it was a sort of deep gratification at learning about one's own capabilities, grim though they might be.

In his guilt at having shot an innocent man, Bill had entirely forgotten that feeling.

Now he was glad to be reminded.

Maybe I can be myself again, Bill thought.

He went to the basement door, unlocked it, and opened it.

"Come on up, everybody," he called out. "You're all safe."

Gabriela, April, Jilly, and Liam all crept cautiously out of the basement.

"What has happened here?" Gabriela asked.

Bill said, "What's happened here is …"

For a moment, he found himself at a loss for words.

Finally he smiled, pointed at Blaine, and said, "What's happened here is … you need to thank this guy for saving your lives. He can tell you the details."

Gabriela and the kids clustered around Blaine, bombarding him with questions. Blaine was starting to come out of his state of shock, and he started trying to explain all that had happened.

Meanwhile, Bill stepped out onto the back deck.

He could see traces of blood trailing through the backyard toward the open gate in the backyard fence. From the quantity of blood, Bill guessed that the wound was serious.

Bill knew better than to hope anyone could follow that trail directly to Hatcher. He'd surely come here in a vehicle and had driven away. Even so, Bill felt certain that Hatcher wasn't going to get very far, not in his present condition.

He took out his cell phone. He'd already put out an alert that Hatcher was in Fredericksburg. The police and FBI probably had roadblocks set up by now. He'd update them that the wanted man was wounded. If he wasn't already dead, he'd be more dangerous than ever.

*

Jenn watched as Amelia Stack was loaded into an ambulance and Judd and Renee Griggs were put under arrest. She and Riley were standing in Coach Griggs's front yard, keeping well inside the area the police had taped off.

Although the danger was over, Jenn's heart was still beating fast and hard, and she felt short of breath.

She could hardly believe what had just happened.

A crowd of neighbors was gathering nearby, some of them looking confused, others looking as angry as the crowd back at the police station. She saw that the media was also arriving, probably following police radio calls.

But Sinard and his men were keeping them all on the other side of the police tape that now surrounded the house.

Jenn smiled a little.

She said, "It's nice of Chief Sinard to keep those people away from us."

Riley grumbled, "It's the least he can do, now that he knows how wrong he was."

There was no doubt about what had happened here. The other girls' cell phones had been found in the basement, all smashed.

The ambulance and the transport vehicle soon left. A small police team was still in the house. Jenn and Riley had answered Sinard's basic questions, but they would have to fill him in on more details.

Riley asked Jenn, "How did you get here from the school?"

Jenn shrugged.

"I called a cab practically as soon as you dropped me off. I knew you were up to something. And it wasn't hard to figure out what it was."

Riley laughed a little.

She said, "That was some pretty good detective work."

Jenn was feeling just a twinge of anger now.

"Riley, why didn't you tell me what you were going to do? Did you think I'd try to stop you? Did you think I'd file an official report or something?"

"Well, what I planned to do *was* illegal," Riley said. "So, yeah, maybe it crossed my mind."

Jenn shook her head.

"Well, you ought to know me better than that," she said. "I thought we were turning out to be a pretty good team."

"We are, Jenn," Riley said. "We really are."

Jenn's anger evaporated at the warm tone in Riley's voice.

Then Riley added, "I guess I also didn't want to get you fired."

Jenn smiled and said, "How many times have you gotten fired or suspended?"

Riley sighed.

"Oh, more times than I can count."

"Then I've got some catching up to do," Jenn said.

They both laughed.

They got into the chief's car that was still in the driveway, with Jenn in the driver's seat. For a few minutes, she just sat there.

"So Renee was the killer," Jenn said. "Who would have guessed it?"

Riley let out a groan of dismay.

"*I* should have guessed it. I've really been off my game. Lucy's death was still getting to me, and I was worried about Bill, and …"

Jenn felt pretty sure of what she was leaving unsaid.

Jenn said, "And you had a new partner to break in. And I didn't always make it easy. Still, I would never have guessed in a thousand years that Renee Griggs …"

Jenn's voice trailed off as she tried to comprehend it. She heard Riley's phone ring.

Then she heard Riley gasp when she saw the name of the caller.

"Bill!" Riley said breathlessly. "Has something happened?"

Riley listened in silence for a few moments.

Then she said, "Oh, my God … Oh, my God …"

Jenn's own nerves quickened. She wondered what had happened to upset Riley so much.

Soon Riley said, "Are the kids OK? What about Gabriela? What about Blaine?"

Another moment passed, and then Jenn could hear Riley breathing more easily.

"Thank you, Bill," she said. "Thank you so much."

Riley ended the call. She didn't say anything for a few moments. Jenn glanced over and saw that her mouth was hanging open from shock.

Finally Riley said, "It was Shane Hatcher. He broke into my house. He killed the two cops who were watching the place. Then he attacked my family at my boyfriend's house. Blaine shot Hatcher, but he got away."

"Is Hatcher seriously wounded?" Jenn asked.

"Bill thinks so—very seriously. They think he might be dead somewhere already. The police and the FBI are all mobilized, searching Fredericksburg, setting up roadblocks to keep him from leaving the city. He's said to be extremely dangerous. If he's seen alive, the order is to shoot him on sight."

"They're sure to catch him, then," Jenn said.

Riley was silent for a moment.

Then she said, "No, they won't. He's far from Fredericksburg by now."

Jenn was startled.

"Riley, what are you talking about? You said he was seriously injured. He can't get far on his own, even in a car. He's got to seek medical help."

Riley shook her head.

"You're underestimating him, Jenn. You must never underestimate Shane Hatcher. I've known him to do the seemingly impossible many, many times. He's uncanny. Sometimes he seems almost supernatural, an evil force of nature. And he's got a will of iron."

Jenn wrestled with confusion as she drove.

"So where do you think he went?" Jenn asked.

Riley fell silent again.

Finally she said, "My father's cabin. And I've got to meet him there."

Jenn gasped aloud.

"Riley, that's crazy. What makes you think he's there?"

"Because I know Shane Hatcher. Better than I want to know him."

Riley began to speak more rapidly and urgently.

"You've got to get me to the BAU plane. I'll tell the pilot to take me to the Roanoke Airport. I'll rent a car there. It's not a far drive to the cabin."

Jenn could hardly believe her ears.

She stammered, "Riley, if you're right … if what you're saying is true … and you go up there … you're likely to get yourself killed."

Riley said nothing.

Jenn said, "At least let me come with you."

Riley turned and glared at her.

"No!" she said sharply.

Then Riley turned and stared ahead.

"I've got to do this myself," she said in a quiet, grim voice.

Jenn started the car.

She said, "Then let's get you to that plane."

CHAPTER FORTY SIX

As Riley drove her rental car up into the hills, she felt strangely claustrophobic.

It didn't make sense to her at first.

Here she was, driving toward her father's cabin through grand Appalachian vistas, breathing in the clean forest air, surrounded by redbud and dogwood trees that were blooming on the wooded mountainside.

She ought to feel free and unconfined.

Instead, she felt cramped and uneasy.

Little by little she realized what was wrong …

Demons.

The demons of her life were closing in around her—demons in the shape of memories of her father. She had rarely visited him during the years he had lived up here. Whenever she had come here, he'd shown her nothing but bitterness. They'd quarreled, and after every visit she'd sworn never to come back here.

And now she could taste that bitterness in her own mouth.

When her father died and left the property to her, she had wanted to get rid of it. She'd offered it to her sister, Wendy, who refused to take it.

Probably smart of her, Riley thought.

Thinking about Wendy reminded Riley …

Wendy lived in Des Moines. When Riley had flown out to Iowa for this case, she'd considered paying her sister a visit sometime before returning to Quantico. But Riley had come and gone twice during the last few days without stopping to even call her.

Probably just as well, Riley thought.

Seeing Wendy would probably just stir up more of Riley's demons.

It couldn't be very enjoyable for Wendy either. After all, Wendy had raised a happy family and lived a happy life. She didn't deserve to be reminded of uglier times in the form of a long-estranged sister.

243

As Riley turned a curve that displayed a view of a beautiful valley, she shivered with an uncanny sense of Hatcher's presence.

He's close, she thought.

As impossible as it seemed, there was no doubt in her mind that he was in the cabin.

A knot of apprehension tightened in her chest.

She found herself remembering how Hatcher had laid claim to the cabin, insisting on hiding out there, and Riley had allowed it. She came to regret her decision when Hatcher murdered an unwary and nosy real estate agent who had been poking around the place.

And now Hatcher had killed two more innocent people—the cops who had been watching her house.

Riley shuddered at the thought.

He's changed, she thought.

Hatcher used to act according to a strange but strict moral code, only killing when it was necessary or justified, at least in his own mind. Riley still found it hard to believe he'd intended to hurt her family. But he wasn't his old self anymore. He was unstable, erratic, and more dangerous than ever.

It's time to stop him once and for all, Riley thought.

Or was it?

Riley found herself turning options over his mind.

If he wasn't as badly injured as she expected, mightn't she just let him go?

She shuddered at the sheer irrationality of the idea.

He was a wanted criminal, and she was a sworn law enforcement officer.

She had done his bidding far too many times as it was.

And yet …

She wondered if she was really capable of bringing him in.

Trying to put her uncertainties aside, Riley followed a bumpy dirt road the rest of the way to the cabin. When the building appeared among the trees, she saw a car parked nearby.

Sure enough, someone was here.

And it was surely Shane Hatcher.

As Riley got out of her car and started walking toward the other car, she felt a rare spasm of fear. After all, she was about to enter the lair of a wounded animal.

Then she put her hand on her weapon and continued walking toward the cabin.

The door was partially open.

She stepped inside and there he was—Shane Hatcher himself.

He looked like some weird apparition, sitting on a chair facing an unlit fireplace, watching it raptly as if a blazing fire were burning there. He was holding a gun in one hand.

Does he even know I'm here? Riley wondered.

Then he said in a hushed voice …

"Riley Paige. As I live and breathe."

Then with a painful laugh he added …

"*While* I live and breathe."

Riley walked closer and got a better look at him.

She saw a pile of bloodstained cloth lying on the floor beside him. Starting with his shirt and continuing with every towel and curtain he could lay his hands on, he had made makeshift bandages. The one he was wearing now was wrapped all the way around his abdomen.

From the bloodstains front and back, Riley could see that a bullet had entered and exited his body. It surely hadn't hit any vital organs or he would be dead by now. Of course, a less strong-willed man would have been dead by now anyway.

He also had a smaller bandage on a shoulder. It looked like a bullet had grazed him there.

Hatcher turned and looked at her with glassy eyes.

"That boyfriend of yours isn't a bad shot," he said, laughing painfully again. "Especially considering that he shoots with his eyes closed. Two out of three—not bad. And this one …"

He smiled and pointed at the wound in his belly.

"'Tis not so deep as a well nor so wide as a church-door, but 'tis enough, 'twill serve."

Riley immediately recognized the Shakespearian quote. It was spoken by the dying Mercutio in *Romeo and Juliet.*

She couldn't help be a little amazed.

Even at death's door, Hatcher just had to make a point of displaying his considerable erudition.

"You're not going to die," she said.

Hatcher's squinted skeptically.

"You don't think so? I'm not sure why I shouldn't. If I'm not mistaken, the FBI has given orders to shoot me on sight. Well, look at me. I'm armed and dangerous. Shouldn't you do it? Shouldn't you put a bullet through my brain?"

Riley felt the wind rush out of her lungs. It was hard to regain her breath.

Why don't I kill him? she wondered.

She suddenly realized she had no idea.

He held Riley's gaze for a few seconds.

"I'd prefer it that way," he said. "I really would. Do you think I want to go back to prison, after the taste of freedom I've had?"

He coughed, and some blood trickled out of his mouth.

"I'll make it easier for you," he said. "Think of all the times when you've abided by my wishes. This is just another one of those times. I *order* you to kill me."

Her hand closed around her weapon.

Do it, she told himself. *It's what he wants, goddamn it.*

But as she looked at him, she couldn't help remember her father, sitting in that very chair and staring into that very fireplace.

Even when her father had been dying—even when he'd *wanted* to die—could she have done the same for him?

Could she have shot him like a dog to put him out of his suffering?

She felt something stirring in her—that weird bond of loyalty she and Hatcher had shared.

He'd helped her in many ways—not merely with insights from his brilliant mind.

He'd actually saved the lives of April and Riley's ex-husband last January when they'd been in the clutches of a vicious killer.

He'd also taught her a lot about herself, about the dark parts of her own psyche.

And in her dealings with him, she'd become something of a monster herself.

She'd defied her own sworn duties as an agent, compromised her integrity, broken trust with people she loved and respected.

It's time for that to stop, she thought.

It was time not to follow Shane Hatcher's orders.

In a growl she said, "You're going to live, whether either one of us likes it or not. I'm going to call the police and an ambulance."

Shane smiled a dark and cunning smile.

"They'll be too late," he said.

Then, with a massive effort, he ripped the bandage loose from his abdomen.

Now the wound in front was bleeding like a river.

Hatcher closed his eyes and lost consciousness.

Riley gasped with horror.

He'd lost a lot of blood already. If she didn't stanch the

bleeding, he'd be dead within minutes.

Let him die, she told herself.

Instead, she put handcuffs on him. Then she rushed over to the window, yanked down a remaining curtain, and started wrapping a new bandage around his abdomen.

Then she got out her cell phone to call for an ambulance and the police in the nearby town of Milladore.

With luck they'll get here on time, she thought.

CHAPTER FORTY SEVEN

The next morning, Riley was walking through the BAU building on her way to meet with Meredith when she ran into Jenn Roston in the hallway. She knew that Jenn had flown back to Quantico just this morning.

Riley put her arm around Jenn's shoulder.

She said, "Hey, girl—how was Iowa?"

Jenn grinned.

"It's very pretty this time of year. Nice people, too. You should check it out."

"I'll have to do that," Riley said.

They both laughed.

Just as they got to Meredith's office door, Jenn stopped Riley from entering.

"Riley," she said, "I heard about Hatcher, how you brought him in. That must have been quite an ordeal for you."

Riley nodded.

She said, "Jenn, I still don't know what the right thing to do was. I could have killed right then and there. Instead, I …"

Her voice trailed off.

Jenn put her hand on Riley's shoulder.

"You did the right thing," Jenn said in a comforting voice. "I *know* you did the right thing."

Riley felt a surge of sheer gratitude toward Jenn. It was strange to remember how, just a few days ago, she hadn't trusted her at all.

Since then, Jenn had covered for her when she'd flown back to Quantico, and then she had saved her life.

"Thank you, Jenn," Riley said in a thick voice. "Thank you for … simply everything."

Jenn smiled.

"Come on," she said. "The chief's expecting us."

As they walked into Meredith's office, Riley saw that there was a rare smile on the team director's broad, dark features. He got up from his desk and shook their hands.

"Well done, Roston. Well done, Paige. Have a seat. Let's get caught up."

They all sat down.

Riley asked Jenn, "What was going on when you left this morning?"

Jenn said, "Well, Renee Griggs has clammed up and won't talk to anyone. But her husband is doing enough talking for both of them, blaming her for everything."

Riley asked, "Did she know about his past, the child porn thing?"

"Oh, yes," Jenn said. "She was engaged to him when it happened. She pushed him into the identity change. She's been using and manipulating him ever since—definitely the dominant partner in their marriage, and always insanely jealous. And she's had good reason to be. He's had quite a few illicit relationships with the girls on his team. One night she made him agree to lure Holly Struthers into the house—just to watch him have forced sex with her, she said. But afterward, she killed Holly. Then she made him do it again and again."

Riley shook her head.

"There are still some loose ends bothering me," she said. "We never found a connection between Katy and Holly. Holly didn't even go to the same school, wasn't interested in soccer. And Camryn Mays had graduated. Why would she have had any contact with the couple?"

Meredith leaned back in his chair.

"I just got a call from Chief Sinard that might shed some light on that," he said. "According to Coach Griggs, Holly was thinking about changing schools at one point. She spent just enough time hanging around Wilson High to meet Griggs, who tried to recruit her for his soccer team. It didn't pan out, but they stayed in touch."

Riley shivered a little.

Unfortunately for her, she thought.

Meredith continued, "As for the older girl—well, it seems that Coach Griggs liked to do a little volunteer counseling on the side, helping kids who wanted to go on to college. That's how she got to know him."

Meredith leaned across his desk and looked at Riley and Jenn with interest.

"This sounds like it was an especially tough case. How on earth did you crack it?"

Riley shrugged a little.

"Angier is a perfect little town," she said. "All we had to do was look for someone who was *too* perfect. The coach really stood out that way—a town hero and an inspiration to his girls."

Riley shook her head.

"But then I dropped the ball. Why didn't I suspect his wife? She seemed even more perfect than he was."

Meredith didn't say anything. Riley knew this was his style. He never consoled agents when they suffered spells of self-doubt. And Riley knew he was wise not to do so. It helped keep his agents up to the mark.

Riley nodded toward Jenn.

"I must say, Agent Roston has got great instincts. I owe her my very life. She's got real promise."

Riley paused for a moment, then added, "In fact, she's got a brilliant career ahead of her. I guarantee it."

Jenn smiled and dropped her head a little.

Meredith held Riley's gaze for a few moments.

Finally he said, "I owe you further congratulations, Agent Paige. You brought in Hatcher—and you brought him in alive. It looks like he'll recover from his wound. He won't be getting out of prison again, that's for sure."

Riley's curiosity was piqued.

"What have you heard about him?" she asked. "Has he regained consciousness?"

"Intermittently," Meredith said. "But he hasn't spoken a word to anyone."

Riley felt an icy chill all over as she remembered the glassy look in his eyes, the deathly tone of his voice.

Hatcher had seemed utterly finished with life.

It didn't matter whether he survived his wounds or not.

He was through with it all, finished with everyone—most certainly with Riley.

Riley wondered …

Will he ever say another word to anyone again?

*

After the meeting, Riley went right over to Bill's apartment.

He looked delighted to see her when he answered the door.

"I was hoping you'd stop by," he said. "Come on in."

Riley walked inside and saw that his apartment looked

remarkably neat. The blinds were open to let in some sunlight, and the clutter she'd seen before had been completely cleaned up.

Best of all, Bill looked more like his old self.

Riley hugged him and said, "I don't know how to thank you. What would have happened if you hadn't checked on my house? Gabriela might have come home to find a dead policeman, or Hatcher might still have been waiting there, and he might have …"

She couldn't bring herself to finish her thought.

Bill smiled warmly and said, "Hey, I was just returning a favor. I don't have the words to thank you for all you've done for me in the last few days. Besides, it made me feel …"

He paused for a moment.

"Well, it made me feel worthwhile again. I know I'm not out of the woods yet. I still hear shots when there's no sound at all. I still see that poor kid I shot falling. I see Lucy's dead body. But …"

His voice faded away.

"But what?" Riley asked.

"Well, something happened to me when I saw what Blaine did. He's really a brave guy, you know. And he reminded me of what I used to be … and can be again, I think."

Riley felt a lump of emotion in her throat as she thought about her own terrible experiences with PTSD. She still suffered from flashbacks from time to time.

"It won't be easy," she said quietly. "It will take time. And it might never go away … not completely."

Bill nodded and smiled.

"That's OK," he said. "I'll be patient."

*

Riley spent much of the rest of the day at home with her family. After dinner, she headed over to Blaine's house. His daughter, Crystal, had already gone upstairs for the night.

Riley was surprised to see everything looking absolutely perfect. She'd heard that Shane had shattered a glass door to get in, but there was no sign that anything had happened.

"How did you get everything fixed up so fast?" she said.

Blaine grinned.

"Pretty impressive, huh? I insisted that the repair company get the new door put in right away. They've worked for me at the restaurant for years, and they're eager to please. Come on, sit down,

I'll get us some wine."

Riley joined Blaine on his living room couch, and he poured them some delicious wine.

Riley looked at him with concern.

"I'm so sorry about what you went through," she said. "How are you holding up?"

"Amazingly well," he said with a shrug. "Crystal is actually proud of me. I've been trying to convince her that I'm not some kind of hero."

Riley patted his hand.

"Don't try too hard to convince her," she said. "She's right, as far as I'm concerned."

Blaine lowered his head and said nothing. Riley squeezed his hand.

"I mean that, Blaine. Do you realize what you did? Shane Hatcher was one of the most dangerous criminals alive. Even the FBI didn't know how to stop him. You stood up to him, you helped bring him down. Thanks to you, he'll never cause any trouble again."

Blaine blushed deeply. He didn't seem to know what to say for a moment.

Then he said, "How about your kids? And Gabriela?"

Riley chuckled a little.

"Oh, God, the kids are *so* resilient. From talking with them, you'd think nothing had happened. They're back to math, soccer, school, chess club, school in general. And as for Gabriela—well, I don't think there's anything in the world that can faze her."

Riley and Blaine fell quiet for a moment. Riley found herself enjoying the comfortable silence.

But then unsettling thoughts started creeping in.

She remembered back when he was her next-door neighbor, and he'd gotten so frightened by the danger she'd brought into his life that he'd moved all the way to this house.

Had any of that changed?

She took a deep, long breath and said, "Blaine ... you know I wouldn't blame you ... if you ran away from me as fast and far as you possibly can."

Blaine smiled and pulled her close to him.

"I'm not going anywhere," he said.

ONCE BURIED
(A Riley Paige Mystery—Book 11)

"A masterpiece of thriller and mystery! The author did a magnificent job developing characters with a psychological side that is so well described that we feel inside their minds, follow their fears and cheer for their success. The plot is very intelligent and will keep you entertained throughout the book. Full of twists, this book will keep you awake until the turn of the last page."
--Books and Movie Reviews, Roberto Mattos (re Once Gone)

ONCE BURIED is book #11 in the bestselling Riley Paige mystery series, which begins with the #1 bestseller ONCE GONE (Book #1)—a free download with over 1,000 five star reviews!

A serial killer is killing victims with rapid speed, and in each crime scene, he leaves an unusual signature: an hourglass.

Its sand is designed to fall for 24 hours—and when its empty, a new victim appears.

Amidst intense media pressure, and in a frantic race against time, FBI Special Agent Riley Paige is summoned, with her new partner, to crack the case. Still reeling from the fallout with Shane, trying to sort out her family life, and to help Bill get back on his feet, Riley's plate is already full. And as she enters the darkest canals of this twisted killer's mind, this just may be the case that sets her over the edge.

A dark psychological thriller with heart-pounding suspense, ONCE BURIED is book #11 in a riveting new series—with a beloved new character—that will leave you turning pages late into the night.

Book #12 in the Riley Paige series will be available soon.

Blake Pierce

Blake Pierce is author of the bestselling RILEY PAGE mystery series, which includes eleven books (and counting). Blake Pierce is also the author of the MACKENZIE WHITE mystery series, comprising six books (and counting); of the AVERY BLACK mystery series, comprising five books; and of the new KERI LOCKE mystery series, comprising four books (and counting).

An avid reader and lifelong fan of the mystery and thriller genres, Blake loves to hear from you, so please feel free to visit www.blakepierceauthor.com to learn more and stay in touch.

BOOKS BY BLAKE PIERCE

RILEY PAIGE MYSTERY SERIES
ONCE GONE (Book #1)
ONCE TAKEN (Book #2)
ONCE CRAVED (Book #3)
ONCE LURED (Book #4)
ONCE HUNTED (Book #5)
ONCE PINED (Book #6)
ONCE FORSAKEN (Book #7)
ONCE COLD (Book #8)
ONCE STALKED (Book #9)
ONCE LOST (Book #10)
ONCE BURIED (Book #11)

MACKENZIE WHITE MYSTERY SERIES
BEFORE HE KILLS (Book #1)
BEFORE HE SEES (Book #2)
BEFORE HE COVETS (Book #3)
BEFORE HE TAKES (Book #4)
BEFORE HE NEEDS (Book #5)
BEFORE HE FEELS (Book #6)

AVERY BLACK MYSTERY SERIES
CAUSE TO KILL (Book #1)
CAUSE TO RUN (Book #2)
CAUSE TO HIDE (Book #3)
CAUSE TO FEAR (Book #4)
CAUSE TO SAVE (Book #5)

KERI LOCKE MYSTERY SERIES
A TRACE OF DEATH (Book #1)
A TRACE OF MUDER (Book #2)
A TRACE OF VICE (Book #3)
A TRACE OF CRIME (Book #4)

Made in the USA
Coppell, TX
22 March 2020

16906372R10142